To Mike
With best wishes
for the future.

[signature] (January 09).

The Back Door

Paul V. Wisely

First published in 1995

Copyright © Paul V Wisely 1995

The moral right of the author has been asserted

*All characters in this publication are fictitious and any resemblance to real persons, living or
dead, is purely coincidental*

A CIP catalogue record for this book is available from the British Library

ISBN - 0 9527180 0 6

Printed in Scotland by BCP-AUP Aberdeen Ltd

Gravic Publishing
8-10 Batchen Street
Elgin
Moray
IV30 1BH

———

It's two years since I first sketched out a short story called 'The Back Door', believing it would make a reasonable screenplay. I then made the mistake of showing my original draft to my business partner, Sandy McIntyre, who suggested I turn it into a novel.

———

ACKNOWLEDGEMENTS

I would just like to express my thanks and appreciation to the people who have helped, encouraged and advised me over the past two years.

Julie T for getting me started.
Davina D for keeping my disks and directories in order.
Jon M for his professional advice and perceptive comments.
Martin F for his support and input.
Jill Dick of The Scottish Cultural Press for her advice.
Tom B for his time and patience as well as his graphic skills.
Stephen B, my brother in law, for his encouragement and support.
Sandy Mc for his insight, support, guidance, professional advice and constructive criticism !
Roddy Lumsden, the Writer in Residence at Aberdeen Central Library, who took on the task of editor for the manuscript. His input and help has been invaluable.

Finally, I have to make a special mention of my family, Alison, Greg, Scott and Megan, for their love, support and patience - I still don't know why they put up with me !

For My Family

Chapter 1

CHAPTER 1

"Good evening Father. I hope you don't mind, but we took the liberty of letting ourselves in."

The priest's eyes widened, straining to see in the half light. The soft, lilting voice in the darkness sounded familiar, but it had taken him by surprise and the intrusion into the privacy of his home shocked him. The little flat overlooking the canal on the Huidenvettersplein was his refuge and no one was ever invited there. He didn't encourage visitors. His business was always conducted in the relative safety of public places. In the shadows he could make-out the outlines of two figures, one standing, one sitting. He clicked on the light and viewed his two guests. He instantly recognised the red hair and beard of the older, seated intruder.

"Gentlemen, my home is your home. Now what can I do for you?" he asked calmly, his voice masking the fear that had spread throughout his body.

"You know Father, I was just saying as we were driving down here that we hadn't heard from you for a while. You seem to be keeping a low profile these days. Still it's good to see you, you look well."

"You've always been a good liar." The priest could make out a smile through the thick beard, but his fear deepened; this was neither a social nor a business visit.

"Father, obviously I need no introduction, but you won't know my young friend here. He doesn't say much, so please forgive his apparent rudeness. He's new to all this and

3

I have to keep him on a tight leash. You could say he's in training. As you can see he's a big strong lad, but he needs the guidance of an old head. You know Father, it's a terrible shame, but in the few months since he's been away from his mother he hasn't been to chapel or confession, so as the evening wears on, perhaps you can give him some spiritual re-direction."

"Somehow I don't think he needs any help from me. Now what brings you all the way down from Holland to see me?" the priest said abruptly.

"Well Father, if you put it like that, we'll get down to business. A few weeks ago we lost a colleague of ours in a brutal murder and we were hoping you might be able to help us trace who may be responsible. We thought that, because of the specialised nature of the incident, a client of yours may have been involved and we hoped you might be able to break a confidence and discreetly point us in the right direction. We all go back along way Father and I'm sure you haven't forgotten your roots. Besides, for the sake of the old days we felt you owed us a small favour."

"I'm sorry, I don't see how I can help you. I know of many things, but I know nothing which may be of interest to you regarding the particular sad episode you refer to."

The priest eyed the younger man at the back of the small room as he toyed with a heavy marble sculpture of the Madonna and Child.

"Please be careful and don't drop that. It's a very expensive piece."

The young man said nothing and returned the figure to its place on the side board.

"Now you'll have to go, I'm very tired and I have a number of early calls to make tomorrow. I'm sorry I can't help you. Have a safe journey home."

The red-headed guest rose up out of the chair.

"You know Father, as we get older we get forgetful and we start believing our powers of recall diminish, but sometimes it just takes little triggers to get the memory banks working properly again."

"I have an excellent memory."

"I'm sure you have Father. I'm sure you have."

Twenty minutes later the priest was alone in the flat. He tumbled out of the chair, his head narrowly missing hitting the cold, blood stained figurine on the floor. He crawled through to the bathroom and hauled himself up so he could sit on the edge of the bath.

4

His breathing was rapid and shallow. His face was pale, his jaw clenched tightly shut. He knew he was in danger of hyper-ventilating. With a considerable effort, he tried to regain his composure and control his breathing. He managed to balance himself against the rim of the peach coloured sink, then with his good hand he turned the cold tap on full. Carefully, gingerly he edged his bruised and swollen hand under the tap. At first he felt the sharp burn of pain, then the soothing effect of the cold rushing water over the damaged and broken skin. The trembling, nausea and panic evaporated slowly.

"Dirty, ungodly bastards!" he mumbled.

******

The five men entered the elegant, oak-panelled room. They were all middle aged or older and dressed as if they had just stepped off the eighteenth at Wentworth, a grouse moor on a Highland estate, or had just tied up at Cowes. The tailoring was bespoke, with blazers and tweeds the order of the day. They were men of wealth and power. Old money. Establishment. They each helped themselves from the pot of freshly brewed coffee which had been positioned on a sideboard in a corner of the board-room. There was no conversation between them, no polite small talk; the only sound was the tick, whirr and Westminster chime of the clock on the mantelpiece of the ornately carved fire place. Close examination of the delicate detail of the carvings revealed them to have a sinister beauty, yet their significance was shrouded in the mystery and symbolism of centuries of secrecy and tradition, associated with a society that had long been accused of indulging in influence peddling. The room smelled of polish, fresh coffee and the kind of strong aftershave that was exclusively formulated and sold from premises on Curzon Street.

This morning's meeting had been convened at very short notice; they had important business to discuss. The political situation they had been monitoring so closely was still fluid and about to change once more. Their sources suggested a political settlement was being discussed in secret and a compromise solution was imminent. The group feared change and now, to counteract the threat that faced them, they would be forced once more to take a proactive interest in influencing the outcome of what were being headlined internationally as *historic events*. As if responding to an unseen signal, each man simultaneously took his delicate china cup and saucer and found his place at the board table.

Sir Arthur Knox-De Vries had flown down from Inverness that morning to chair the meeting. He didn't particularly like working on the Sabbath and had curtailed a short hunting and fishing break to be there. He had considered having a discreet word with the other members of the Randolph Group at Temple later in the week, but there was no guarantee they would all be present and this meeting could not be delayed. Decisions had to be taken, plans had to be made. It had crossed his mind, but on further consideration, a formal board meeting any time between Monday and Friday was out of the question; it would only draw interest from certain quarters and besides there were always far too many distractions during normal office hours. His dark brown eyes gleamed, then his lips tightened as he returned his cup to its saucer. He pushed back in to the soft, red, cracked leather of his chair and for a moment his eyes panned round, with the slow deliberation of a surveillance camera, at the gallery of framed sepia photographs, oil portraits and coats of arms that adorned the panelled walls. They were pictures of the founding fathers of what he referred to as 'the Firm', hanging there in a lasting tribute to their long and loyal service. They had all served the company man and boy, commencing with a junior posting overseas, usually after a period in the Armed Forces, before returning to London, their power base and a seat on the Board. The financial strength, power and influence of today's firm was a lasting tribute to their guile, foresight and ambition. The male lineage of the Knox-De Vries family was well represented. They all had the same dark eyes. Genetic inheritance is the phrase they use. Breeding.

Sir Arthur was 62 years old. He had a ruddy, almost rural complexion, his cheeks red with tiny broken blood vessels and, below his eyes, a network of furrows and lines. His hair was grey and impeccably groomed, but his eyebrows were dark and bushy. He was not a particularly handsome man, but like so many of his kind he had the aura and inherent arrogance of the landed classes. Gentry. He had been immersed since childhood in the ways of his family, their beliefs, their traditions, their history. His father had been a distant man, but since boyhood he had instilled in him a sense of duty to Family, Crown and Faith and he bore his ancestral burden with ease. It had been a life of purpose and pageantry. At five years old he had been sent to boarding-school, whilst his father circled the globe, establishing and consolidating business interests in the remnants of the Empire.

Sir Arthur Knox-De Vries was also Chairman of the exclusive and somewhat mysterious Randolph group, which had been formed by his great-grandfather in the early 1900's, as well as holding official chairmanships and directorships on the boards of financial, investment and construction companies, based not only in London but overseas, primarily in those countries once coloured red in the atlas of his childhood. The controlling interests in these organisations were invariably held by his family. He was also a very successful corporate lawyer and this, coupled with a very shrewd and ruthless business brain, had helped him amass considerable personal wealth in addition to what he had inherited. Many years ago he had been advised by senior colleagues in the legal profession to turn his back on the family business and study for qualification to the Bar, but to him there was only one career path and he was always destined to stay in the City. It was his duty. Born into wealth and privilege, he was the undisputed head of the family, by right, by temperament, training and instinct. A man of resourceful competence, who exuded a quiet power, he inspired among his relatives, colleagues, business associates and peers - respect, admiration and fear.

He turned his attention back to the meeting and the job in hand. An observer may have noted that there were no documents on the table, no secretary sitting unobtrusively in a corner taking notes. No formal minutes were recorded. Pens and paper were conspicuous by their absence for a meeting which only had one item on its agenda.

The laconic Knox-De Vries stood up and welcomed his four associates, apologising for the unscheduled disruption to their weekend. He then began a brief speech that concisely summarised the intelligence he had been passed less than twenty four hours earlier. He was eloquent and direct. He did not have to spell out the implications and ultimate consequences of what he had learned.

Of course, the hereditary Knight knew exactly the course of action he would ultimately take but, as was his management style, he politely asked for suggestions from his fellow directors. Their opinions were valid. He liked their involvement, their commitment to a project. He preferred to have everyone singing from the same hymn book. His hymn book.

"Well, gentlemen, are we agreed, we call Mr Richardson?" His voice was both quiet and disciplined, concealing a capacity for decisive action.

He looked round the table at the four other grim faces and each in turn nodded his approval.

"It will, of course, be very expensive, as I do not think he will be able to carry out this particular project alone and we will also have to consider the 'heat' of the most recent assignment he performed for us in our negotiations. Are we prepared to meet his price? I'm sorry gentlemen, that sounds a little trite, a little tacky for a professional such as Mr Richardson. Please allow me to re-phrase - his consultancy fee. Should he accept?"

He looked round the table once again and the four faces of the quorum signalled their agreement. Sitting directly opposite the chairman was the pale, deeply lined face of the Right Honourable Jeremy Barrington. He began to speak - his voice deep, refined and perfectly cadenced.

"Well, here we are again gentlemen. I feel we are almost there. Personally, I do not care what Mr Richardson's price is, I strongly propose we take steps to get him operational now. We all have far too much to lose if this ill-conceived process succeeds and the action we have taken thus far will have been in vain. To make matters worse we are even having to witness and suffer the ignominy of the Americans and their hill-billy President getting in on the act, promising all this 'peace dividend' balderdash and claiming it all as a Foreign Policy success. It'll finish us over there, if we're not careful. Personally, I find them all dreadfully tiresome. As we all know, they have absolutely no sense of history, they are without tradition and they constantly meddle and interfere in world affairs way beyond their jurisdiction. It may be acceptable to behave as they do in the backwaters of Haiti, Panama and Grenada, but this is an English problem and it is only fit and proper that Englishmen should be the ones to prosper from its solution.

"Like you, my fellow and esteemed members of the group, my forebears served with Cromwell in the campaigns of 1649 and 1650 and they were rewarded for their loyalty and bravery, with estates and lands. They also swore an oath to preserve their Faith, our Faith. I for one cannot stand back and let these uncouth 'colonials' step out of the shadows and lay claim to investment opportunities that are ours by right. In addition to what we have learned today, I have also heard stories, stronger than mere rumour, that emissaries of the Bishop of Rome are also at work, weaving their spells and incantations among the people, as they too try and claim the credit for what they are suggesting was, all along, their initiative. In my opinion, what that amounts to in real terms is a Vatican plot. It has all become most unacceptable and, as if to compound this situation, some of our own Royal Family have recently alluded to a defection to the Papacy. As a nation we have lost our way, it is therefore behest on groups like ours, as guardians of our heritage and beliefs, to turn it around. We must take action, we cannot allow all that we stand for to be destroyed, even threatened by these treacherous, ungrateful beggars. I suggest we move swiftly so that we take advantage of those who are already dissident to the political moves that are afoot and that we disrupt, derail and destroy this process, or indeed any process, that seeks to germinate in the future." Barrington paused. His face was flushed. He had never before addressed the group in such a way. The others just looked at him. There was silence. He continued, "I assume you intend to use the Liechtenstein account? Do you need to transfer any funds?"

"No, we are well covered."

"Sir Arthur, can you share with us how you came by this invaluable information?"

Knox-De Vries ignored the question, but he was generally pleased with the sentiments he had just listened to being so vehemently expressed. There was so much at risk, but there was still time.

"Thank you gentlemen. Leave the arrangements to me and I will contact you all again, once the project is underway. I am confident we will reach a satisfactory conclusion, and the status quo will be maintained. Any questions?"

The only sound was the ticking and whirring of the clock. Silence implied consensus. He therefore adjourned the meeting.

"Thank you for your time. Enjoy the remainder of your week-end gentlemen," he said. As they filtered out, he stood at the door and shook each man by the hand.

Within five minutes the board-room was silent and empty, leaving no trace, other than a tray of neatly stacked crockery, that a meeting had actually taken place there. Two of the group rushed away in a chauffeur driven Daimler to be at their golf club for a challenge match with a Law Lord and an influential back-bench Tory MP. The third man sped away in his Bentley Mulsanne Turbo to his Buckinghamshire estate, to celebrate his eldest grand-daughter's engagement and Barrington just walked away in the direction of his mother's London address in Belgravia.

Sir Arthur was last to leave. He hailed a black cab that took him to a penthouse apartment he kept in London, on Park Lane. It was an expensive leasehold, but it served his purposes well, both in terms of location and prestige. He sat quietly in the back of the cab, concealing, with some difficulty, his impatience. He hated delays, technical or otherwise and this cabby seemed to be on a go slow. He glanced at the headline of a tabloid newspaper, that had been left in the car: THE EDGE OF THE ABYSS: CIVIL WAR LOOMS. He permitted himself a smile. If his strategy worked it would be 'business as usual' within a few weeks. For a brief moment he contemplated asking the cabby to find a shop so he could buy a packet of cigarettes, but his willpower fought through. He was not a weak man. He had been off the weed for five months and ten days exactly and he felt physically better, but at certain times of the day he had to battle with a gnawing craving. However, the option of attaching nicotine patches to his arm was undignified and therefore unacceptable to him. Time was not on his side and his instincts told him he would have to mobilise Richardson immediately, or at the very least get a commitment from him that he was prepared to accept the assignment. He wanted to drive things along but, on this occasion, as in past dealings, even with all the power and wealth at his disposal, he knew Richardson was not a man who would be pushed.

It was now late morning and the traffic was light, as Londoners and tourists sheltered from the thunderstorm that seemed to have permanently settled over the capital and over Knightsbridge, Kensington and Mayfair in particular. The black Hackney cab, its wipers struggling to cope with the deluge, dropped him off just a few feet from the pillared entrance, but even in the short time he was exposed to the downpour it made its presence felt on the shoulders of his khaki coloured Burberry, darkening the coat in a two-tone effect. He acknowledged the friendly wave of the concierge as he entered the marbled hall and then took the lift to his 5th floor suite. He entered the apartment, disabled the alarm and walked to the window and for a few minutes he watched in awe, with a child-like fascination, as the thunder rumbled and the lightning forked over the park and the West London skyline.

*****

The phone rang in the pretty riverside cottage, shattering the library-like silence. Piers Richardson carefully marked his place, put his book down, rose from the high backed leather chair and walked over to the table by the window. As the phone rang, he stood for a moment and watched a cat crouching almost out of sight under a large, mature hebe, waiting patiently and silently for an opportunity to strike. A sparrow skirted the shrubs and the lawn, then landed on the damp grass, only feet from the watching eyes. The cat waited. The sparrow, nervous at first, grew in confidence, but then something caught its eye. It may have been the movement of the breeze through the bushes, but it suddenly took off for the safety of a telephone wire, high above the garden. The bird had flown. The cat waited, never revealing its position. There would be other opportunities. Richardson picked up the receiver, but said nothing.

"Mr Richardson, this is Knox. I have just returned from a meeting with my people and we'd like to see you. We have an overseas opportunity that may be of interest. I must confess it is linked to your recent work and is of vital importance not only to myself, but also to my colleagues, as a point of principle and to prevent further US Dollar imperialism. Does your schedule permit you to be available tomorrow to talk further?"

"No. I have some personal affairs to attend to. However, I am available on Thursday. Your office or the Park?"

"Yes, my office, 11am, if that's convenient for you. As per our previous arrangements, I will refund your expenses, as well as paying for your time."

There was a slight delay before Richardson came back on.

"No, let's make it the Park. Usual place, by the children's play area." Richardson's cold black eyes narrowed as he said it.

Yes, that rendezvous would be more convenient, as he could coincide it with a long overdue visit to the Harrods Food Hall and their Fine Wines Department. Knox-De Vries on the other hand was a little perturbed by the delay. Monday would have been better, but at least he had a commitment from Richardson to meet and discuss the matter. He had been more than just a little concerned that Richardson would turn him down, as it was only six weeks since they had last engaged his particular specialist skills. This was now the third time they had contacted him in seven months and Knox-De Vries did worry that they were increasing their exposure by using him again, but it was a calculated risk, a risk he was willing to take.

10

Richardson said nothing. Without any discernible change in expression, he replaced the phone, returned to his chair, picked up his book and continued reading. The cat remained crouched, silent and hidden in the shrubbery. Waiting.

Richardson didn't particularly like his client, in fact he was dismayed by the way that, in spite of their great wealth, Knox-De Vries and people like him, this so-called Randolph group, continued to profit from conflicts they were safely isolated from. His one other great dislike was America. In fact he despised the 'good old US of A', 'period', with its self-assuming role as the world's policeman, its bastardisation of the English language and, more importantly, the fact that, as a country, it had never experienced 'modern war' on the home-front, on its own back-yard. Europe, Africa, Asia, Latin America had all suffered, but not Uncle Sam. They had of course fucked up so many times on other people's turf and, as a fighting force, the US Military had never impressed a man with his pedigree. However, the reality was that he had undertaken work for Knox's organisation in the past and they had not only proven to be very secretive, but also very generous and prompt payers. Only recently he had carried out an assignment on their behalf and some months earlier he had arranged for a device to be detonated in the Republic's fair city which had aroused a storm of public protest, indignation and outrage and had greatly increased the pressure on what was already a powder keg situation. This latest call offered an opportunity to work with them again, as well as undermining a Foreign Policy coup and investment bonanza by the White House and Wall Street. He would no doubt accept the assignment, at a vastly inflated fee, but he also sensed an urgency and concern in the voice of Knox-De Vries and he allowed himself the pleasure of delaying the meeting. His personal thoughts aside, the Richardson modus operandi was never to question the motives of his clients, but Knox's people confused him; they seemed to have no obvious political ambitions, their targets normally chosen on the basis of a business need and not any political or military expedient. He was bemused by their rituals and always insisted on a firm, conventional handshake when being met by anyone associated with their secretive little group.

Richardson read on for an hour or so, then he scribbled a coded note in his diary to remind himself of the appointment.

*****

"So that's it then, you're going..." She wiped away the tears that were streaming down her face.

I closed my eyes and nodded, then prepared myself for an attack, either verbal or physical...or both.

"You're a bastard, a selfish, self-centred bastard," she snapped, "I don't know what I see in you. I must be a fool, and I can't help but feel that the year's investment, in fact it's probably longer than that, that I have put into this one-sided relationship has been a complete waste of time. I don't know what planet you're on, but one of these days you are going to get a shock and you'll find there are more people on this earth, than Paul bloody Robertson."

Claire turned and stormed out of the flat, doors slamming in her wake. A few moments later, I heard her car start up then speed off down the road. I sat for a moment, relieved that the expected tirade of abuse had not been too bad. I adjusted the cushions on the settee and went through to the study. This was very much my room, my den. The walls were covered with some framed photographs from my footballing days, from school all the way through to my time in the Highland League. My old school cricket bat stood proudly in the corner along with my tennis and squash rackets. By the window there was a picture of me looking into the corrie of Lochnagar on my first trip up the mountain. It had been presented to me by an ex-colleague who had taken it, then had it enlarged and framed. There was no one else in the picture, just me and the dark brooding crags of Lochnagar. Friends often said it was a cold, lonely picture, but I liked it, it had great sentimental value. My desk was there, my old leather Captain's chair, my PC and shelves heavy with books. I found my checklist and I used it to check off against what had and what still had to be packed. Jeans, chinos, ties, pants, socks, toilet bag, shoes, polo shirts, everything seemed to be there. I quickly checked my suits and jackets, zipped up the holder, put my passport and £250 of Norwegian Kroner on the roll-top desk and made a call.

"Hello, can I have a taxi right away, please? Yes, going to the airport."

I gave the taxi firm my address and telephone number then hung up. I put my case and suit holder in the vestibule, checked the back door and then made sure that all the windows were locked and the water was switched off at the mains. It had been bitterly cold and frosty over the past few nights and I didn't want to return to burst pipes.

The taxi arrived within ten minutes, which was surprisingly responsive. I put my passport, cash and flight tickets into my jacket pocket along with the trip itinerary. I kissed Hannah's photograph and left. The journey to the airport took about twenty minutes and passed in silence. I always went with my instincts with taxi drivers and would either make polite conversation with them or decide that they were assholes and not take them on. This one was a pure asshole. He was smoking even though there were signs clearly indicating that the car was a no smoking zone. I asked him to put the cigarette out which he did reluctantly. He made some sort of mumbled comment which I didn't quite make out, but I flashed him a look that contained more than just mere contempt. In retrospect, asking him to stop smoking was a mistake, as his body odour was infinitely worse.

12

As we drove over Anderson Drive, the city's inner ring road, I thought of Claire. I felt sorry for her. I knew I had let her down but I felt I didn't really have a choice. I would sort it all out on my return.

We arrived at Dyce airport and the car pulled up at the passenger drop-off point. I shivered when I got out of the taxi. The wind had got up and it had started to rain - sometimes Aberdeen could be a cold place.

I paid the driver and at the last minute I asked for a receipt. That usually pissed them off, but this was a trip where all reasonable expenses were recoverable as long as they were supported by the appropriate documentation. I picked up my gear and went into the terminal. Our party was travelling on the 14:20 SAS flight so I went to the desk and checked in. As I was going through the standard security questions regarding the carrying of electrical goods and the packing of your own case, I felt a hand on my back.

"Fit like Robertson? I thought it was your name on the official list. I was glad to hear that you were coming to 'La Norvege zero point' land for this piss-up as well. I didn't want to be stuck with these boring chocolates for the whole week-end."

I turned slowly and saw Roy Calder. Roy was an Information Officer with the Council and a useful contact. He was pot-bellied, follically challenged and on a good day he was a bit of a laugh, but on a bad day he was a lecherous slap head who would hump anything with a pulse or, as he proudly claimed, 'he'd shag a stab wound!'

"Have you got a kilt?" he asked, his face so close to mine I could smell the alcohol on his breath. Start as you mean to go on Roy, I thought. I shook my head and turned away. He was too close. He was in my space.

"Oh Nightmare! You should have hired a kilt, the babes in Norway just love a bloke in a kilt. They can spot you a mile off and they know you're fresh meat. You won't pick up anything without a kilt. This thing's a babe magnet. By the way, I think I'm sharing with you when we get over there. Oh, and a wee word of advice, buy your drink now from the Duty Free, 'cos it costs a fortune over there. The idea is to get pissed on your own bevvy in your hotel room before you go out. Dinna' worry, stick wi' me and I'll keep you right."

I had to laugh, partly out of pity for Roy because he was a bit of a loser in the looks and style department and partly because of my own misfortune at having to share a room with a pervert!

Maybe this trip was not such a good idea after all and for an instant I could see Claire barking at me on my return with that old, smug, 'I told you so' lecture.

The flight to Norway left on schedule and passed without any major problem. Roy, who had managed to get himself a seat next to me, scoofed back three gin and tonics, his own quarter bottle of wine and mine, but fortunately the flight was too short for him to become a real pain in the butt. Our one-sided conversation consisted mainly of what he intended doing to the female population of Stavanger. I despaired at the thought of his sad portrayal of the 'Tartan be-decked Scotsman abroad'. Although not a rabid Nationalist, I was fiercely proud of my country, a patriot and a Scot first and foremost, but his type irritated me, as they did nothing to enhance our image. I started to doze, partly to escape from Calder and partly to mull over the situation with Claire. The aircraft was battling against a head wind as we started to cross high over the oil and gas fields of the North Sea. I felt my eyes closing and my mind slipping back to the situation I'd just left. Claire was well pissed off with me. For the second year in a row she would be without a partner at the annual Law Society Ball. She alleged that I had said, no matter what, I would go with her this year, but I genuinely had not foreseen this opportunity to cover a story in Norway. What had happened was that a group of Local Councillors from Aberdeen and some members of various Scottish Fisheries organisations were travelling to Stavanger on a cultural and trade visit. The main purpose of the trip was to encourage discussion and networking amongst the Scottish and Norwegian fisheries groups. Normally I wouldn't have touched it, but I got a whisper that a couple of key MPs and several Scottish Office bureaucratic fat cats were going to be going over as well, which coincided neatly with a corruption piece I was investigating on one of them. Nothing too heavy, just an MP having a 'few jollies' at tax payers expense - that sort of thing. It also had the added advantage of being held in Stavanger, which was where my younger brother, Stephen, had been transferred to by his company, an oil industry service company. He had rented an apartment just outside the city and had been in Norway for about five to six months. He phoned me from the office at least once a week and according to reports he had settled in fairly well and was keen to see me when I got over. It was strange, but having fought like cat and dog throughout our boyhood and teens, we had now become good friends and we had grown remarkably similar in looks and behaviour.

As far as the Law Society Ball was concerned, I was pleased to be missing it. Making polite conversation with the senior partners from Claire's firm and their wives and listening to the inane bleaterings of the young, up and coming, male solicitors was not my cup of fur! Apart from the odd exception, I was not a great fan of the legal profession.

At work, Claire was pushing hard for a senior partnership and the 'old boys' on the Firm placed a great emphasis on stable domestic relationships for their more highly regarded people. She was 34 and had joined them immediately after graduating from University. She had covered all the various departments, before carving herself a niche as a very sharp and competent court solicitor who was not afraid to take on cases and clients that some of her more experienced colleagues were, to say the least, reluctant

14

to touch. We had been introduced about two years earlier by an associate at a dinner party, although I knew of her from some of my own acquaintances.

She was aware I had played semi-professional football and for a few years I had even played in the same team with a colleague of hers (a nice bloke and one of the few solicitors I liked!). Looking back, and without meaning to sound too vain, I think she had been instantly attracted to me and, as was my style, I had played on being the shy, somewhat distant, vulnerable charmer and it seemed to hook her. We had been going out together now for just over twelve months but, somehow, even though we were at times physically very close, she had not broken through the front and emotional armouring I always put up and, if the conversation ever came round to subjects like moving in together or getting engaged, I would just laugh or clam up, as these were issues I was happy to avoid. I still didn't feel ready to get back into a serious relationship and a major commitment with anyone. I guess I was fond of Claire, she was attractive, stylish and smart and she was also a very useful contact as far as the Aberdeen business community was concerned, but there was something missing between us, the all important spark, that little bit of alchemy where you instinctively know someone is right for you.

For a lot of guys, going out with and marrying Claire would have been regarded as a major coup. She was a fully paid-up, life-long member of the Lucky Sperm Club. She was typical silver spoon. Private, fee-paying girls school, rich friends, exotic holidays and a fixation with people's social backgrounds. Without putting too fine a point on it, she was a snob and I'm still not sure how I managed to slip through the fine gossamer mesh of the socially acceptable net. Her father was a wealthy man, a former senior partner in a firm of Accountants. He was now retired. He was a likeable enough old guy and she was very like him, very clever, arrogant, shrewd and obstinate. He wasn't the sort of man I ever felt I could get too close to, we had so little in common really; he was a rugby man and regarded football with disdain. It was all a bit too working class for him. He had, however, given me some free advice on property development, particularly in Spain, where he had one or two interests, but what he was advising me to do called for financial resources, which pushed it way out of my league. His character was so different to my own dad.

At work, Claire prided herself on being able to become detached from the trauma and stress of her cases. She never became personally involved, but with me I think it was different. She was an only child and was used to getting her own way and, since I had come on the scene, she viewed me as a bit of a challenge, even though she never felt completely secure with me, or in our relationship. She was always asking if I loved her, especially after we had made love, but I never said the words. Sometimes I would laugh it off and I would say 'of course I do', but I never actually said it and although it wasn't intentional on my part, I'm sure it hurt her like hell. Of course, saying something like that is easy, meaning it...well that's a different matter.

For my sins I work as a free-lance journalist, although for the last five years or so, the bulk of my income has come from several small time, but highly lucrative, speculative investments in the Aberdeen property market. After being kicked out of College, ('Course Terminated') in the early eighties, I hadn't known what to do. In the end I just fell into work with an oil major and stayed there, fighting against the dangers of becoming institutionalised and the inevitable brain death. I think it was Paul Getty who said that you never get rich working for someone else and I had always believed in the logic of his words and I had treaded water for a few years, waiting for the circumstances that would allow me to jump and go into business for myself. The oil industry has, on the surface, been good for Aberdeen, but working directly in it had just induced frustration and disappointment in me.

I stay in a spacious, ground floor flat in a treelined avenue in the city's West End, where the second bedroom has been transferred into my study. It was to have been a nursery. The style of the interior of the flat was still very much Hannah's. Her influence was everywhere. She had been the driving force behind the stripping of the floor boards, the doors and the skirting boards, back to the natural wood. It had been bloody hard work. Hannah had been responsible for all the skilful work and I had done my fair share of the graft. The final effect was worth the callouses and the blisters, not only in terms of the cosy, stylish home that had been created, but also in the way it enhanced the character and the value of the property. Claire kept some things there, but she had never moved in - I had never asked her to and I think we both knew that it probably would never happen. She would stay over most weekends, or on the odd occasion on weekdays, if we had been out, but I still needed space and independence and, to be honest, she never pushed it. I'm sure she thought it would be much easier if we moved in together. Her friends expected it and constantly joked about it, but it was non-negotiable as far as I was concerned and any attempt by her to get a discussion going on the subject just led to strained silences between us. She hated that. She would have preferred to have had some sort of intellectual debate, a verbal joust, with me the journalist, supposedly clever with words and she, the smart-assed lawyer, as sharp and incisive as anyone in the city's legal fraternity. I would never give her the opportunity and if I sensed an argument on the subject building up, I would just back off and retreat into myself. I couldn't be done with all that shit. Mind you, I certainly would not have fancied going up against her in court! 'Hell hath no fury' and if she scented blood, she would have no compunction about going for the jugular. She could be a real head-fuck when she wanted to and during one particular one-sided verbal onslaught, out of sheer frustration she had slapped me. I just stared at her, but said nothing. The incident was enough to split us up for a few weeks, until she had weakened, called and we got back together again.

The voice of the Captain announcing our descent into Norwegian airspace, brought me back into real time.

We landed at Stavanger or, more accurately, at Sola Airport. It seemed ironic that it was used by the German Luftwaffe as a base to raid Scotland, particularly Aberdeen, during WW2. I think the worst raid Aberdeen suffered was in 1943, when a flight of twenty five bombers raided from Stavanger, killing ninety-eight people and injuring over a hundred more. The house next to where my dad lived as a boy was bombed, taking a direct hit and one of his neighbours was killed. His school did not escape damage and one of his teacher's was seriously injured whilst on fire watch duties. My mum had her own experiences of the war and even though she was just a little girl she remembers the bombers attacking the ship yards where her brothers worked.

On arriving at Sola, the excitement levels in the camp had increased and there was a noticeable surge in light-hearted banter, as our Aberdeen contingent was met by representatives of our Norwegian hosts once we had passed through customs control. After a few congenial handshakes and muttered welcomes, they invited us to board a bus that would take us to the SAS Royal Hotel in Stavanger.

The dark grey of Aberdeen had by this time given way to broken sunshine in Norway, although it was still cold and breezy. The journey from Sola did not take long but somehow I felt that I liked the place. I liked the look of the wooden houses with their balconies, the well maintained gardens, their flag poles and their pennant style national flags fluttering in the breeze and I loved the countryside and its tree covered hills. The driver then explained over the speaker system that we were taking a slight detour, as we turned off the dual carriageway en route to town. We drove up past the site of an ancient Iron Age settlement and as we came over the brow of the hill, by the Ullandhaug TV tower, we marvelled at the view. The city of Stavanger, the islands and fjords spread out before us and in the distance snow-dusted mountains rose vertically out of the sea. Our hosts were pleased at the reaction they were getting and they sat smiling smugly at each other at the front of the coach, as the Aberdeen group muttered their appreciation of the view.

*****

Sir Arthur had arrived early. He did not want to jeopardise or prejudice the meeting by being late. Richardson was not the kind of man you kept waiting. He was always fastidious and punctual. Knox-De Vries casually looked around. The park was quiet. There was no sign of Richardson. He sat down on a bench and placed the black attaché case securely between his feet. He pulled the lapels of his cashmere coat in at the neck, then watched three young Arab children in the fenced-off play area, as they moved from swing to climbing frame to roundabout, under the alert and ever watchful eyes of their nannies and body guards. A grey squirrel plucked up the courage to venture over and scuttled to within a few feet of the case, sniffing and foraging for titbits. Sir Arthur watched it for a few seconds, surprised by its tameness. He looked at his watch, it was 10.59 am.

"Good morning, Sir Arthur, what can I do for you?" The voice was deep and incisive.

Knox-De Vries was slightly startled, he hadn't seen or heard Richardson approach.

"Ah! Mr Richardson, its good to see you again."

As Richardson stepped round to the front of the bench, the squirrel, sensing danger, scampered off for the safety of the nearest tree. Even with all the wealth and power at his disposal, Knox-De Vries was wary of Richardson, a man who radiated a skin-piercing chill of menace.

"Thank you for agreeing to see me at such short notice. Before I begin to explain my current requirement, can I just congratulate you on behalf of the group for the excellent work you carried out in France."

Richardson remained silent and unmoved by the praise, as Knox-De Vries went on to outline his latest project.

"Well Mr Richardson, what do you think?"

"Obviously, what you have requested to be carried out, can be done, but it requires exact planning based on the supply of credible intelligence information. It is going to be very high profile, the fall-out from this one will be even more intense than before and I will need the assistance of at least six trusted colleagues. What timescale are you working to?"

"To achieve maximum effect in my opinion, I would suggest before the end of the month."

Richardson raised his eyebrows and made a few mental calculations.

"Very well, I will take this on. My fee will be trebled and thereafter I do not wish to hear from you or your organisation again, is that clear? Furthermore I will require some advance working capital to fund some upfront expenses. At some stage I will have to make a short trip to Belgium, to meet with a religious acquaintance of mine who specialises in the provision of project hardware."

Knox-De Vries knew that Richardson's trip to one of the Low Countries would not be for the purposes of any spiritual cleansing. His soul had been given up as lost, a long time ago.

"I've taken the liberty of assuming you'd accept and the initial funds you require are here. On the subject of fees I accept your terms without condition and I will abide by all previous arrangements."

"In that case our business is concluded." Richardson snapped to attention, then turned and marched away.

"Good luck!" Knox-De Vries called after him.

Sir Arthur rose to his feet and walked away from the bench, in the direction of Park Lane, his hands seeking warmth deep in the linings of the pockets of his Crombie. He was now quietly confident that the entire operation would be planned and performed with the ease and surety of a highly trained, professional team.

*****

The hotel we had been booked into was indeed the SAS Royal. It was a fairly recently built building which overlooked old Stavanger, a quaint community of original wooden houses, painted white, with red roof tiles and narrow cobbled streets that had stood there, aged and stubborn, for hundreds of years, huddled closely together as protection from the harshness of the Northern winter. In direct contrast, the SAS as it was known, was very modern. It had a very clean and clinical marbled foyer that overlooked a restaurant area, housed beneath a glass atrium. Each floor of the hotel had been designed in the style/theme of a country: Norway, Japan, America and Italy. All the floors had internal balconies overlooking the atrium void which had been decorated with the flags and banners of the particular country it purported to represent.

As previously advised, no, I think warned is a more appropriate description, I was booked into a twin room with Roy on the Japanese floor. We completed, then signed the registration forms, were each given an electronic key card and we took the glass lift to the third floor.

Our room was large and faultlessly clean, although at first sight you certainly did not get the impression that you had walked into a geisha house in Kyoto! Some low black furniture and a couple of water prints of Fuji, certainly not Hokusai originals, were the only indication that we had been transported to the Land of the Rising Sun.

Roy and I unpacked our respective cases and suit holders and he held up his kilt against his flabby torso. He had hired a full Bonnie Prince Charlie outfit and it was obvious that he couldn't wait to wear it.

"Well, what do you think?" he asked.

I nodded my approval, held up my thumb and said sarcastically,

"You'll look great, Roy, I guess you'll be fighting them off."

By the look on Roy's face, he sadly, but obviously agreed with me. I am a great fan of the kilt as our national dress, it's smart and impressive and I have worn it many times, at weddings and other functions, but like so many other things Scottish, I hate its misuse and misrepresentation.

The trip itinerary had scheduled an introductory reception in the hotel that evening for an hour or so with several Norwegian dignitaries. The rest of the evening was free. There was to be an early start the next day when we would attend a commemorative service at the graves of three Scottish commandos who had been sent on a mission into occupied Norway during the last war. They had been informed on by Quisling collaborators and as a direct result they had been captured, tortured, then murdered by the Nazis, their bodies unceremoniously and callously dumped in the fjord. At great personal risk, for fear of Nazi retribution, some local people had retrieved the corpses and their remains had been laid to rest in a local church yard by the people of Stavanger, who had tended the graves ever since. There was also to be a series of talks on the state of the respective Norwegian and Scottish fishing industries.

Having a couple of hours to spare before the evening's festivities began, I decided not to join Roy in the bar. Instead I nipped down to the hotel pool for a swim. The facilities in the Hotel's Health Club were first class. There was the now obligatory sauna and steam room, a fully equipped gym with both free weights and a Nautilus system, a solarium and a warm, kidney shaped pool. The gym was unused, but a family of four sat laughing and chatting in the jacuzzi. I took advantage of the pool and easily swam thirty lengths. Sometime later I returned to my room and lay on the bed. I called Claire but there was no-one in, only the answer machine offering its invitation to leave a message.

"Claire, it's me. I've arrived safely, the views over the fjords toward the mountains are something else and the hotel's OK, I'll call you later. Bye."

I hated answer machines. I'm sure everyone does, but the gesture eased my conscience slightly.

I switched on the television and went channel-hopping with the remote control, through umpteen channels of crap, both English-speaking and foreign, before settling for a re-run of the classic American sixties programme, 'Bewitched'. Elizabeth Montgomery, who played the lead character Samantha, was a fantasy figure for me when I was a young boy and I dreamed of one day having a wife like her. She looked great and just by twitching her nose, she could give you anything you wanted. I kind of liked that idea (read into that what you want!)

I must have dozed off, but about an hour later I was woken by Roy coming back into the room.

"I've been speaking to a guy in the bar and he's told me there's a few good places to go tonight, so once we get shot of this lot, we can hit the town and check out the talent."

By 'this lot' I assumed he was referring to his lords and masters, the Councillors. "Sounds good," I said, playing him along.

I rolled off the bed and opened my case, found my Filofax, looked up Steve's number and dialled. The ringing tone was different to what I was used to in Scotland and I worried that there may be no-one home. Just as I was about to replace the receiver, I heard Steve's voice.

"Hello."

"Stephen, it's me, how are you doing?"

"Fine, when did you get in?"

"A few hours ago, we've just been getting settled in. I'm staying at the SAS."

We chatted on the phone for a couple of minutes as I described the group I was with, the flight over and my hotel room. Steve knew the SAS very well, having stayed there for a couple of weeks when he first moved over, before he rented his apartment. We arranged to meet that night at 10 pm, in a place called Newsman. Steve thought that the place would appeal to a hack like me.

I stripped and prepared to shower and shave. It had been a couple of years since I had played football seriously. I had kept myself in shape and carried no excess weight, but I could hardly have claimed to be at the peak of honed physical condition A daily regimen of press-ups and stomach exercises had been a habit I developed when I played and before showering, I quickly completed a circuit of a hundred press-ups and a hundred sit-ups. My body felt lean and hard, although not quite in the wash board abdomen class and it still carried traces of a Majorcan sun tan. Claire and I had holidayed on the island at her father's villa. The weather had been great, the villa luxurious and the setting perfect, high up on a hill, in its own grounds overlooking the Med, but the ten days had been fraught with Claire's petty rows and tantrums. I laughed to myself as I remembered that during one of her many mood swings at the villa, she had poured a pitcher of martini over me because I had forgotten it was the anniversary of our first meeting and to be honest it hadn't even registered with me as a milestone date. She had even made me sleep in one of the other rooms for the night - something I did without protest.

I showered, shaved, examined my face in the mirror for any tell tale signs of ageing, then dried myself off. I dressed smartly in a pair of beige trousers, Jaeger blazer, blue oxford button-down, a Boss tie and my trusty Timberland deck shoes. The reception was scheduled to begin at 7.30 pm and I was ready in good time. Roy, who had been ready for ages and had been down bevvying in the bar, had come back up for some extra cash and was wearing his kilt. After rooting around his case for his wallet, he left the room with me. We had just got into the lift and the doors closed behind us when Roy, being the refined and charming type, dropped his guts.

"You animal!" I said, disgusted with his behaviour, "that's putrid!"

"Better oot than in is what I always say," came the inane, defensive reply, a huge grin, creasing his reddened, podgy and unrepentant face. Sad.

To my horror, the lift stopped at the first floor and the family who had been in the jacuzzi stepped in. I felt totally embarrassed, but Roy was unperturbed. The parents remained impassive, but the two kids sniggered and exaggerated coughs all the way down to the ground floor. I could only glower at Roy, sickened by his moronic behaviour. As we got out of the lift, he volunteered his thoughts on the forthcoming proceedings.

"I hope to fuck this doesn't go on too long!"

Although I agreed with him, I would never have told him. As it was, the speeches of welcome were not over long and I made it very obvious to everyone that I was listening intently, taking copious notes as each speaker got up and soporifically delivered their presentation. The speeches over, we broke up and the food and drinks were served. The food, albeit pretty to look at, was a little bit lacking in substance, a sort of rye bread and prawn offering, no more than hors d'oeuvres. If you ate enough of them they did take the edge off of any hunger pangs. I could, after all, always get something later.

At 9.25 pm, the party broke up and the Norwegians bade us farewell and I was now effectively 'off-duty'. I finished my beer, shook hands with several of the Councillors, before setting off for the centre of Stavanger and my meeting with Steve. In perfect English, a very statuesque and quite stunning receptionist gave me instructions on how to find Newsman. I thanked her for her help and left the hotel. I'd only gone fifty or so metres down the hill toward the town centre when I heard the unmistakable clatter of leather brogues on the cobbles and Roy's dulcet tones cutting through the peace of the evening.

"Hold on a minute! Wait for me! Where are you going?" panted Roy.

"I'm meeting my brother for a beer. Come if you like."

"Aye, I'll do that, then maybe the three of us can go hunting babes! I didn't know you had a brother over here."

I smiled to myself. I knew that my younger brother would not mind the company, but I also knew how Steve's mind worked and that his first impression of Roy would be...clueless git, where did you find him? We Robertson brothers could spot a 'tube' at over a hundred paces and our tolerance threshold for people who did not meet our acceptance criteria was very low. I have always had a fairly strong perception of what was and what wasn't acceptable in terms of people's behaviour, their dress and sense of style and, with females, what was attractive and beautiful and what wasn't. I always felt I had an instinctive eye and could spot the difference between those wearing plastic shoes and those wearing genuine leather with the first once-over. To me, first impressions always mattered.

We walked on down the hill from the SAS, past the main Post Office and the Breiavatnet lake to our right and then across to the city centre itself. A beautiful, medieval Kirk, the Stavanger Domkirke, positioned on a slight rise, stood like a sentinel at the entrance to the sentrum, overlooking the fjord, or Vagen as it was known, the waters of which cut right into the heart of the town. An American navy communications vessel en route to a NATO exercise was berthed there, its massive, grey bulk dominating all the surrounding vessels and buildings.

Carefully following the receptionist's instructions, we walked through the market place, past the statue of the Stavanger author Alexander Kielland, then on through the narrow streets, passing several young girls who all either laughed or shouted something at Roy. The poor guy was in his element, but sadly on another planet.

"I told you these Norwegian girls love a guy in the kilt, they're probably all dying for it. By the way, where the fuck's this pub? I'm suffering from alcohol withdrawal, I'm gasping for a beer."

I just smiled and said nothing.

A few paces further on, we came upon Newsman's which was situated close by a number of other pubs and discos. We entered Newsman's and were given a friendly greeting by the doorman. It was about 10.05 pm and the bar was busy, even though it was a Thursday night. It soon became apparent why it was called Newsman's; the walls were adorned with various framed front pages of international publications such as Time and Life magazine, with their banner headlines covering everything from JFK's assassination, the D-Day landings, Neil Armstrong in 1969, Lennon's murder, Gorby and the collapse of Communism and the Berlin Wall. It was all interesting stuff and I would have loved to have taken the time to have studied them in greater detail, fascinated as I was by the trivia of general knowledge. They also had several old typewriters hooked or nailed up on the walls and shelves filled, end to end, with leather bound books and tomes above the booth seating which helped enhance the effect.

"Well, what do you think of my local then?" It was Steve. We shook hands and I gave him a pat on the back.

"How's the oil industry, then?" I asked.

"Its a load of crap, as you well know, but I can't complain too much, as it keeps me in beers and labels!"

Steve was worse than me when it came to buying clothes.

I turned round, "Steve can I introduce you to my room mate, my inside man in Aberdeen's corridors of power, the Summerhill stallion, the rampant Roy Calder. Roy's going to join us for a few beers."

Steve shook Roy's hand and I could see he had already begun to form an opinion. Steve glanced at me and winked and I knew what he was thinking. First impressions!

"I suppose you'll know where all the talent is Steve. Where's the best place to go huntin' beaver?" asked our kilted Don Juan, as he fumbled about with his sporran, "they're there, thank fuck! I thought I'd forgot my rubbers."
Roy's comments merely served to confirm what Steve was thinking and we both laughed. Whose protection were the condoms for?

"What's so funny? What's the joke?" asked Roy innocently.

"Nothing for you to worry about Roy, sometimes we Robertsons just think funny things."

Steve ordered two beers and a diet coke for himself and we spent the next hour or so chatting about Stavanger, the local football team, the oil industry and some background to the trip Roy and I were on.

"It seems to be a really busy place in terms of night life," I commented.

"Yes, it is now, but about ten years ago there was only one pub! In the old days, when they'd got fed up raping and pillaging, the only industry was the sea and fortunes were made in shipping, fishing and canning, but since Stavanger became a centre of the oil industry, pubs and clubs have been springing up everywhere. It was by all accounts a bit of a 'hick' town and I've heard it described, by some 'expats', as Fort William with oil, but that's unfair in my opinion. It should be busy in town tonight, there's a Yank ship in the Vagen and the streets will soon be crawling with refugees from a Brat Pack or a Spike Lee movie!"

"Yes, it's some size of a ship. I couldn't help but notice it on the way here."

"They've actually had the QE2 moored here, the water is so bloody deep, but as I said, tonight the place will soon be full of crew-cuts, good ol' boys and ghetto boys."

"And there's plenty of *ugly* women going about," I said sarcastically. Steve raised his eyebrows and nodded, then changed the subject.

"How are you getting on with the property business? Any new projects coming up?"

"Things are OK, I've got a couple of small deals looming, you know, buying houses and getting long term leasing deals on them and I've also got my eye on a couple of sites with great potential which I'm following up on, but I'm keeping that fairly close to my chest, for obvious reasons - you can't trust anybody these days." There was no way I was giving away information like that in front of a council employee! "Have you spoken to mum recently?"

"Yeah, I phoned the other day. Her and dad are finally committing to coming over in the Spring. I'll take a few day's leave when they're here and show them round."

"Good stuff, I bet the old man won't believe the prices over here!"

"I don't even think about it now, but I couldn't believe it when I was first over. I'd go out for a quiet pint with the lads and end up spending a fortune. What's the weather been like in Aberdeen?"

"Awful, the last couple of weeks have been bloody 'Bertie' and it was a bit 'Mork and Mindy' when we left".

Roy interrupted.

"*Bertie, Mork and Cindy*, what are you two talking about?"

Steve laughed and began to explain, in a slightly exaggerated 'bools in the mooth', English accent.

"We're discussing the inclement weather you're having in Aberdeen. 'Bertie Auld' means 'cauld' and 'Mork and Mindy' is..."

"Windy!" said Roy, as the penny dropped. You could see him trying to remember the phrases for his own use back in Aberdeen.

"How's Claire?" Steve asked.

"Pretty good...I think?"

"That sounds ominous, I bet she's not exactly delighted that you're over here." Steve grinned. He knew Claire would be well pissed off with me, and that pleased him. He quite liked her, but he hated her arrogance, and her extreme views on politics and feminism. More to the point he had never got used to me being with someone else since Hannah had died.

"It's the Law Society Ball on Friday. She's hacked off because I'm not going to be there."

"Didn't you miss that last year?"

I grimaced and nodded.

"I bet you're not exactly popular, but you will go for the career-minded, social climbing type."

As the conversation grew too personal for Roy to understand, he ordered another round and suggested that after they were finished we go on somewhere else.

We drank up and Steve led us downstairs in to a lower basement bar which I hadn't realised existed and from there out through a fire exit in to a yard at the back of the premises. We dodged some empty kegs of beer, some broken crates and a large offshore container. On pushing open a battered and paint peeled door we found ourselves in a place called the Fun Pub. The result of five months' local knowledge and a few boozy nights out with the lads in the project team had produced this alternative route in and somehow I knew it wasn't an official entrance.

Steve turned to Roy and commented with more than just a hint of sarcasm.

"Here you are Roy, this is a place where the girls will just love a guy in a kilt."

"What's it called?"

"The Fun Pub."

"The *Fud* Pub! That'll do me. I'll probably have to get my knob out at some stage," Roy laughed. Steve just looked at me.

The pub was packed. It was long and narrow in shape but opened up at the back, where two blokes were doing their best to shoot a game of pool while everyone else danced and bopped to the music. The music, which was the pub's outstanding feature, was loud, very loud, and I could feel the bass vibrate through my chest. Very little money had been invested on fitting out the bar but, judging by its popularity, refurbishment plainly wasn't an issue. The atmosphere was brilliant and reminded me greatly of a wee pub in Ibiza called the Pink Panther that opened at mid-night and as soon as the music started it used to just bop!

"Great place, great record," I shouted to Steve.

It was the Smiths' "This Charming Man" being blasted out of the speakers.

"Yeah, this place is jumping tonight."

"Music always sounds better when the volume's given a bit of welly."

We literally fought our way to the bar and I ordered a round. There were only two barmen on duty, but they handled the orders that were being shouted at them from all directions with good-humour and ease.

True to form, Roy was in his element and after some minimal coaxing from Steve and myself, he actually climbed up on to the pool table and gave an impromptu Highland Fling. He had by this time dispensed with his bow-tie, his waistcoat was open and his shirt was unbuttoned, revealing his sweating, hairy paunch. People were shouting and applauding, but I felt it was more out of pity and embarrassment for him than admiration. As I've said before, he was a stereotype reinforcement of the 'Drunken Jock/Brigadoon' brigade. My dad would have described him as a bit of a 'Neep'. I had previously experienced that 'Neep' mentality at Wembley for a Scotland-England game in the late seventies and what I'd seen then did not make me proud. The romantic notion that we were there as some great invading Highland host soon disappears when you see a broken glass being stuck in someone's face, or grown men urinating in the street in full view of women and children, or an open razor being brandished in the confined space of a railway carriage. Nowadays my blood was stirred by the sight of the Scottish rugby team and their pre-match rendition of 'Flower of Scotland', with the massed backing of a capacity Murrayfield crowd.

27

"Struth!" I panted, almost spilling my drink.

"What's up?" asked Steve.

"You know that girl who's been eyeing us up?"

"The one who was standing by the pillar? Bit on the chunky side? With shoulders like a member of the Chinese ladies swimming team. Eyeing YOU up to be precise!"

"Whatever, but that's the fella, well, that sophisticated young lady, with the convent upbringing, has just walked past me and tried to stick her finger up my poop chute!"

"Unless you fancy your chances, I'd say it's time to exit stage left," laughed Steve, "before you get us into any trouble with the local girls."

At 11.50 pm we left Roy and the Fun Pub and went to a nearby club called, quite simply, New York. It was full of young trendy Norwegians and a smattering of 'expats'.

Steve, who was driving, was on soft drinks, and as I was working the next day there was no point in getting rat-arsed, so I too had a Diet Coke or Coke Lite, as they call it in Vikingsville. Coping with a hangover was not a family strong point. It wasn't just our looks we had inherited from our Dad.

"You must have some life over here lad?" I said, as yet another very attractive girl passed us on her way to the bar.

"You forget that I'm a happily, almost married man and besides Jane would cut my balls off if she thought I was playing away from home," smirked Steve and he continued, "but you're right, a man could get into serious trouble over here."

I knew exactly what he meant.

We both laughed and ordered another couple of diet cokes, just as a group of four girls came towards us.

"Hello Stephen."

I looked at Steve and raised my eyebrows. Steve blushed and laughed and then introduced me to Sissel his secretary. She then introduced her friends, Anja, Silje and Wenche and explained that they were having a bit of a reunion as they had all been at school together and this was the first time they had all met up in years. As I shook hands with Anja, our eyes met and we held our gaze for a few brief seconds.

Steve offered them all a drink, but they all politely refused and returned to the dance floor.

"Sissel seems nice," I said.

"Yes," agreed Steve "too bloody nice!"

Steve chatted on and I listened, my back to the dance floor. Sometime later Steve disappeared off to the toilet and Anja, by far the prettiest one from the group of four approached me.

"Hi, have you seen the others? I seem to have lost them." Her English was perfect and her accent was well...you know what I mean.

"No, I haven't, sorry...eh! would you like a drink?"

"Yes, please can I have a Farris."

I just looked at her, she could see I didn't know what a Farris was.

"It's a mineral water," she laughed.

I nodded, turned to the bar and bought her a drink. She noticed that I wasn't drinking and she offered me a drink from her glass. I hesitated, then shyly accepted. I took a sip of the ice cold water and lemon and thanked her. I liked her immediately.

"Do you work in the oil industry?" I asked naively.

"No, Sissel and the others do. I work in Oslo at the University for Professor Bjorn Pederson. I'm his Research Assistant. This is actually the first time I have been home for some time. It's nice to see my family and friends again," she explained.

Anja Andresen was 24, tall, slim, blond haired, had perfect skin and lips with a wonderful bee-sting pout. A classic Scandinavian. The name of her boss meant nothing to me, but I assumed by the reverential way she talked about him that he was some big shot and reasonably well known in Norway.

"I don't know where the girls are, maybe they've gone home?" She looked at me, smiled and shrugged.

Just then Steve appeared. He glanced at his watch.

"Look its getting late, I'll have to go and get a taxi...you coming?"

"No, I think I'll hang on." I said it without hesitation, but not daring to look round at Anja.

"Well tell you what, give me a call at the office tomorrow and we'll arrange for you to come round to the apartment. See ya later."

Steve left and I was alone with Anja. She seemed to sense my boyish unease.

"Would you like to dance with me?" she asked.

I hesitated, then nodded. She placed her glass on the bar, took my hand and led me to the dance floor.

When the record finished, the pelvically rhythmic beat of Marvin Gaye's "Sexual Healing" began and Anja looked at me, but I averted my gaze.

"If you don't want to dance with me it's alright," she said.

I gently took her hand.

"No, it's not that." For a moment I thought of Claire; what would she be thinking if she knew I was out dancing with a young, beautiful Norwegian girl, with my brotherly chaperon having already left the scene of the crime - guilty no doubt.

"It's OK, I'm glad you asked me to dance."

The great man was followed by Phyllis Nelson's "Move Closer" and then Jane Birkin's "Je t'aime". It's funny, most people remember "Je t'aime" for the somewhat orgasmic sound effects but, when you're actually dancing to it, it has a genuinely lovely melody and string arrangement.

Gradually, my shyness and unease passed and I relaxed in to the dance. I opened my hand and my fingers entwined with Anja's. We didn't speak, we just moved slowly around the dance floor, our bodies coming closer and closer, until we were dangerously close.

When the slow music stopped, I eased myself away from Anja's hold. She smiled, took my hand and led me off the dance floor. Sissel and the others were waiting for us at the bar.

Sissel asked where Steve was and I explained that he had decided to go home. She looked disappointed.

30

"Anja, we're going back to Per Christian's for a party, are you coming?"

Anja turned and looked at me, but I avoided catching her eye.

"No, I don't think so, I'm a little tired, you all go and I'll call you tomorrow."

Sissel, Silje and Wenche said something in Norwegian to Anja, then they all kissed and hugged her before they said goodnight to me and left.

"You should have gone with them," I said.

"No, I'm not really in the party mood. I'm tired and its time for me to go home."

For a moment I thought about Claire, then suddenly I blurted out.

"Can I walk you home?" I asked sheepishly. The classic, corny, old fashioned cliché.

Anja laughed, "No it's alright, you can't walk me home." Before she had even finished her sentence, I felt a warm blush of embarrassment wash over my face, but she continued.

"You can walk me to my taxi though. My parents stay near Madla, a few kilometres from the sentrum and I don't think you'd thank me if I took you up on your offer and we walked there."

"Madla! That's where Steve stays," I stated, hoping to impress her with my knowledge of the city and its suburbs.

Anja smiled then said, "Come on then let's go, walk me to my taxi."

We left the club and walked along by the Vagen. I dodged to be on her outside nearest the road and I explained that my mum had always told me that gentlemen always walk on the outside. Anja giggled approvingly at my 'olde worlde' manners.

"Not many Norwegian men would do that." She sounded disappointed.

We walked to a taxi rank outside the Atlantic Hotel directly opposite the Breiavatnet Lake, but there was a long queue.

"Where are you staying, Paul?"

"The SAS."

"Oh, that's a nice place. Instead of waiting here, I'll walk up the hill with you to the hotel, it's not far and I can get a taxi from there."

"Are you sure?"

"Yes, it's alright, besides I can't let you walk home all by yourself in a strange town. You'd probably get lost."

She laughed at her own joke and took my arm. I didn't object. I didn't feel uncomfortable and we walked slowly up the hill to the SAS Royal. We traded on our backgrounds, or rather she told me about her life. She talked constantly, I didn't say much. She told me about her job in Oslo which she obviously adored and how exciting life was working in the Faculty of Political Sciences. She explained that she had a great working relationship with her boss, the Professor, and that she got on very well with his wife and two children. He was apparently an authority on some issue like international politics. She had left Stavanger a couple of years or so earlier, after graduation and following the break up of a long term relationship. She came home only rarely. Her parents and younger brothers still lived in Stavanger, but they were leaving for a holiday in the States on the Monday, so it was nice to come home and see them before they left as well as meeting up with her old pals. I interrupted when I could and I explained the reason for my visit to Stavanger. By this time Anja was holding my hand.

"Your hands are cold," I said.

"I know, but I have a warm heart!"

It was one of Hannah's sayings. Spooky!

All too soon we arrived at the SAS. After crossing the road, we stood outside the entrance to the hotel and I broke the silence that had grown between us.

"Do you want to come in and I'll ask the receptionist to call a taxi for you?"

"No, it's alright, I'll be able to wave one down from here...you go in if you like."

"Well, it *is* past my bedtime, but I think I'll stay and make sure you get safely into a taxi."

My manners and concern, mixed with my shyness, seemed to charm her and I hoped she was as attracted to me as I was to her. We stood in the shelter of the hotel entrance and she took my hand and touched the gold ring on my finger.

"Are you married?" she asked, looking directly at me, "it's always the married ones I seem to fall for." She paused, then added reflectively, "The nicest ones are always taken."

I shook my head and looked away, before explaining.

"I was married but my wife died three years ago."

"I'm sorry, I didn't realise."

I didn't think she thought it possible for someone to be a widower at 29.

"It's OK," I said softly.

Just then a taxi pulled up and Anja stepped forward and opened the door. I handed her a 100 Kroner note but she just smiled and handed it back to me. She kissed me gently on the lips, pushed her hand through my hair, climbed into the taxi and was gone. Fortunately I had managed to slip the note to the driver. It had been a chance meeting, and now I was left standing outside the hotel collecting my thoughts and feelings. A complete stranger, a very beautiful stranger whom I had met less than three hours ago, had danced with me, shared a drink with me, had kissed me goodnight before disappearing off into the Stavanger darkness. I felt different. I shivered, then turned and walked into the foyer, said goodnight to the girl on reception and took the lift to the Japanese floor. Roy was already in bed, his kilt lay in an unkempt heap on the floor. I switched on the bathroom light and undressed, folded my clothes neatly and went to bed. I wasn't ready for sleep. Too much excitement. Too many worries. Christ! I didn't even know her last name or even a phone number. I resigned myself to never seeing her again and I felt the pain.

In Aberdeen, Claire had come home after dining out with some colleagues. She played her answer phone messages, muttered the word bastard and went to bed.

Chapter 2

CHAPTER 2

The telephone rang at exactly 7.30 am with my alarm call. I jumped out of bed and quickly completed a hundred odd press-ups. I thought of Anja and it saddened me to think I would never see her again. Still, I was a few years older than her and she probably hadn't even liked me that much. I tried to push her to the back of my mind, but the memories were still too fresh to go away and they continued to flit in and out of my thoughts, disturbing me. Haunting me. The alarm call had also woken Roy from his slumbers.

"What happened to you guys last night? One minute you were in that Fun Pub place, then you'd gone."

"It got too lively for us, Roy, so we left. We did try and find you but you were deeply engrossed with some big, red haired bird."

Roy seemed to find my explanation acceptable and he began to recount his attempted seduction of the red head. It seemed that he had not had a successful night, although he had found a perverted consolation in the 'hundreds' of girls who wanted to know what he had under his kilt!

I showered, dressed in a dark, softly tailored suit, white shirt, Ralph Lauren tie and black Churchill brogues. My clothes were dark and sober as I did not know what to expect when we went to the graveside. I waited for Roy to prepare himself for the day

34

and we went down to the front door together.

The morning light was grey and flat, the sunshine of the day before having given way to a light drizzle, but it wasn't cold. I nipped back up to the room for my raincoat and got back to the foyer as the coach taking us to the cemetery arrived.

There must have been around fifty of us standing over the graves of the three young Scotsmen who had died all those years ago, fighting for the freedom of this foreign land, struggling to rid it of the tyranny of National Socialism. The local Mayor and the Church of Scotland minister who had travelled with us, delivered their eulogies, then the group stood, heads bowed for a minute's silence. The proceedings were solemn. The faces of those who had gathered were pale and serious, their hair dampened by the incessant drizzle and the all enveloping mist of the Haar. The stillness and the silence of the morning was eventually broken by a lone piper playing the heart tearing lament, 'the Flooers o' the Forest', which I think originally commemorated the grievous loss of life of tens of thousands of Scots at Flodden, its message no less potent here. I thought about the terrible waste of life and I made a mental note to research their mission and their subsequent deaths when I got back to Aberdeen. I thought too of the ones who had been left behind in Scotland. The wives, the girlfriends and most poignantly of all, the mothers. They would have waited and waited and waited for their boys to come home. The words of the Andy Stewart song, 'Scottish Soldier', crept into my mind and although they had not been buried among 'Highland hills' or 'Island Hills', these Scottish soldiers had been laid to rest with a view of distant, rugged mountains. It was, I thought, an appropriate and fitting substitute for their native Scotland.

The music drifted, the last mournful notes fading away into the morning air. I felt sad. Pathos. Many of the men standing there may have wanted to, but they did not succumb to tears. It's hard for men to cry in public. The minister was now speaking, but I didn't really hear him... 'At the going down of the sun and in the morning, we will remember them. We will remember them'. The drizzle had become heavier, the cloud lower. It all seemed to suit the sombre mood of the morning. I looked around at my cold, damp colleagues, convinced it had been a good decision to take my coat. The service over, we boarded the bus which took us back to the hotel. It seemed to me that it would have been quicker to walk back, but the prevailing weather made this an impractical option for many of my more inappropriately dressed colleagues.

After lunch, the next item on the itinerary was a trip to an oil industry fabrication yard. We were shown around the facilities in small groups and although I took some notes I was distracted. I kept thinking about Anja. In fact, I don't even remember any of the details of the visit, although the majority of our party were in awe of the sheer size of the operation they had seen and being the bunch of boring, self-important farts that they were, I couldn't help but cringe every time one of them opened his gub and spouted out the most ludicrous and inane questions. Maybe, that's a little unfair, as very few of them had any real oil industry knowledge, other than what the Region and District Councils fed them in their bulletins, plus the parochial coverage in the local dailies and, most importantly of all, the fact that they lived in Aberdeen, absorbing the influences of 'Europe's Oil Capital'. Some of these guys actually believed all that tosh and still used cliched and hackneyed expressions such as 'Black Gold', 'Oil Bonanza' and the rest, when talking shop with the yard's reps. The 'Topsides' modules of a Production Platform were currently under construction at the yard, its artificial lighting and metallic bulk blending in surprisingly well with the natural surroundings of sea and rock. As the guide proudly led us round the yard, I wondered what the hell had gone wrong in the UK and in particular in Scotland, where indigenous companies had not, in the main, taken advantage of what opportunities had arisen. My experience was that Scotland was merely a base office for Dutch, French, American, Italian and Norwegian companies. We had welcomed them in with open arms in the late sixties and seventies, and as a result we had pissed away our home advantage.

After our tour of the yard, we again boarded the bus and we were taken to view the offices of a local, family controlled, Stavanger shipping company, which over the past twenty or so years had diversified into the drilling and production business, both in the Norwegian and the UK sector of the North Sea, as well as overseas. I didn't know much about the ship-owning business, but I had always held the impression, it was an industry of great tradition, with gentlemen players and rogues. This firm was conservative with a small 'c' and strictly on the level. Their offices impressed everyone, especially the views from the upper floors which looked out uninterrupted over old Stavanger and over the fjords to the mountains. I thought it would be a nightmare place to work, given the scenic distractions. I knew I would never get anything done. In the vast open plan reception area, there were several glass display cabinets, each housing an exact, scaled down replica of the company's tanker and rig fleet, both past and present.

We were given a brief video presentation on the history of the company, from its earliest beginnings to its present position as a very cash rich, asset based organisation which would shame its UK counterparts. The place oozed with an understated air of success, seeped in a tradition of generations of shrewd and conservative business acumen.

We returned to the hotel at about 5.45 pm. While the fishery executives and council representatives went into session, I went to my room, changed and went down to the pool. I should have attended the meeting, but I couldn't be arsed. As I came out of the lift by reception, the receptionist called me over and informed me that she had taken a telephone message for me. I hoped it would be from Anja, so I was a little disappointed to see that it was from Steve. He was going to pick me up at seven and take me back to the apartment. I glanced at my watch and decided to give the swimming pool a miss. I took the lift back up to my room, changed into my jeans, a dark blue polo-shirt, my Timberlands and my favourite RL deck jacket.

Surprisingly enough, for a man who didn't usually know the meaning of the word punctual, Steve appeared promptly at 7 pm and we drove out to Madla. He drove his car effortlessly through the streets, having acquired a sound knowledge of the layout of Stavanger and its satellite villages and suburbs and by now he was well used to the differences in driving between the UK and Norway, although he did fire off a salvo of expletives at a female driver who cut out on him at a junction.

"Who had the right of way there then?" I asked.

"Fuck knows!" he laughed.

"By the way, Sissel was asking all about you today. How did you get on with her mate last night?" he asked sardonically. I feigned memory loss.

"Which one was that?"

"The very pretty one in the red dress."

"Oh her! I think she disappeared off in a taxi, just after you left," I said dismissively and immediately changing the subject, "Are you still into your jogging?"

"Yes, I often take one of the routes up through the trees where the TV tower is," he explained, pointing to the large white tower on the tree covered hill we had passed in the coach on the way in from Sola.

"You get a fantastic view from up there. I tell you what, why don't we go for a run up there before you go back to Aberdeen?"

"That'll be fuckin' right!" I said, fighting images from my footballing past when I used to go through the hellish nightmare known as 'pre-season training'. Every year, in preparation for the new season, we would get physically thrashed with boring, repetitive running exercises. Up hills, down hills, up sand dunes, down sand dunes. It always used to kill me and I invariably ended up breathing through my arse. Mind you, somehow I always managed to save a bit for the game at the end of the session. Hannah always had a laugh at the state I was in when I came home from a training session, ashen faced, unable to speak, barely able to move. Steve also knew what I was like and laughed.

We motored on down the hill before turning off the main road by the primary school and onto the lane that led to Steve's place. His apartment was fairly modern looking from the outside and to be honest quite unappealing, but once inside it was great. It had spacious rooms on two levels, all laid out with wooden floors and on the upper level the dining area had glass doors that led out onto a balcony with great views over the fjord to Sola airport and the sea. Steve explained that the water we could see was the Harfsfjord and on its shoreline, although he wasn't exactly sure of the accuracy of his version of the story, it was said that a great battle was fought by the armies of three Norse Kings, in a time long past. There was now a permanent memorial there, symbolising the swords of the three Kings who, on calling a truce at the end of the battle, plunged their swords into the ground, then made a pact never to fight again, thus uniting their divided lands and creating the Norwegian nation.

Jane, Steve's fiancee, was pleased to see me. We were fond of each other. I was comfortable with her. She was very pretty, had a wicked sense of humour and she kept Steve in line, as well as running around cleaning up after him and keeping him organised. Having missed the evening meal, I was ready for several cold beers and the home-delivered pizza that had been ordered. As we ate, we chatted about life in Norway and it was fairly evident that things were going well for them and would soon get better now that Jane had picked up some temporary work which would give her an interest. I got the impression that Steve had forewarned her about the Claire situation, as it was diplomatically never mentioned. We spent about two and a half hours together, then I said I'd have to get back. Jane, who hadn't been drinking, offered to drive me back to the hotel. I said I would as easily get a taxi, but she insisted.

The journey back to the hotel seemed quicker than the journey out and we soon arrived outside the SAS.

"What are your plans for tomorrow?" Jane asked.

"I've got to attend a civic function in a hall at the Atlantic Hotel tomorrow afternoon, then it's back to Aberdeen late on Sunday. Tell Steve I'll give him a call to arrange a time for us to meet before I go back."

Jane said goodnight and I thanked her for putting up with me for the last couple of hours. She drove off back to Madla and I thought about her and Steve. My younger brother was very successful, the oil industry had been good for him. He was earning good money and he was obviously happily involved with Jane. I wasn't envious. As brothers go, we got along fine.

I waved and watched as the car disappeared, before turning and going into the hotel. My heart seemed to skip a beat, as Anja approached me.

"Hei, have you had a good day in Stavanger?"

38

"Yes, it's been OK," I answered.

I then gave her a quick summary of the day's events. I described to her the solemnity and sadness of the scene at the gravesides of the three soldiers, the trip around the yard and the shipping company offices and finally the pizza and beers with Steve and Jane.

"I hope you don't mind me coming to see you, but I wanted to return your money."

"You didn't have to do that," I replied, "I just felt bad about leaving you to go home in the taxi on your own."

"You're too nice...here is your money." She held out her hand with the note.

"Sorry, I can't accept it, but I 'll tell you what, you can use it to buy us a drink if you want?"

Anja laughed, "OK, I do that, but I just want a coffee though."

I led her through the hotel foyer to the Chicago Bar and ordered two white coffees. The young barman grinned and set about making our order.

"I'm glad you came, have you been waiting long?"

"No, maybe ten or fifteen minutes, in fact I was just about to leave when you came back."

"I'm glad you didn't."

The barman carried our coffees on a tray to the table and Anja duly paid him. She played with her spoon, toying with the froth in her cup and every now and then she would look up at me and smile. Sometimes she would catch her lower lip between her perfect teeth. There was a naturalness about this girl, not just in her outstanding looks, but in her expressions and the way she moved and acted, that provoked and awakened all sorts of thoughts within me.

It felt good to talk to her and be near her. For some reason I had felt a dull ache inside at the thought of never seeing her again, but that had now evaporated and gone.

"What are you doing tomorrow?" she asked. "Do you have any free time?"

"Late afternoon I have to attend a reception in the Atlantic hotel, but apart from that, the day is mine."

"Would you like to go for a walk tomorrow? I'll take you to a nice place that has an art gallery, a cafe and some nice walks along the beach."

"Hmm, I don't know you that well," I frowned "I don't know if a nice, quiet Scots boy like me should go away with a strange and mysterious, beautiful Norwegian girl I hardly know."

"Fuck you!"

She rose up out of her seat as if to leave. Her response startled me and I realised that my adolescent attempt at wit and charm had failed miserably and I grabbed her hand. Maybe I had offended her and for a few seconds there was an injured silence.

"I'm sorry, I was trying to be a smart-ass...name a time and I'll be ready."

"Is 10.30 too early?"

"No, sounds good."

"OK, I have to go now."

I took her hand and we walked to the door of the hotel.

"Do you need a taxi?"

"No, it's alright, I have my car, it's parked over there."

She pointed to a dark blue Volvo estate, overtaken by the years, sitting under the trees on the other side of the road, outside an oriental rug shop.

"Don't laugh," she pleaded, "that's my baby. She got me all the way up here from Oslo yesterday."

"I like your car," I said nodding my approval.

We crossed the road hand in hand to the car. It had seen better days and I would have hated to guess the mileage. She had left it unlocked and I opened the driver's door for her. Anja sat in the car and smiled up at me.

"OK, I see you tomorrow. Take a warm jacket, it might be cold."

I wanted to kiss her and hold her, but I didn't. The fear of rejection was a fear I wasn't yet prepared to risk, so I decided not to make a move and just closed the door. Anja turned the key in the ignition and the engine roared into life. She casually waved good-bye, swung the car round and drove off.

I went back into the hotel. The reception area was quiet, but there were one or two people in the bar. The thought of a late night drinking session with these guys didn't impress me, so I returned to my room. Roy wasn't there and his kilt was also missing. I went to bed, flicked through the satellite channels with the remote, but after five minutes of MTV, then CNN and then MTV, I switched off and eventually fell into a light sleep. I vaguely remember Roy falling into the room a few hours later, but I ignored his drunken mutterings.

I woke and rose early next day and after the usual exercises, I showered, dressed and went down for breakfast. The girl on reception politely said good morning as I walked into the restaurant area. I was just about to sit at a table by the small fountain, when two of the councillors called me over and invited me to join them. They then broke the news that the party of Scots MPs, Fisheries and Scottish Office officials would not now be travelling over. Some crisis in the Commons had caused the Party Whips to recall everyone to London. What a bastard! They were the real reason I had made the trip over. I wanted to nail one of the officials over allegations on the misuse of organisational funds. Bastard! Bastard! Bastard! It would just have to wait. The week-end would now just have to be a bit of a holiday. Claire would be pleased. The waitress poured me some tea then, from the 'help yourself' breakfast buffet, I had some cornflakes. This was followed by some sausages and bacon that were, to say the least, just that little bit different to what I was used to back home in Scotland. I then spent a quite un-enthralling thirty minutes with my councillor friends, discussing with them what a success the trip had been and I suggested they would have to reciprocate and invite their Norwegian colleagues over to Aberdeen. They thought this was a marvellous idea. I put up with them for a further twenty minutes. It's quite amazing, but it's the apathy of the rest of us that allows people like them to get into positions of power. They eventually excused themselves from the table and headed into town to do some sight seeing and some shopping. To be honest they were arsewipes, but I suppose they were harmless arsewipes!

I took the lift back up to the Japanese floor and opened the door of our room, only to be greeted by the retching sounds of a seriously hung over man emanating from the loo.

"Everything alright in there?" I said, sniggering to myself at Roy's zombie-like figure slumped over the WC.

It was difficult to comprehend the pained response. I checked to see I was carrying enough money, then I shouted a good-bye to Roy before taking the lift back down. The weather was a little brighter, but showers were forecast and there was a stiff

41

westerly breeze blowing. I had taken Anja's advice and had put on a jacket. I hovered around reception and the foyer, trying and probably failing to look cool. Trying not to constantly look at my Tag. She was after all only four minutes and thirty seconds late! Roy's unfortunate condition had prevented me using the toilet in the room, so I decided to take a chance and go to the loo in the Leisure Centre, as I was desperately needing a pee. Pre-date nerves. I jumped down the stairs, did what I had to do and was back in no time, but as Sod's Law would have it, Anja was waiting for me when I returned. She was sitting patiently in the foyer, on a beautifully restored barber's chair, its red leather in perfect condition, its chrome and brass work polished and gleaming.

Anja stepped off the chair, walked forward and kissed me.

"Hei! Are you ready to go?"

"Yes."

She took my hand and led me to her car. I didn't think of Claire and I didn't see the blood-shot eyes of Roy following us as we left the hotel. Today she was dressed in a navy blue turtle neck, faded 501s held up by a thick black leather belt and a pair of desert boots. A red Helly Hansen jacket was thrown over the seat in the back. She looked great. Great in the kind of way only foreign girls look...both beautiful and alluring and the way they wear their Levi's...it was almost too much for a clean living Scots boy who had led a very sheltered life. She had the kind of looks that usually attract a salvo of jealous comment from certain British females; you know the kind of things, 'they're not so keen as us on personal hygiene' or, 'they don't shave their armpits you know'. My only comment to all that is "Bolleaux!" - which is continental for Bollocks!

As usual, Anja did all the talking, but every now and then I would interrupt with some sarcastic quip. Sometimes she would laugh, sometimes my attempt at humour would somehow get lost in translation and the remark would just sail over her head, without a reaction.

"Tell me about Norway, Anja."

"Sure, I do that."

It was an obvious question, but it not only touched a nerve, it was like pressing a start button. She proceeded to tell me about the country, its people, their Royal Family (who seemed to be a little bit more in touch with reality, than the English lot) and the fact that she actually owned her own national costume. It had been a present from her parents and was very expensive because of the time and effort spent on the intricate embroidery and the silver decorations. It wasn't uncommon for people in Norway,

42

especially females, to have their own national costume and she went on to explain that she wore hers every 17th of May, Norway's National Day. It's the biggest day of the year in the country's calendar, as all over Norway the people celebrate their independence from Sweden. It wasn't a day to show off military might, it was a day to celebrate the country's traditions and its past, as well as its future, with the emphasis of the celebrations being on the children. She would also wear the costume on other special or formal occasions at the University in Oslo.

It was becoming increasingly obvious to me that these Norwegians were very nationalistic and fiercely proud of their country and its history. I told her that ever since I could remember, I had been fascinated by Norse mythology. As a boy I had read stories about Beowulf, Grendal, Thor, Balder, Odin, Loki, Valhalla, the Valkyries, Asgard and Midgard. She seemed to approve. I also tried to describe one of my favourite piano pieces of all time, a piano duet by Grieg which I didn't know the name of, but my efforts to give her a vocal rendition foundered miserably. She failed to recognise the tune and we both laughed. I did manage to name five famous Norwegians, believe it or not, five Norwegian cities and some Norwegian football players. I guess she was pleased that I knew more about Norway than she had expected and she was probably relieved that my knowledge of Norwegian history did not revolve around the Hollywood version and the movie, 'The Vikings', with Kirk Douglas and Tony Curtis.

"Your English is very good," I said, with more than a hint of jealousy of her bi-lingual skills.

"Do you think so? As a subject, we are all taught English at school and I once worked as an au pair for a family in London during my summer holidays which helped and besides a lot of the work I do on behalf of the Professor at the University is in English."

"Put it this way, your English is better than my Norwegian!"

"Maybe, but you have such a nice Scottish accent and I have no trouble understanding you. If you want I could teach you Norwegian sometime."

"Yes, I'd like that."

"Well just to get you by in the meantime, you can say 'Vaer sa god' which can mean lots of things, such as, 'here you are', 'may I help you', 'you're welcome'. You try it, 'Vaer sa god'."

"Vaer sa god," I repeated.

"Well done, that's pretty good."

We turned off the main coast road south and then travelled or perhaps more accurately, we bumped our way up a long pot-hole ridden dirt track which Anja's car only just survived. She parked the car in the parking area and we both got out. The strong wind coming in off the sea whipped and tugged at our hair and bodies.

"Come on, I show you some Norwegian paintings," she said enthusiastically.

We crossed the car park, which already held several other cars and we entered the largest of the buildings. The gallery was an old, converted barn or outhouse which had recently been refurbished, with new wooden floors, white washed walls and wonderfully restored and stained, wooden beams. Paintings, all originals, were hung in no particular order on the walls, everything from oils to water-colours, from landscapes to seascapes, still lifes, sketches and a couple of abstract works which were too obscure for my tastes. They were all by different artists and I was amazed at the price that was being asked for some of them.

As we walked through the gallery's rooms, Anja would touch my hand, or my hair. It felt good, I felt close to her. If she liked a painting, I would nod and agree and vice versa. She seemed to have a knowledge about art and the arts in general, she oozed class and had a completely effortless style. I watched her move round the room.

"Do you want to go for a walk along the beach before we go for coffee?"

"Yeah, sounds good," I replied.

We left the gallery, after spending some time browsing at the books and prints that were on sale in the shop. We followed the path to the dunes then we were on the beach. The wind was blowing harder now and the sky had darkened. Large waves crashed and pounded the sand and rocks along the shore. We walked in relative silence, oblivious to the elements, happy in each other's company. I put my arm around her and she rested her head on my shoulder. I was relaxed, but the silence had let the voices in my head mutter their warnings. Don't hurt me they pleaded.

We walked for a few hundred yards along the edge of the surf, leaving a footprint trail in the soft, wet sand. I bent down picked up a piece of driftwood and drew our names in the smooth sand. Anja watched, smiled, then walked on. It was a scene reminiscent of a Claude Lelouch film. I threw the stick into the sea and ran after her as the breakers washed away any trace of our names.

I decided that, even though I was feeling like a teenager on his first serious date, there was no way I was going to let myself fall for her, or at least not let her know that I had

44

fallen for her. I worked on the belief, that the deeper you fall for someone, the greater your emotional vulnerability. The two things were directly proportional. When your heart was in someone else's hands, the propensity to get damaged rose dramatically. Getting too close might just end up with me being hurt and I didn't want that. That wasn't my style. I had previously made the mistake of building hopes and dreams and I wasn't going to get burned again. I had seen the warning signs. We walked along the lonely, windswept beach, before turning and making our way back along the path that led to the car park. As we walked over some shingle and pebbles at the foot of the dunes, Anja bent down and picked up a small, white stone with a feint red grain running through it and handed it to me.

"Here you are, a present from Norway."

"Thanks!" I said, as I slipped the cold, smooth pebble into my pocket.

"Coffee?" she asked.

"Yes, good idea, it's bloody chilly out here."

I looked back out over the brooding North Sea. A coaster was making heavy weather of the waves several miles off shore. I watched the spray clouds as its bow dipped and crashed into the foaming crests of the swell. I studied the scene for a few seconds, but as my eyes followed the progress of the little ship, as it headed northwards along the coast to some unknown destination, my thoughts had turned to other things.

"What are you thinking, Paul?"

"Nothing," I lied, "let's go in."

Somewhere, tucked away deep in my thoughts, I had a notion of perfect love, a kind of fairytail love with happy endings, but I had never really believed that it could exist. I looked over at Anja and I guess this was the way I'd always dreamed it would be. When Hannah had died I thought my life had also ended, but now there was Anja and I wondered if she would be the one to fill the void.

We made our way back and we entered the little coffee shop and sat down at a table by the window. It was good to get out of the wind. Like the gallery, it too was a converted farm building. It had exposed brick walls and about eight or nine tables of varying sizes, which were covered in either red and white or blue and white checked, gingham table cloths. You could describe the place as rustic. It was tastefully decorated with strategically placed antiques and bric a brac. We ordered coffees and smiled at each other across the table.

45

"I have to go back to Aberdeen tomorrow, I..."

I hesitated, I didn't know what else to say. She leaned over and touched my hand.

"I know...I know," she whispered.

I knew I wanted her, I knew I wanted to be with her, but these were like new feelings for me, I was so used to keeping everything hidden away, the kind of character who was an expert at compartmentalising their emotions, always building the front, fearing the slip that will cause exposure. I just wasn't sure how to play it. Soon I would be returning to my life in Aberdeen and I wanted to play it cool, as if it didn't matter, but it did and I was hurting. I hardly knew her, yet I was feeling vulnerable already.

"I have to go back to Oslo on Monday. My family go to the States in a few days and I'm back to work on Tuesday," she explained, "I'm going to miss you."

Her words just jangled in my head.

I caught the eye of the young waitress and she refilled our coffee cups. I sat gazing out of the window toward the sea, reviewing my thoughts and feelings. I just wanted to be with her, to make the moment last as long as I could. I hated having to say that it was time for me to get back to Stavanger and prepare for the reception. Once more there was a silence between us, but it was during these silences that so much was said, either by our eyes or the tenderness of our touch. She held my hand tightly across the table and her eyes locked in on mine, her mouth a sad little 'o'.

I paid the waitress and we walked back to the car. I opened the door for her, but before she climbed into the driver's seat, she pulled me to her and held me tightly, her body pressing against me. We kissed. First only a soft and gentle caress and then we held each other in a long and passionate kiss. I held her face gently in my hands and looked deep into her eyes, desperately seeking a sign that told me she wanted to be with me as much as I wanted to be with her. We kissed again and she bit my lower lip. I couldn't remember feeling so turned on just by a kiss for years. We broke from our kiss and held each other very tightly. I found myself looking past her, into the vastness of the world beyond. I was sure I could hear her say, "I know, I know," but there again, maybe it was only the moan of the cold wind that continued to blow in off the blue-grey sea, bending the couch grass against the hard-packed sand of the dunes. We broke away from our hug and Anja swallowed hard. Her eyes were moist. I kissed her again and tasted her tears upon my tongue.

*****

Now that I knew the big nobs weren't coming over, the reception was a bloody ordeal. More speeches, from just about everybody in the hall, some folk dancing and a light buffet. During the course of the event, I was introduced to a Norwegian businessman who was quite fascinating. He had set up his own fabric maintenance business in the late seventies and after years of success in Norway, he was now looking to expand into the UK sector and ultimately the Far East. He was your proverbial, self-made millionaire, his success however achieved without the benefits of being part of a shipping dynasty. The offshore market, he explained, was getting more and more competitive, with cost reduction initiatives meaning he was working on margins that were becoming tighter and tighter. What he was saying didn't surprise me, it was a dog eat dog, more appropriately a 'rat eat rat' business. The back-stabbing and political in-fighting that goes on is rife throughout the industry and at times you can surface from a meeting with an imaginary chalk mark etched on your back. Everyone seemed to have their own hidden agendas - colleagues, bosses, clients. I tried to work on the old Don Corleone adage, 'keep you friends close and your enemies closer'. Maybe I'm unjustly critical of the oil industry and it's like that in any walk of life. I scribbled a few notes. I admired people, especially the entrepreneurial type, who had made money out of the oil industry. It gave me great pleasure to think that the tables were being turned and just for a change it was the oil companies who were being shafted. In the main, just exactly how these guys got started in business was usually a grey area and I'm sure that with a bit of digging, the odd skeleton would come tumbling out of the woodwork; wealth and position now having given them an opportunity to turn their backs on the dodgy deals and illegalities of the past. By mid-evening, the party, for want of a better description, was still going strong and I slipped quietly and secretively out of the hall. My luck unfortunately didn't hold and Roy Calder accosted me just as I was leaving.

"Where you off to then?" he asked pointedly.

"I've got to see a man about a dog."

"Oh aye, is it that blonde dog I saw you with this morning? You're a dark horse, you boy."

"Steady Roy," I said through clenched teeth, as I felt my hackles rise. He was a real jerkoff at times and I felt like giving him a slap for referring to Anja as a 'dog'. He suggested we meet up later on to do a bit of 'clubbing'. I said that it was a great idea and I would see him later, even though we made no firm arrangements, but I had no intention of spending my last night in Stavanger with him.

I returned to the SAS and called Steve from my hotel room. I explained that something had cropped up and that I was busy that evening. I apologised for not seeing them and I suggested that he and Jane should arrange to come over and see me tomorrow before

I left and I would treat them to lunch. I then picked up the phone to call Claire, but I never made the call.

I had arranged to meet Anja in Newsman and she greeted me with a smile and a peck on the lips. We stood at the bar and I ordered a couple of beers. For some reason, conversation seemed difficult and there were some long silences between us. Although I liked my own company, in certain circumstances conversational silences made me feel awkward, but with Anja it was different. Words were not important. A glance, a smile, her touch were all that I needed. I stood hands in pockets, desperately wanting to hold and touch her, but again I was trying to play it cool. Never wanting to commit myself, never wanting to breach the Paul Robertson code. Every now and then I would catch her eye and she would smile at me. She looked great, dressed in a beige two-piece trouser suit and striped top, her hair falling onto her shoulders. She looked better than anything I had ever seen. So natural. No make up required.

We left the now crowded Newsman and found ourselves out in the street. It was full of young Norwegians out on the town, having a good time. There were plenty of drunks going about, but the atmosphere was good humoured and although there was no obvious undercurrent of violence, there was a conspicuous police presence. A few people stopped to speak to Anja and she introduced me to some of her former school friends. Several of these girls were a little drunk and were obviously making suggestive remarks about me or us, but because it was in Norwegian, Anja said it was better that I didn't know what they were saying.

Around midnight we went down into a basement night-club and found a table in the corner of a raised seating area. I ordered a beer and Anja had a Farris. We kissed, we talked, but most of all we kissed. We both knew it was maybe our last night together and we didn't want it to end. The club was mobbed and I was relieved we had found seats. Anja explained that it was a fairly new place and attracted a more 'trendy and cosmopolitan' crowd. Judging by some of the characters going about and the substances they were smoking, she was being very diplomatic, but I think I know what she meant.

After about an hour, a young male Norwegian tapped me on the arm and began to talk to me. I didn't understand him and gesticulated my lack of comprehension by just holding out my arms and shrugging. Anja bailed me out and began to converse with him. The guy shook my hand and offered, in broken English, to buy us a drink, which we politely refused.

"What did he say?" I asked. Anja laughed.

"He wanted to know if we were in love, because he thinks we look so good together."

"What did you say?"

"I told him...I told him we were just good friends."

"Good answer. I can handle that."

We both laughed, then rose from our seats and made or way to the dance floor. We danced for a while, then the DJ announced the slow records that would bring the evening to an end. We moved slowly round the floor to Roxy Music's "Avalon" then the evening was over with Crowded House's "Don't Dream its Over". It seemed an ironic title given the circumstances.

Soon, too soon, the house lights came on and we were the only couple left on the dance floor. Reluctantly, we stopped dancing and went back to our seats. Anja picked up her bag and we drifted out with the others as the staff carefully placed the chairs upside down on the table tops and swept away the debris that had accumulated on the floor.

"When I get back to Aberdeen, I'm going to make up a tape with all my favourite slow songs and send it to you, just so you won't forget me," I said.

"Please, I'd like that," she smiled.

It was raining quite heavily when we got outside. Anja asked if I was hungry, silly question really at that time of night. We walked through the narrow streets, holding each other close, trying to stay warm in the chilly rain. We joined the queue for pizza and I ordered a large slice with extra pepperoni and mushroom, a second slice of 'Quattro Fromaggi' and a can of Coca Cola Lite. I paid the guy behind the counter, then felt a tap on my shoulder,

"Hey! Are you English?"

I turned round and was face to face with two young lads, maybe in their late teens or early twenties. I looked them up and down, then turned my back on them to pick up my change. Anja picked up the pizza slices and the can of Coke.

"It's time to go, come on Paul," but the question was repeated.

"Are you English?"

I felt my fist clench around my car keys.

"No!" I replied curtly, then calmly, I explained, "I'm a Scot!"

My fist tightened round the keys. One, if not both of these young turks was going to get a helluva smack in the face if they came at me.

"Paul, come on, ignore them," she then turned to the two lads and said something in Norwegian and left. It seemed to have the desired effect.

"Ah! Scottish! We like Scotland, we like Kenny Dalglish, he's our hero."

"Very good, boys," I said as I brushed past them. The threat had passed. Anja was outside waiting for me.

"You OK?" she asked.

"Sure, no problem."

We walked a few yards down the street and sheltered in a shop door way, sharing our food, sharing the cold coke. It was oddly romantic, no intimate candlelit dinners for two here, I thought. We eventually left the shelter of our doorway and headed back through the still busy town centre to the nearest taxi rank. The taxi service in Stavanger is first class, there appears to be an abundance of taxis; they're very efficient and they even take credit cards. We were picked up in no time and I asked to be taken to the SAS. I would have preferred to walk, thereby prolonging my time with Anja, but that would have been selfish and inconsiderate, given that it was raining much heavier now and very cold.

I wanted to ask Anja to come in for a coffee and maybe she wanted me to ask her, but I didn't. We swapped telephone numbers and kissed good-bye. We held each other for what seemed like ages.

"I won't forget you Paul," she whispered then she left in the taxi. She looked back and waved only once, before turning away.

I had tried to stay in control, to stay cool, but she'd only been gone a few moments and my stomach was knotted and I ached for her. 'I won't forget you' she had said, but that was no consolation. No comfort.

I looked down at the note she had given me. It contained her name, her address and her home and office telephone numbers in Oslo. She had signed it Anja H. Andresen. I wondered what the 'H' stood for. I closed my eyes and wanted to be with her. "Don't dream its over," I whispered to myself.

I didn't sleep well that night, the events and voices of the day still whispering in my head. Next morning I woke up lonely, not completely rested and I just lay in bed, considering the thoughts and feelings that had so disturbed my sleep. I decided to give the church service a miss. Unfortunately, Roy had made a similar decision and I had to endure the gory details of his exploits of the previous night. In basic terms, our bald and kilted Lothario, had 'picked up' a middle aged divorcee and had his wicked way with her in the truly romantic surroundings outside the hotel kitchens. So passionate, more like bestial, had been their 'lovemaking', that they managed to knock over a couple of dustbins. Still he seemed pleased with himself, the experience had obviously given him a buzz and reinforced his belief in the pulling power of the kilt!

"This, eh, 'lady' you were with last night, was she a bit of a babe?"

"Was she fuck! What a beast! She could hardly walk, she just sort of waddled, with her big arse heaving from side to side, like two Buckie trawlers in a storm. Mind you, I love big tits and her paps were like a dead heat in a Zeppelin race, and nipples! Fuck me, she had nipples like cigar butts."

When I looked over at Roy, he seemed to be fiddling with himself.

"I'd better go and have a shower, I can still smell her on me! Wee word of advice - if you ever meet her, never eat chips out of her knickers!"

"What?"

This guy had bags of class and I laughed loudly as I pictured the scene he had described in my head, then I thought' of Anja and the time we had spent together and I felt a kind of emptiness rush over me. I asked myself who had the right idea in all this, Roy the shagger or me, the dreamer?

Roy passed by my bed on his way to the bathroom,

"She even asked me for my address so she could write to me. I couldn't believe it, I just told her to awa' and shite!"

Steve and Jane's eventual arrival was a pleasant distraction and we went for a walk through the old town. I wanted to tell them all about Anja, but instead I encouraged them to tell me more about Norway. They had never heard of Professor Pederson.

"What do you want to know about this Pederson guy for?" Steve asked.

"No reason, just a name I overheard in conversation."

I changed the subject and they continued to tell me about their recent experiences. They really liked the city, the people and the way of life. It was a lot less pressurised and more laid back than Aberdeen and people were heavily into spending time, quality time, with their families. It appeared that nearly everyone was a skier, a runner, a sailor, a hill walker, a footballer, a hand-ball player or something. Sporting activities played a major part in their life styles. The only hole in their Norwegian life, and their only real complaint, was the apparent lack of choice in the supermarkets. Jane was without doubt missing the food section of M&S. Eating out was certainly expensive compared to the UK, but Steve was on such a good 'expat' package, it didn't unduly worry him. Overall they gave Norway and Stavanger a rave review.

"We're really looking forward to May, that's when the country has its National Day and they say, weather wise it can be the warmest month of the year in Stavanger, so we're hoping for lots of barbies and boat trips," Jane said, "and in two weeks time, we're even planning a long week-end in Sirdal for some skiing, if there's more snow."

"Skiing, you lucky beggars, I haven't been on skis for years. I'd love to come back and see you both, because you're making me very jealous of your lifestyle over here. It sounds great." I meant it, but I also had a more pressing need to return.

"Well, do it....bring Claire."

Jane offered the comment in all innocence, but the mention of Claire's name reminded me of the uncertain welcome that awaited me on my return to Aberdeen.

We walked along the waterfront, then back into the narrow streets of the sentrum. It was virtually deserted, the same streets that had been just heaving the night before were now empty and quiet. We stopped in by a cafe bar for lunch. It was a typical, white timbered building which was perched high on some kind of mound, near to an (I guess) observation tower that overlooked the Vagen. I had an excellent lunch of chicken enchiladas before we walked back to the SAS. I said good-bye to them both then nipped back up to my room to finish packing and to prepare to checkout of the hotel.

The bus arrived to take us back to Sola. We thanked our hosts and posed for a souvenir photograph, then we left. The bus reverberated with the excited buzz of Aberdonians who had been well impressed by their week-end visit. I leaned against the cold window and dreamed. Workwise, the trip had been a bit of a non-event for me, but the chance encounter with Anja had aroused feelings in me I thought I had locked away. At Sola, we checked in and put our luggage through baggage control, then we all made our way to the International departure lounge. Roy and one or two of his cronies got wired into the booze, after it was announced that our flight would be delayed for a couple of hours due to technical problems. I had a wander round and bought a book about Norway from the Duty Free shop then sat at a table by myself, flicking through the pages, not really concentrating on any articles or pictures. I had thought about buying Claire a present or something, but she wasn't into any of the gifts on display and I didn't really want to make a peace offering.

I could hear Roy's mob in the background. He was holding centre stage and his shallow followers listened intently, interrupting with the odd ribald comment as he re-described the love scene against the kitchen wall. Poor bastards! They just didn't have a clue. Being a loner certainly has its advantages and I hoped I would never ever become one of the lads.

The return flight back to Aberdeen passed in a haze. It would be nice to get back home to the flat, but part of me was still in Stavanger. Soon we were over the east coast of Scotland and all the familiar landmarks came into view. It was chucking it down in Aberdeen and everything seemed grey and sad.

I shared a taxi into town with Roy. He wasn't going directly home, but was heading for a pub not far from where I stayed, for a few more beers. He asked me to join him, but I declined. It's strange, but the first thing I did when I got home was call Claire. She wasn't in and I didn't leave a message.

Chapter 3

CHAPTER 3

Monday morning was cold, wet and thoroughly miserable and just about mirrored my frame of mind. I felt scunnered. My time with Anja felt like a million years ago and the fact that I hadn't been able to reach Claire also pissed me off. I got up out of bed, went through to the kitchen and opened the fridge. I hadn't slept well. I took a long gushling swig of fresh orange juice straight from the carton. Hannah would never have approved.

I breakfasted on tea and toast, then read the local morning paper, which had been delivered some time earlier. I turned immediately to the back pages to catch up on the weekend's football stories. I flipped through the rest of the paper, then went back through to the bedroom and as I was sorting my clothes out, I picked up a sweater and for a fleeting second, I could smell Anja's perfume lingering in the woollen fibres, where she had rested her head. I closed my eyes, then slowly opened them. I then went through' to the study, sat down on the old leather captain's chair, switched on my PC and began to work through my notes for an article I was researching. I had recently bought some new hardware, with a Lotus Smartsuite software package, which gave me spreadsheets, graphics, a WP, a fax macro and various other attachments. I only ever used the WP and the fax, as I didn't have the patience or the inclination to read an instruction manual on how to use the other functions. Reading technical manuals has never been my cup of fur, I just can't be arsed. Hannah used to do all that sort of thing for me, then give me a step by step fool's guide. Mind you, since she had died I still found it hard, even struggled to work the timer on the video to pre-record programmes. I've always been completely handless and non-technical, not quite a Luddite, but about as much use as a Magpie presenter. Certainly in today's cyber-world, I was digitally impoverished, yet I knew all these guys who got a hard-on just talking about CD-ROM's, Megabytes, Gateways, Internets, SmartIcons and all that crap! They were the types who probably helped their dads tinker with the engine of the car when they were kids! Sorry, it's just not my scene man! Mind you, I bet they couldn't kick a ball properly!

I lost myself in my work and the morning soon passed. I called my solicitor to arrange a meeting to discuss some properties I wanted to buy and then lease out. Then I called a couple of the news offices in Edinburgh and Glasgow to see if they had anything for me. The best offer I had was to try and investigate and follow up on a piece on a safety issue offshore. A drilling company had experienced a fatality on one of their rigs and they were being accused of negligence and mis-management by the burgeoning offshore Union activists and the guy's family. To make matters worse, it was further alleged that the American owned company was trying to cover it up. Since Piper and the Cullen Enquiry, the word safety in North Sea terms twitched the respective sphincters of Oil Major and Contractor service company alike. I was keen to do the story and investigate my former masters. The oil industry is, as I said, a dirty business, especially on the contracting side. Deals done on the back of fag packets, 'brown envelopes' being furtively dished out under tables, 'it's not what you know, it's who you know' and some over-zealous corporate entertaining, which I'm sure neither the Tax man or the wives knew about.

To be honest, it was no longer as obvious as that, given the fact that most of those on the take had developed ever more elaborate and sophisticated methods to cover their trail. Thinking about it just pissed me off. I'm very much in favour of fair competition and when you bid for a contract, you can only hope that you are competing on a level playing field but, time after time, after submitting what we thought were first class documents, offering a quality service at a highly competitive rate, we would find that we didn't win the work and that a deal had been cut and dried, even before the tender documents had been issued in some cases. In the States, large companies are only now beginning to put a value on the damage done by these so called 'information brokers'. One of these days I would do some digging, talk to some people and expose the reality of it all.

*****

Richardson spent two days shut away from the outside world, cocooned in the stillness and isolation of the cottage, studying the subject matter of his project and planning the most appropriate method of attack. On paper it was a straight forward assignment, but the need for preparation had been drummed into him at the Regiment and he had now been classically conditioned into the habit of planning everything down to the most minute detail. Nothing should be left to chance. The case he had been given by Knox-De Vries in the park two days earlier had contained £15,000 in cash, used notes, and a large A4 manilla envelope. Inside the envelope there were twenty five pages of information relating to his target, timings, personal details, location and most importantly the name and telephone number of one of Knox-De Vries' contacts who could provide whatever back-up information was necessary prior to Richardson arriving in situ. He had absorbed all the details of the documents within the first reading and having completed the outline planning phase he now needed to identify, select and short-list those associates most suitable for this kind of work. He pulled a floppy disk from the hidden drawer of his desk and accessed the information he needed. He then dialled eight private telephone numbers one after the other. He was unsuccessful with three of the calls, but of the five he did contact he was more than satisfied that their experience would be good enough. Each one of his hand picked team possessed a toughness and ruthlessness that was absolute. He had not eaten since breakfast, such was his concentration and now as the hours crept into early evening he entered the kitchen and prepared a light meal of grilled sole and steamed vegetables, before returning to his study. After a further two hours of double checking his preliminary plan, he decided he had, had enough for the night. He examined all the doors and windows of the cottage before switching on the alarm and retiring to bed.

Piers Richardson was 43, the only son of Brigadier Clive Richardson and his wife, Olivia. He had followed his father's career almost to the letter, same school, same college at University and then the regiment. At school he was always in the top band academically and at University he obtained a 2nd Class Honours Degree in History and a rugby 'blue'. Their career paths only differed in that his father remained with the colours until he had retired, but the younger Richardson had been invited to join the intelligence services.

In early the eighties while serving under cover behind enemy lines in the South Atlantic, he was posted as 'Missing in Action', feared dead. Through sheer bad luck, he had in fact been captured by a small group of Argentine conscripts. He had been held in an isolated farm building, starved, tortured and sexually assaulted by his three captors before making his escape. He later returned to the barn where he had been held and coldly executed each of the young Argentinians with a single shot to the head, even though they had offered to surrender to him. With the help of Burgoyne, a trusted junior officer, he was able to dispose of the bodies, and cover up his crime.

It was during his period in captivity that his mother, a manic depressive, took her own life, unable to cope with the apparent loss of her much loved only son. Two years later, the Brigadier collapsed while walking alone in the Austrian Tyrol. He had suffered a massive heart attack and had lain for two days on a rainy, wind swept mountainside before he was found. He died later in an ambulance on the way to the hospital. A professional soldier and fighting man all his days, it was a not a fitting or glorious way for him to leave this life.

Piers Richardson had left the Army the year after the ignominious death of his father and had gone into business for himself, as an arms and security consultant. He was financially secure on account of his inheritance, his army pension and being left the family home; he had also spent three years in the Gulf on a very lucrative consultancy contract, personally advising a prince on security, defence and intelligence matters. Richardson had subsequently returned to the UK in the late eighties when he had embarked on a new career that had given full reign to all his skills and training from his Special Forces days. He had carried out a number of assignments for clients from the Americas, Europe, the Middle East and the Far East. He was perfectly type-cast for the role; he had no family ties, no political affiliations, no loyalty to Queen and country. He was a man without a conscience. For those who did not know him, he teetered on the brink of misanthropy, yet he was regarded in certain circles as a very effective and professional operator, whose services did not come cheaply.

Richardson woke next day as usual at 6 am. He rose immediately, such was his self-discipline and went down into the basement gym and put himself through a punishing workout of martial arts and boxing training that involved a makiwara and a speed ball. He then breakfasted on tea and toast and prepared to greet his five guests, whom he expected to arrive at various times throughout the day. He had taken a calculated security risk inviting the group to his house, but by late afternoon everyone had arrived. By mid-evening the conclave was in session.

"Gentlemen, thank you for coming. I trust you are all well."

Apart from Richardson, the assembled group contained two other Brits, a German, a Dutchman and a French-Canadian. The little tryst knew each other personally and professionally and they engaged in some cruel barrack room banter, before they were called to order by Richardson.

"We have been asked to take on a little project in Scandinavia, all the details are in the folders in front of you. Spend the next hour studying the contents, then we'll meet in the library for a further briefing. By the way, details of the financial arrangements are also in the folder and, given the nature of our assignment and my recent dealings with our clients, I have, shall we say, negotiated a premium fee for our services. You have the run of the house, please feel free to help yourself to tea, coffee or fruit juice... no alcohol. We will re-convene in exactly one hour. Dismissed."

After two days of fitness training, briefings and preparations, the group split up and left for various destinations in Europe. They would all meet again in Oslo on the following Thursday.

Richardson telephoned a private number in West London and confirmed that his preparations were complete and that he was leaving first of all for Belgium and then north to Norway. He ended the call by giving details of a bank account number in Geneva and hung up. Richardson then called a number in the Norwegian capital.

"This is Richardson, I will meet you a week on Thursday for lunch, please book a table at the Annen Etage and do try and reserve a table by the window."

"Of course, Mr Richardson, that won't be a problem. I have also arranged the hire of the vehicles, just exactly as you asked."

"I trust you will have the photographs, documents and the plans I requested."

"Yes, of course, Mr Richardson, everything will be ready, just as you listed. I am very thorough. I am sure you will not be disappointed."

Richardson replaced the receiver, secured the cottage then left for Heathrow. He had some business with a Quarter-master in Bruges, before he could travel onto Oslo. His supplier, a former priest, had been closely involved in gun-running, initially for a cause he passionately believed in, before the passion waned and he realised he could make substantial amounts of money going into business for himself and supplying both sides.

*****

Monday became Tuesday and Tuesday became Wednesday, and Thursday came so slow. Each day the same as the other, except that, on Wednesday morning the phone rang and I rushed to pick it up. I hoped it would be Anja, but it was just the local journal letting me know that the game scheduled for that evening was off. I used the free evening to tidy the flat and do some chores. When I finished I went for a jog. I wasn't a keen jogger, but I would sometimes go for a run when I wanted to clear my head. I changed into a grey Adidas sweat suit and tied a blue and white cotton, cowboy style neckerchief round my head as a bandana. I had seen a picture of a guy dressed exactly like this in the first ever copy of GQ I had bought and I thought it was a great pose. Claire hated the bandana, but Hannah had liked it. She used to fuel my ego by agreeing it made me look very Ivy League, a Yale or Harvard 'preppy' out for a jog on campus.

I jogged for a few miles, trying to make sense of a head full of jumbled thoughts, hopes and guilt. As one of my old team mates would say, 'my head was full of slamming doors'.

On the one hand there was Anja; I hardly knew her, but I knew I wanted to be with her. Then there was Claire, and although we had not talked since I had got back, I still felt guilty and wasn't yet sure I could give her up for someone who was really no more than a stranger. Claire and I had been together for almost a year and a half and during that time I had been reasonably faithful.

On Thursday morning I met with John Derrick, my brief, and we signed the papers that made me the new owner of two newly built houses in the suburb of Cults. I had already lined up a deal to lease the properties to an oil company and they wanted immediate occupancy. It was good business. They paid excellent rates, quarterly in advance, and would commit to a five year deal for a fully furnished let. I had six other properties leased out on a similar basis and four flats rented out to students.

"Once I've had the documents registered, I'll send a copy to you and hold the originals here in the fire safe."

"No problem, but don't be in too much of a hurry, because knowing you, you'll probably include your fee note!"

"A man has to live you know, I've a business to run, overheads to cover," he joked.

John was a hard working, conscientious solicitor. He had broken away from the stuffy restraints of one of the more established firms and had set up in partnership with a female colleague. He specialised in conveyancing and she did corporate law. I had used him for several years. He had more in common with me than some of the other solicitors I had unfortunately come across over the years, and from a business point of view, I trusted him implicitly. He was in many ways the antithesis of my normal opinion of members of the legal and accountancy professions. As a rule I saw them as the parasites of the business and commercial world and their existence annoyed me.

"I didn't see you at the Law Ball last Saturday," he said.

"I was in Norway."

"Business or pleasure?"

"Business of course," I could see in his eyes he was fishing for more details than that.

"Actually it was a Council junket, but I enjoyed it. In fact I combined it with a visit to my brother Steve who's based there now."

"Interesting. By the way I saw Claire and she was looking *very, very attractive.* I think she was having to fight off the advances of an old friend of yours, Gordon Hazeldine.

You know the guy, flash bastard, Porsche and a house in the Den. Just recently, I've heard he's got himself involved in a deal to develop some green-belt land for student accommodation, although the locals are pissed off by the application and are likely to object."

"What are the chances of that getting through Planning, if it's green-belt?" I quizzed.

"For a Jack-the-Lad like you, very difficult, but you know Hazeldine, he moves in the right circles, his nose is up all the right arseholes and I've heard whispers he has a backer, some wealthy bloke, who wants to break into the property game and as you can obviously imagine, he has an inside man in the Planning department. He seems to have a finger and various other parts of his reptilian anatomy in a lot of pies these days."

"Everybody's at it. It's almost becoming as big a rat race as the oil business."

I knew Gordon Hazeldine alright, and we shared an intense mutual dislike for each other. He was a slimy bastard, so I changed the subject and asked John to keep me posted of any griff he got on the progress of the Hazeldine deal, or on any new planning applications or potential sites that may become available.

"By the way, have you managed to get that garage owner to respond to my offer letter yet?"

"I phoned him yesterday and he was about to go on holiday...Torremolinos or something, but he has promised to get his solicitor to respond when he returns. I've taken a diary note and I'll chase it up."

"He's a fly bastard. Pretends to be a doddery old git, but he's as sharp as a tack. We've shaken hands on the deal, he'd better not let me down now."

"Don't worry, I'll keep on top of it. Anything else?"

"No, I don't think so, this is already costing me too much money already."

I left. John was a straightforward guy, he'd never knowingly breach a professional confidence but, off the record, he had given me one or two useful tips, shall we say. He would keep me informed.

Property development was never going to make me an enormously wealthy man, but several deals over the years had given me a reasonable portfolio of substantial assets, cash in the bank and a pretty good income that more than supported my journalistic tendencies. If I had to depend on writing as a career, I'd have been on skid row by now. I preferred to be selective in the stories I covered and the publications I would free-lance for. On the business side, I had opportunities in the past to take major speculative risks in property, but my natural tendency toward caution had proven right 90% of the time. There was one guy who had suggested a particular deal, three or so years back, which the canny Aberdonian in me declined to get involved in. It was the right decision. In the long run the property thing was only a means to an end. This deal with the garage owner could be a big one. The timing would be perfect, if I could get John to conclude the bargain and the application went through planning at the first attempt. Any delay would be problematic, as I sensed the arse falling out of the Aberdeen market within the next twelve months. I had identified the site some time back even though there was still an operational business being run there. I just approached the owner. It turned out he was thinking of retiring so I made him a provisional offer. We had shaken hands and Jon had followed up with a formal letter. It was a great location, the business having been sited there for over fifty years and all I wanted to do was get the planning permission for a hundred or so flats and up to six shop units and sell the deal on to one of the big construction companies. It was a great opportunity for me if it came off. The cash generated would allow me to do something I had always intended doing: to take some time out and disappear up to a cottage on Deeside or a gite in France and write a novel. I had the germ of an idea in my head that I hoped to research and develop. It was good to dream.

That afternoon, I called in by the local radio station to catch up on the latest gossip and local news. One of the girls who helped in the newsroom had become a good friend. Kate was one of the very few people who could read me like a book. She could see right through my moods and my defensive barriers and she would slap me back into place if I ever got too carried away with myself.

"Hi, Paul, how was Norway?" she asked.

"Good, very good. The official trip was very boring, but overall it was alright and it was good to see Steve."

"Did you behave yourself?" she quizzed.

"Of course, you know me."

"Yes exactly, Mr Robertson, I know you and there's no way you've gone over to Norway and not got up to something."

"I'm sorry, but I have absolutely no idea what you mean, please elaborate," I said coyly.

"Look Paul Robertson, I know what you're like. You play at being the 'boy next door', but you're just a rebel."

I just listened, with an embarrassed grin on my face, as Kate continued.

"You pretend that you think you're not good-looking, but you know fine that females, with the exception of me of course, find you attractive and a little bit of a honey and the worst thing is, all this politeness and shyness crap you come away with seems to work! It's such an old and worn out script, but you keep getting away with it and I bet they fall for it every time. Poor bitches, hasn't anyone told them this is the nineties?"

"Is Semple in, Kate?" I asked politely, doing my best to stop myself breaking into a wide grin.

She laughed.

"Ron's busy at the moment, do you want a tea or a coffee while you're waiting?"

I said that tea would be fine and she soon returned with a large, chipped mug brim full of tea and a couple of digestives. She knew how I took my tea - weak, one sugar and a splash of semi-skimmed. It tasted surprisingly good. Far better than it looked in the badly stained cup.

Kate had been with Northeast FM since she had left school. She hoped to make a career in journalism and news broadcasting and without any formal qualifications, she was more than willing to start at the bottom and learn her trade. The radio station milked her enthusiasm for the job and certainly took a loan of her, often asking her to work long, extra hours without pay. I was quite fond of her, in a brotherly sort of way. True, we flirted with each other, but it wasn't serious and the relationship had the advantage of, as she put it, our sexual incompatibility. I think I know what she meant by that, as she was always reminding me how much older than her I was. Every now and then I would ask her to help me research some work, even though I didn't need to. She was enthusiastic and certainly had a raw talent in that she saw things very clearly. Issues were black or they were white. She didn't believe in bullshit, shot from the hip and didn't take prisoners.

Kate was only 19, slim, petite, not unattractive and with a dress sense which verged on the trendy. She was worldly wise to say the least and I enjoyed listening, sometimes open-mouthed, to stories about her nights out with the girls, even though on occasions I couldn't believe how naive I was and how sheltered a life I had led compared to what she got up to! I told her briefly about Norway. I wanted to tell her more. I wanted to tell her about Anja, but I decided to keep that episode to myself. I had always had a problem sharing confidences, sharing my inner most thoughts, even with a friend like Kate.

62

Ron Semple eventually surfaced from his office. He was Head of News and Current Affairs and the station's acting Sports Editor. I had done a few bits and pieces for him, mostly with a sports angle, because of my former footballing days. He was in his 50s, had a full head of greasy greying hair and wore dark, heavy rimmed bi-focals, perched on the end of his nose. He had experimented with contact lenses, but he kept leaving them in overnight when he was pissed and in the morning he would wake up, looking like a mixie rabbit, unable to open his eyes. The lenses had now been consigned to the waste basket. In winter he wore a baggy turquoise cardigan and you always felt it could do with a wash. He spoke with a very pronounced guttural 'r'. I loved it when he was doing a spot on radio and he would produce sentences heavy with alliteration of the letter R. Ron had never played football at any level. His working knowledge of the game was therefore limited to the standard range of journalistic clichés, but there again he was no different to his more illustrious colleagues from the central belt who, in my opinion, knew S.F.A. about football: the irritating little gits with columns in the national tabloids who summarise on the radio or, worse still, actually work in front of the cameras.

Ron shook my hand firmly when he saw me and we made some light conversation regarding the current state of Scottish football and agreed we'd both rather watch the Serie A on a Sunday afternoon or as a second choice, the top games in the Premiership in England.

"Do you miss playing?"

"Ron, you ask me that everytime you see me."

"I know, but you never give me an answer. I'll get you fixed up you know. How old are you? I bet you're still under 30, that's far too young to have hung up your boots, especially where you played. Sweepers should be able to play until they're 40!"

"Aye, aye, I know...I packed up too early, heard it."

"Have you been over to Pittodrie recently?"

"No, 'fraid not. I only go these days if someone invites me and I don't have to pay. I'm not a fan anymore, I'm a critic, so I don't enjoy it."

"Aye, its not been great, this past wee while. Are you busy or do you fancy doing some work for me?"

"Sorry, too busy, I only came in for a free cuppa."

Ron was well aware of my abilities as a journalist. He had seen the work I had done for the Sunday broadsheets and the more highbrow monthly publications and it often embarrassed him to offer me some of the assignments he had on the board, but I accepted he had a duty to give his regular reporters the pick of the work. Although I preferred to write on more important issues, some of the local news items could be just as rewarding and, if I took something on, he knew he could rely on me to produce a piece that had a degree of quality, sporting or otherwise. On a couple of occasions he had used my free-lance articles ahead of his own people.

I said good-bye to Kate and promised to meet her one night for a drink. I left the building and started to walk back to the flat. As I walked back along the wide tree-lined streets, past the solidly impressive granite town houses and villas that bordered the North and South Dens, quite unexpectedly a memory flashed into my mind of a so-called Careers Guidance talk I'd had in my second year at the Academy.

"University material and a fair sportsman," the advisor said, as he flicked nonchalantly through my file. "Hmmm, rugby player?" he peered at me over the glasses, that had slipped half way down his nose, "no, definitely more of a footballer. You're far too handsome a young man to be a rugby player."

'Too handsome!' Holy shit, is this guy a shirt-lifter or something? I smiled.

"Well son, what are your plans? University, then into the legal or the accountancy profession?"

"Well no, actually someday I want to be a journalist or a writer," I answered honestly.

" Oh, a writer? A budding Enid Blyton eh?" he said sarcastically. I was convinced this guy was a wanker. I wondered what he'd say next.

"Look son, you've obviously got a good head on you, take my word for it and forget any aspirations you have of being a reporter or a writer - it won't pay the bills and it'll more than likely damage your liver. Get your Highers, get a degree, then get into a profession. Join the golf club, the Round Table and have a family."

I just sat and listened, as he mapped out my future.

"Your History and English marks are excellent. I think Law would suit you...any questions? No? Off you go then, oh and eh, can you tell the next person to come in," he said as he closed my file.

"Thank you for your time and advice," I said, as I got up to leave. He didn't raise his head, he didn't even acknowledge me. Rude bastard, he had little or no interest in me

or the other school kids in his Year.

I left the little interview room confused and deflated. I never discussed my career aspirations with anyone again.

*****

When I arrived back at the flat I checked the answer phone. There were no messages.

That evening, Claire came round unannounced. She rang the door bell and just breezed in to the flat. She had obviously had time to think things over and she was very matter of fact in telling me she was only there to pick up her things. I'm not sure if she wanted me to talk her out of it, but it was her choice to go; I wasn't going to stop her. I wasn't pushing her out. I thought about asking her if she had enjoyed the Law Society Ball, but realised that discretion was probably the better part of valour and decided against it. Claire gathered up all her gear, including her toothbrush. It didn't take long, then she asked me to call her if she had forgotten anything. She called me a bastard, again, and for a few moments I felt like one. I had never planned to hurt her. I wasn't even sure I wanted her to leave. Well, not entirely sure. After Claire had gone I looked at a TV magazine to see if there was anything of any note on the box. There wasn't, so I decided to work on the compilation tape I had promised to send Anja.

Anja. Her memory still quickened the pulse and I found myself whispering her name. I hadn't called her; I didn't want her to think I liked her. I didn't want her to know how much it hurt to be away from her. I was torturing myself. Although I wasn't a subscriber to the 'treat 'em mean - keep 'em keen' school of thought, I hated the idea of being emotionally vulnerable by showing my feelings. It had happened before and I had got hurt, even with Hannah in our early days. I know this sounds a bit sentimental, like the lyrics of a song, but sometimes if you're cut deep enough, the wound never really heals and the scars are always there to remind you never to get cut again. That would just be careless. I didn't ever want to surrender control. I wished it would be different with Anja, but I guess you can never really feel completely secure about someone else's love, someone else's feelings. There's always a hint of doubt, a tiny nagging voice, that asks, do they feel the same as I do? Maybe not, so be careful. Be careful.

I had grown deeply cynical, but I had survived before. I would just have to live with the pain. They say it gets better with time. The only contact we would possibly ever have now was when I sent over the tape. I poured myself a wee Macallan into a cut crystal tumbler that had come from a wedding present set, given to us by former colleagues. I took a tentative sip of the 'cratur', savouring its rich, warming Speyside smoothness. Sheer nectar! Eighteen year old Macallan. Wonderful stuff! Steve had given me the bottle before he moved to Norway. It only had one dram out of it, but he had been told that he would have to pay the full duty if he took an open bottle into the country. He thought, to hell with that, and gave it to me!

I pulled out a mixture of vinyl and CDs and got started. Most of the tracks I taped were a bit on the sentimental side, real wrist-slashing stuff. They all either had outstanding lyrics or a great melody. What the hell, I was never going to see her again, so for once I could wear my heart on my sleeve. My selection was inspired by loneliness and self-doubt. I taped for ages, not fully realising how long it would take, eventually going to bed in the early hours of the morning. I lay in bed and first of all thought about Claire and the fact that she had taken her things, then I thought about the tape and felt pleased with my efforts. I would send it off to Anja the following day. Sleep was difficult. During the day, I could keep my mind off her, when work occupied my time, but the night was different.

Unusually for me, I had forgotten to set my alarm and next morning I overslept. I was in that state, bordering between light sleep and consciousness when I thought I heard the phone ringing. I fumbled about for the cordless next to my bed. I eventually found it and held it to my ear.

"Hello, Aberdeen...39823," I mumbled, almost forgetting my number.

"Hello Paul, it's me." The voice was bright, the accent was foreign.

I regained my senses immediately.

"Hi, its nice to hear from you, how's life in Oslo?"

"It's good, a bit cold, but at least the sun is shining."

"Are you busy at work?"

"Yes, I guess so. I'm helping the Professor to research and prepare for a talk he is giving to some very important businessmen here in Oslo about Norway's possible entry into the European Union."

"I did think about phoning you, you know...honest, but I didn't want to be thought of as a pain in the arse!"

"You should have called and you're not a pain in the ass. If you were I'd soon let you know."

There was a brief silence, then she hit me with it.

66

"Paul, I was wondering if you would like to be my guest at a weekend event the Professor is hosting next week, over here in Norway. He has invited a number of friends to spend a few days at a lodge in a lovely part of the country, north-east of Stavanger. I will have to work some of the time, but it should be fun. He knows I have been working very hard, so as a reward and a thank you, he asked me if I'd like to bring someone. I tried almost everyone I knew, but they couldn't make it, then I remembered about you! I understand, if you say no."

I didn't hesitate. I wanted to, but I didn't, I didn't even refer to her little attempt at a joke.

"When do you want me to come over?"

It was great to hear from her again and I looked forward to returning to Norway.

"Next Thursday? If that's alright? I realise it's a bit short notice. The Professor has told me to say that it will be an informal weekend, with a few selected guests and that the only things I should ask you to bring, are a pair of walking boots, some warm clothes and an open mind!"

"Look, Anja, the whole thing sounds great, can you give me a few more details."

"Ja, OK, I do that."

We talked for over twenty minutes as she gave me some general information about the trip. We arranged that I would come over next Thursday morning and that she would pick me up from the airport. There would be an approximate one and a half hour drive to the house and I would meet everyone the following day. The Professor and his wife Nina would already be there, as they were flying up from Oslo on the Wednesday to prepare. She told me that I wouldn't need to worry about food or anything like that, as it would all be taken care of. Once again she re-emphasised the need to take my boots and some warm, casual outdoor gear. She was obviously very excited by the trip,

"You may be intrigued and surprised by some of the guests. I'll call you Monday to see if everything is OK, bye."

"Bye, be good and take care."

She was gone. Bring an 'open mind' she had said. What the hell was that all about? Christ, don't tell me it's a kinky, partner-swapping weekend! I dismissed that interpretation and I decided it must be the English equivalent of a Norwegian phrase which did not necessarily translate well, but I could have been missing something. I came to the conclusion it would be a weekend in the country with a group of chinless

Norwegian academics. I developed this mental image of a group of Open University presenters wearing big woolly jumpers and boring the arse off me. I shook my head to erase the thought.

I called Steve at his office and told him I was coming back over. He quizzed me about the reasons for the visit, but I told him it was business and that I would call him when I got to Norway. I had a bath, shaved, got dressed, then went into town. I decided not to take the car, as the tasks I had to complete could all be conveniently done on Albyn Place and the West end of Union Street, which was within easy walking distance of the flat. The morning was cold but clear and in the gardens and on the cars, there was a crisp white covering of frost. I popped into the Travel Agents, booked an open return to Stavanger and topped up what Kroner I had left.

I had got used to and quite enjoyed my own company, but there were times, I have to admit, I missed the interaction and 'crack' of the office and the lads in the football team. Having completed my allotted chores, I walked back toward the flat, along the path through the gardens by Rubislaw Terrace. It was only 11 am and I felt I needed and deserved a caffeine hit, so I changed course slightly and wandered up Queen's Road to the cafe for a cappuccino and, in a complete loss of will power, a bacon roll. I stayed there for an hour, sipping coffee and reading a copy of The Economist and the latest edition of the Big Issue which I had bought from a guy in town. Just before noon, the first wave of clones, the office workers and business types started milling in. I debated whether or not to stay and have lunch, or just head home. I decided on the latter, as having a full lunch in addition to the bacon roll was not good for the waist line. I said hello to a couple of surveyors, I'd had dealings with as I left. I was back in the flat within five minutes, then spent some time sorting out my mail.

That afternoon I planned having a drive out the Deeside Road to Banchory, as I had wanted to have a bit of a walkabout and check out some sites. I called a mate of mine, a guy called Jim Melville, an IT consultant who was 'resting' in between contracts, to see if he wanted to come with me, but he wasn't in so I left a message on the dreaded answer phone. Sometimes it seemed that everyone now had an answer phone or their own fax. Jim was older than me and still single, even though legend had it he was a bit of a ladies man. We had played football together for several years, before he had decided Aberdeen was too small a place and had jacked in his job and taken off around the world. He had virtually disappeared for fourteen months and apart from the odd post card, he had kept his whereabouts and adventures pretty close to his chest. Since coming back to Aberdeen, he had been doing consultancy work at tremendous day rates and I got the impression he was building up another stash so he could disappear off again. The two of us got on very well and, much as I loved Aberdeen, I sympathised with him, given the type of character he was and his need to express his Wanderlust. Jim was a mate, and also a very useful guy to have at your back if you were out in town and there looked like there was going to be some bother.

The youthful detective had settled in quickly to his new assignment following his transfer from the Met, but for some reason he was a bit apprehensive about approaching the Commander. Nervously he knocked on his boss's door. There was no response. He had prepared himself for the expected barked, 'yes, come in', but was surprised by the silence. Strange, the boss was a workaholic, he was always in.

"You looking for the Guv'nor?" The voice was pure barrow-boy.

"Yes, that's right. Is the Commander in the office today?" he asked in a voice that, in direct contrast, carried the refinement of his public school education.

"He's not in, mate, he's off on a jolly down to Hereford for a meeting with the boys in the *Regiment*. What is it?"

"It's a file from our colleagues up in Vauxhall Cross, they're just alerting him about the movement of some suspected mercenaries they believe are heading for the UK...I don't know if it's high priority, I just thought I'd let him know."

"Well, in that case just you leave it with me, I'll have a look at it and if it's important, I'll see that he gets it Monday and I'll tell him about your exceptional initiative. You've just been transferred to the Branch haven't you?"

The young lad wasn't listening,

"Can't we call him or something?"

"Look mate, the Commander is in discussions with the Embassy Blowers right now, so the last thing he needs is a wet knickered kid disturbing him with what is probably yesterday's news. You see son, you'll soon learn that the spooks in '6' rarely share their goodies with the likes of us."

"Just you see that he gets it."

"Yes sir! No sir! Three bags full sir! You can trust me sir!" he bleated sarcastically.

The young officer reluctantly handed over the file, glowered at his so called more experienced colleague and left. He was angry and embarrassed. Why were some policemen such fuckin' prats!

The week-end passed slowly. I just stayed in on the Saturday evening. I micro'd an M&S meal for two, cracked open a bottle of wine and settled down to watch the box. It was a hell of a boring way to spend a Saturday night. The TV shows on offer couldn't hold my attention and I dozed intermittently. Eventually I surrendered to weariness and went to bed. On Sunday morning, I read the papers then went out for lunch with Fraser McDonald, an old school friend. We had known each other for years and we always had a laugh when we got together. Fraser was one of the few people I completely relaxed with and I considered him a true friend. He was there at my wedding and was there at Hannah's funeral. For years I had been accused of being arrogant and emotionally aloof by those who didn't know me, even though I put it down to shyness, but with Fraser there was no need for pretence, conversation was always easy. He worked for an oil company and had spent some time working in the Middle East for a few years on 'expat' status as a cost engineer. He was disillusioned with his job, just as I had been when I was a faceless number with one of the oil majors. We would often meet for a few beers and scheme as to how we would make our fortunes. We had come up with a couple of possibilities, but I doubted that they'd ever fly. Every venture it seemed needed a wad of capital just to get started. He was one of the very few people, who had been supportive and had said I was doing the right thing when I packed up my job to become a free-lance journalist and property tycoon! I met Fraser as arranged and we managed to get a table in the corner of the conservatory, from where we could observe all the bar's comings and goings. A waitress approached our table while we were studying the menu.

"Hi, would you like to order a drink?"

"Yeah, pint of lager for me; Paul what are you having?"

"Purdey's please." I had developed a taste for the stuff a couple of years back. It was no longer considered fashionable to drink it, but so what, I liked it.

"Thanks, I'll be back in a few minutes to take your food order."

The girl smiled at us and left. We both watched her walk away; she was wearing a short skirt and had a great set of pins.

"Nice under-carriage," Fraser commented, before he turned on me, "You off the drink then?"

"No," I answered "I'm just looking after my body you can't be too careful at our age...are you still playing rugby?"

"Yeah sort of, I've injured my back, so I haven't been turning out for the Firsts."

Just then the waitress returned with our drinks and we gave her our order. I took a sip of my Purdey's, while Fraser put the pint glass to his lips and took a long, deep draught. Typical rugby player, I thought to myself. Hates a beer!

"Are you getting any physiotherapy for your back?" I asked with genuine concern.

"Yes sure, there's a cute wee Thai girl who comes round on a Sunday night and walks all over my back in her high heels."

Just as I was foolishly about to ask how he got in touch with her, he added.

"And then she gives me head...it's very therapeutic and only costs a fiver!" he explained, completely dead-pan.

I just about choked and spat my drink out at his comments, which had been inadvertently delivered as the leggy waitress returned with our starter. She gave me a strange look, as if I was laughing at her. Fraser's face had gone red and she returned to the waitress station with an indignant air. She seemed well pissed off.

"Bloody women, they're so touchy! You should see the ones I have to work with. I didn't know PMT lasted 365 days a year!"

"I know what you mean. I worked in an office full of women and individually I got on reasonably well with all of them, but when it came to their relationships with each other, shit! It was like being cornered by a coven full of rabid Rottweilers, but mind you, that's maybe a wee bit unfair on Rottweilers!" Fraser snorted a laugh.

We composed ourselves and I remarked that the girl might not return to wait on our table. We were both a little embarrassed; we hadn't meant to offend her. Fraser changed the subject

"Oh, by the way do you remember a guy called Euan Graham at one of the rugby club 'smokers', a couple of months ago? I introduced you to him."

"Yes, I remember him," I said, an image of a Neanderthal flashed across my mind, "big, solid guy, with a neck like Mike Tyson's...bit of a boring git, personality of a crow-bar and if I remember, I think he works for the police."

"Not exactly, but close, it's Special Branch, but that's the fella. He's usually based out at the airport. For a 'Fed', he's a real hard beggar - I'm glad I play on the same side as him. He's the sort of beast that does a fair bit of damage when he arrives at rucks, a right belligerent bastard. In simple Aberdonian terms, he's a radge. I don't know whether you pissed him off the other week, but believe it or not, he was asking all about you in the Club after yesterday's game."

"Oh aye, is he an arse-bandit like? Do you know what he was after?" I said trying to look disinterested.

"Nothing much really, nothing too strange, just personal sorts of things. He knows we're mates, obviously saw me as a credible and reliable source."

"That'll be the day!" I said, in my best John Wayne 'Searchers' drawl.

I racked my brains. Why would the police, let alone Special Branch, have any interest in me or my business dealings. I didn't do drugs, I wasn't involved in any scams and besides, since the Council, God bless them, had stopped giving out 95% grants for converting tenement flats in the mid-eighties, all my deals had been strictly above board. It then occurred to me, I bet Claire's playing a little game. Hell hath no fury...yes, it had to be that - she had a lot of contacts with the local Polizei and she'd be playing games in an effort to get back at me. Fraser saw through my mask and sensed my discomfort.

"Of course, I told them you were a right bad bastard and that you had been kicked out of college for drug dealing."

"You're fuckin' joking?" I sneered.

Fraser cracked up.

"Course, I'm winding you up...I told him you're a member of 'The Sons of Wallace', an extreme Scottish Nationalist group who go about threatening to burn out all the English white settlers in the Grampian area."

"Aye, aye."

"Relax, I said you're a good guy really, under all the protective layers. He seemed satisfied."

I wanted to ask more about this guy's interest in me, despite Fraser's assurances that everything was alright and that it was probably just nosiness on Bain's part. He didn't convince me, but I said nothing. Throughout our meal and during the rest of the day, these enquiries about me by a bloke from Special Branch, unofficial or not, intrigued and troubled me. I sat in front of the telly reading through my new book on Norway, unable to completely settle.

First thing Monday morning, I checked my diary. I had a few appointments in the afternoon, but I rearranged them for the Tuesday and used the day to scribble some notes and do some research for an article I was working on.

The phone didn't ring and I felt a little anxious. I made a sandwich for lunch, then realised I needed some milk. I switched on the answer phone and popped out to the local newsagent for a pint of semi-skimmed.

I hadn't been out of the flat for five minutes but, as chance would have it, Anja had called. Sod's Law. I looked at the flashing red light and pressed play,

"Hei, it's me, I have some more details about the trip. I have to go out to a meeting right now, but I'll call you later. Bye, take care." I rewound the tape and played the message again.

I couldn't believe she had called when I was out, but there wasn't much I could do about it now. I ate lunch, went through to the living room and played the compilation tape. I sang every word and what I didn't know I made up. When it came to some particular songs I would play them a couple of times, especially if they made me think of Anja.

She eventually called back a couple of hours later. We didn't talk for long, just enough for me to confirm my flight times and for her to say she would meet me at Sola.

"Bye. Take care and be good," I said.

*****

In the hushed, respectful silence of the board room Sir Arthur Knox-De Vries stood and addressed the other members of the Randolph Group.

"Gentlemen, thank you for coming, I will be brief, but just before I begin, can I just say, I appreciate the efforts you are all making at this time, however let's get down to business and the reason we are here. As you may be aware, Mr Richardson accepted our assignment though, sadly, he insists this will be the final time he will work for us. This is regrettable, but I can perhaps understand his motives.

"I have requested that he carry out the project as expeditiously as possible, before the end of the month in fact, but the final details of the timings will be his affair.

"To coincide with and therefore maximise the effect of Mr Richardson's work, I have taken steps to arrange for a confidential Government Document to be leaked to the media, at or around the time of his strike. The selective leaking of the contents of this document will undoubtedly provoke outrage among certain elements who are already isolated by their own fears and paranoia. They suspect a sell out of their position and I believe the phrase they are using is 'a derogation of sovereignty'. The leaking of this as yet incomplete document will be seized upon by the mass media and the revelations will, I am certain, magnify the impact of Richardson's work and should ensure the complete undermining and eventual destruction of an already precarious political process. I am confident that once this leak breaks and news of Richardson's work filters out, then any hopes of peace in the shabby working class streets and ghettos, however tentative, will be decisively wrecked."

There were grunts of approval.

"Gentlemen, a round of applause for Sir Arthur, for the way he has masterminded this very difficult situation for us. I am sure his plan will avert the serious threat that was looming from across the water."

"Thank you gentlemen, there is really no need," De Vries said calmly, "but, we should not get too carried away, after all, Mr Richardson still has to complete his assignment. Does anyone have any questions? No? Then thank you for your attendance. I do not think we need to meet together for some time, as I am sure the media coverage will more than keep you informed. Good day."

Moments later, the board room had emptied. The clock on the mantelpiece whirred and chimed and the eyes of the faces in the portraits gazed down, as they always did.

*****

Tuesday and Wednesday came and went. Workwise, I had been unproductive, but I did receive a cheque from the 'Times on Sunday' Scottish edition for a piece I had written on the decline of the north-east's white fishing business and the local skippers' concerns about interference from Brussels Eurocrats, but I was distracted, my mind was elsewhere. I spent the bulk of the remaining two days preparing for the trip, making sure everything was washed, ironed and ready for Thursday. I also spent a few hours just driving round town, with the radio turned up loud, looking for potential sites for flats, houses or small retail units. It was something I had always enjoyed doing and one or two had come to lucrative fruition, but it was a task that was becoming harder and harder, as the 'bigger players' monopolised all the obvious development opportunities. Like so many of my peers, I was having to look beyond Aberdeen for sites that were cost effective to develop.

On Thursday morning the alarm went off at 6:45 am and I rose immediately. It's funny, but it's so much easier getting up in the morning when you're in the right frame of mind. For years when I worked in the oil industry, getting out of bed in the morning was a chore and I would lie in for as long as possible without making myself late for the office. I had sussed out very quickly that the whole 'oil thing' was a game. It offered limited opportunity for career progression and unless you had set up your own business and were screwing, rather than being screwed by the oil companies, there was no chance of ever earning really big bucks. As I said, I quite admired some of the so called entrepreneurs who had made fortunes providing goods or services to the majors. I also knew full well there were a few skeletons rattling about in the cupboards, relating to how they got their start in the business. I had kept a file of the various snippets I had picked up over the years and it was a subject which required further investigation.

I had a quick look out of my bedroom window, to check the weather. The sky was blood-red, an impressive 'shepherd's warning' and I worried that I might be flying into a storm. Air flight turbulence and changes in cabin pressure usually fucked up my ears for days. I completed a set of weights, sit-ups and press ups, showered and packed. As usual I had left everything until the last minute, but I began working my way methodically through my ever dependable checklist and soon everything was ready: my well worn Rockport boots, my new Red Wings, Timberland deck shoes, a couple of Devold jumpers, my Dark blue Patagonia ski-jacket, Berghaus fleecy, etc, etc, etc, as Yul would say. I hoped I would have enough clothes. I had started to get into hill walking a couple of years earlier, so I had some bits and pieces, but my good intentions had never come to much. It hadn't managed to fill the gap left by my giving up football, although I had also bought a mountain bike and that was good for a blast up in the hills every now and then.

I packed my case, which was an old fashioned, leather one and over thirty-five years old. Hannah had searched every antique shop in and around Aberdeen until she found it and had given it to me one Christmas. It was covered in original Airline stickers and was of deep sentimental value. I was very proud of it and was secretly pleased that the Philistines among us did not appreciate its timeless style. I carefully and neatly filled my case with the bulk of my stuff and a black pilot's case with some smaller items. I was just about to call for a taxi when the phone rang.

"Hi!" I said as I snatched up the handset.

"That's not how you usually answer the phone."

Shit! It was Claire.

"Were you expecting a call from someone else?"

"No, no, sorry about that."

"Look Paul, I've been doing some thinking and I'd like to take you out for dinner on Saturday night, I need to talk to you."

I had never been a good liar, but on this occasion it just flowed naturally.

"Sorry Claire, that would have been great, but Andy's asked me to go down to London. He thinks he might be able to set me up with an interview for a job with a Sunday heavy. They're looking for a part-time correspondent for the north-east of Scotland and Andy's hoping I can get a crack at it."

"That's excellent news, I'll keep my fingers crossed for you."

She was very polite, wished me good luck and asked me to call her when I got back to let her know how I'd got on. It was very easy to like her when she behaved like that, but I was in the shit now. Things had been made relatively easy for me with regard to the Norway trip, because of Claire's decision to go, but now, having been caught off guard, I had started to dig a hole for myself. That was going to take a little bit of explaining when I got back. The bit about the interview was partly true, but it wasn't likely to happen for at least a couple of weeks. What the hell, what was I worrying about? I was a free agent, Claire had been the one to walk out. If it was a problem, I'd cross that bridge when I got back. Still, I wasn't comfortable lying.

I called a taxi. The driver rang the door bell a few minutes later. I kissed Hannah's photograph, whispered an apology and left for the airport. On this occasion my driver was a friendly, witty bloke and we chatted easily about football. On arrival at Dyce I even gave him a tip, which he politely refused at first, then accepted when I insisted he take it.

Having checked-in, I had some time to kill before the flight was called. I walked through the main waiting area and went in to the newsagent and started aimlessly thumbing through some mags: GQ, Esquire and the Face. My eyes then turned to the rows of paperbacks and I pulled a couple of the most recent thriller titles off the shelf and read the synopsis at the back. I was debating whether or not to buy one when my flight was called. I returned the books to their places when the familiar cover of a paperback from my past caught my eye, jogging into place some vivid memories. It was a book called 'The Pearl'. Not the John Steinbeck classic, but a compilation of Victorian erotica that had done the rounds at school when I was in First Year. It had been a quite memorable introduction to the world of sex for a lad in his early teens. I grinned as my mind recounted the stories and the various adjectives and nouns which had been used to describe and refer to the male and female sex organs and the 'sex act'.

I left the shop and walked toward the entrance to the International Departure lounge.

As usual the metal detector bleeped as I went through and I was frisked and as usual, it was the metal frames of my glasses that had caused the problem. I had fairly good eyesight, but years of working under fluorescent light and at VDU's had made me susceptible to headaches and the optician suggested that because I had a slight prescription, glasses would be beneficial for me in the long run. I had bought a pair with Armani frames and they were good for a pose. Once I'd satisfied security that I wasn't a terrorist threat and I wasn't carrying anything I shouldn't have, I proceeded into the departure lounge. I always had a chuckle at these people in their tasteless uniforms, with their moustaches and tattooed forearms...the men weren't much better. I had a quick run off, before handing in the tear-off section of my boarding card and making my way to the plane.

There were about fifty passengers on the flight. Suits mostly. Suits that hung limply on the hunched shoulders of nondescript, sad little men who all longed for the day they could escape from the snare of The Job and working for someone else. The oil business - international travel, glamour? - all just crap really. It's a dirty bastard of a business. Of course the boys at the top of the heap, they were in the main alright. Money, power, kudos and all the 'invisible' benefits and trappings that go with corporate and executive snobbery, but a few rungs down the pecking order, the cannon-fodder below them, the worker bees, were all trapped in The Job. Family commitments, mortgages, just making enough to get by, suffering from a lack of recognition, having to be nice to 'clients', always having to put on a show, creating the right impression, talking in the 'buzz-word' of the day. It was worse in the 'contracting' sector. I had worked in both and now, as cost-reduction became the order of the day, if the customer said 'jump', you said 'how high?' However the way the industry was going, even the bosses were no longer safe. Rationalisation, re-engineering, right-sizing, all the new phrases for good old-fashioned job-cuts were taking their toll and it was the 'Executive' levels who were now also in the firing line.

Working for the large corporation had always sat uneasily on my shoulders and I used to spend hours, days even, dreaming and scheming my way out. It was all a game. I had been there, hated it and I thanked God I was free from all that. Property development provided the cash, writing provided the creativity, freedom and contentment.

It's all a bloody game and if you're not fortunate enough to be playing with your own ball, then the workplace is a tough old place and you just have to play to someone else's rules. Society's changing, the days of careers and jobs for life are slipping away. In my opinion, the ideal situation is to have 'fuck off' money, but people like that are few and far between.

I checked the seat number on my boarding card and found myself sitting beside a female Petroleum Engineer, who was heading ultimately for Bergen, where she was based. A graduate of Heriot Watt in Edinburgh, she was originally from Bath. She sounded a bit posh at first, but turned out to be a bit of a laugh. I enjoyed her company. When the conversation turned to more mundane issues, it transpired that she was extremely career minded, but I wondered if her naive enthusiasm of the present would be dulled in the future as the career promises of her employers failed to materialise and her aspirations faded into cynicism. She had been in Bergen for eighteen months and we discussed the differences between life in Scotland and Norway. Her description of the city of Bergen made me keen to visit one day. She gave me her business card and asked me to look her up. We touched the ground at Sola and, just before leaving the plane, I wished her all the very best with her career. I retrieved my case from the conveyor belt, passed through customs without a hitch and stepped out into the main concourse of the airport public areas. Although Dyce was currently being re-furbished, Sola was light years ahead by comparison in terms of style and the practicality of its layout.

Anja was standing there waiting. She was in her 501's again, but something was different. She walked toward me and we hugged and kissed.

"You're wearing glasses," I said vacantly, "You look great in them. You almost look intelligent!"

"Hey fuck you! You know you are terrible."

She did look great. She was wearing stylish, wire-framed specs, with small, neat lenses, that suited her perfectly. I found her irresistible.

"I like your case," she said, "it's very you."

"Thank you," I said, smiling back at her, "I think that's a compliment."

"Is it genuine Louis Vuitton?" she asked with a giggle.

"Well slap my thigh, Norwegian sarcasm or is it wit?" We both laughed.

"How was the flight over?" she asked, as we made our way to the car.

"It was good. I met this really nice girl, who was in the aisle seat next to me. She was on her way to Bergen, where she works as some kind of Engineer. Anyway, being a gentleman, I offered her my seat so she could sit at the window and we just got talking. She was alright, smart and funny."

"By the sound of your voice, I'm surprised you didn't stay on the plane and fly up to Bergen with her!"

"The thought did cross my mind, but then I remembered I promised to fit you in this weekend. Still she gave me her phone number."

Anja shook her head and said something in Norwegian to me, which made her laugh. I put my cases in the boot and we set off. I gave the dash board an affectionate tap and told her how much I liked her car. She explained that it been her father's and that she had bought it from him several years ago and in a year's time it would be so old that it was exempt from tax, or something. Somehow the old car just suited her. It wasn't exactly this year's model and close examination revealed some evidence of rust and some mis-matched primer had been used to touch up some marks and scratches. The seats had been patched in places, but it got my vote.

The red sky of the Aberdeen morning had so far borne no ill and the sun was shining brightly against a background that was clear apart from a few small cloud puffs that were sent scudding across the distant mountains by the light breeze. I put on my Wayfarers and looked across at Anja, who nodded approvingly as we continued to head north and east away from Stavanger. We had been driving for about three quarters of an hour when I asked,

"What's the plans for this weekend then?"

"I can't say. It's a secret. You'll find out when we get there."

"Bloody Norwegians! My brother Steve said you never could get a straight answer out of them," I quipped.

By now we were well out of Stavanger and the scenery was, for want of a better cliché, breathtaking. It was almost Alpine, but with a harder, rawer edge. More wilderness than just biscuit tin beauty. We were making our way along roads that clung perilously to the steep mountains, overlooking lush narrow valleys and fjords, which had been gouged, bulldozed and furrowed into shape thousands of years ago by glacial action. Every now and then Anja would have to switch the car's lights to full beam as we entered yet another tunnel, hewn from the solid rock. Sometimes on exiting a tunnel we would pass through a torrent of water, crashing down from the mountain and onto the road. In fact there was water everywhere, from the sea fjords, whose long crooked fingers stretched for miles inland, piercing the bare mountains, the valley floor, criss-crossed with fast flowing rivers and burns and everywhere you looked there seemed to be waterfalls. Spectacular cascades of white water and spray pouring down the mountain sides, covering the pale granite of the cliff walls in a lace like veil. It was as if the frozen heart of Norway itself was melting.

"What do you think of my country then? You had better say something nice."

"It's stunning. If I was wearing my romantic Scottish writer hat, I would have to describe it as 'a dream of rock and water - a bold, heroic land'"

"That's nice - I like that."

"It reminds me of parts of Scotland, particularly an area called Torridon, in the west. I feel at home here."

"I'm glad you feel that way."

The next few miles passed in relative silence then, without really thinking why, I idly asked her, "What does the 'H' in Anja H. Andresen stand for?"

"Why?" she asked suspiciously.

"Just curious, but the note you gave with your phone number had Anja H. Andresen. I just wondered..."

"It stands for Hilde," she said softly, with a casual unconcern. She didn't turn round, her eyes concentrating on the road ahead.

"Hilda!" I mimicked, the way she had pronounced it, trying not to sound like the Chef in the Muppets. "Hilda as in Ogden, as in cleaner woman, as in hair curlers, flying ducks and a 'muriel' on the wall," I laughed aloud, expecting her to be confused by my connection.

"Are you making fun of me?" she asked.

"No," I said, stifling a giggle.

"The Hilda you refer to from Coronation Street - yes we do get that in Norway - is spelt with an 'a', my name is spelt with an 'e'," she explained indignantly.

"Oh! Sorry, I stand corrected. Hilde, eh? Hilde with an 'e'," I smirked.

"I'm very proud of my name you know, it was my grandmother's."

I think I had hurt her feelings a little bit.

"Sorry, I'm just joking Anja, it's a nice name...honestly. It's, it's...very Norse and it suits you."

"I accept your apology, you sarcastic Scottish bastard."

Changing the subject I asked, "What kind of music do you like?"

"I like everything really," she said, "rock, pop, dance music, some opera and classical pieces, what about you?"

"Me? Oh, my taste is pretty eclectic, it..."

"I'm sorry, what is that word?"

"Eclectic? I think it means it's not exclusive. I borrow from many sources is the dictionary definition."

She smiled, she had a new word.

"I like the same things as you really. I don't have the patience to play whole albums or CDs so I tend to just pick out and play individual tracks, whether its rock, soul and like you some opera and classical 'greatest hits'. I'm certainly no buff, but I do have a few favourites, like "Au fond du temple saint" from the Pearl Fishers, "Oh mio babbino caro", from Gianni Schicchi, "Ebben ? ne andro whatever", from La Wally, "Belle nuit", the duet from the Tales of Hoffman and the Bailey's advert and of course, "Un bel di", from Madama Butterfly. I used to like "Nessun Dorma", but doesn't everyone? Since Italia 90, its not exclusive anymore. Like so many other things we become too familiar with, it brings with it a degree of contempt. There is also a song, I think its called the 'Shepherd's Song', but I'm not 100% sure, which was used years ago as backing music for a Dubonnet advert. I don't know if its from an opera, but it's so good, so dreamy. There are probably others, but I can't think of them. I also like soul music, Otis Redding, Al Green, some rock music, again mostly individual tracks. I also like to get mellow and self-indulgent and listen to Frank Sinatra, Ella Fitzgerald, the songs of Cole Porter,...Christ, there's so much, I've even liked and I don't know whether I should admit this or not, songs by Abba and that Norwegian lot, A-ha. Maybe your country should have entered them in the Eurovision song contest."

"Yes, very funny, I'm sure. There's nothing wrong with either of those two groups, you know and just for the record, my favourite songs by Abba are "Knowing Me, Knowing You" and "The Day before you came" and may be "SOS"."

"That's a good call, I'll go with that."

"What about movies? What kind of movies do you like?"

"You're putting me in the spot now, but again, it's a bit of everything. I have a soft spot for old, classic black and white films, like "Some like it hot", "The Thirty Nine Steps", or as Tom Hanks referred to them, 'chick's movies', weepies, like

"Casablanca", "Now Voyager", "Camille", "Brief Encounter", I also like a good Western, a good Hitchcock type thriller, the odd French or foreign movie..."

"'Now Voyager', which one was that ?"

"It's an old Bette Davis movie, where she plays the part of a frumpy spinster who, when she's re-covering from a breakdown is advised to go on a world cruise, as part of her rehabilitation and therapy. On her travels she meets and falls in love with a married man. It's very moving and very sad and the theme music is great too."

"Is that the one where the guy, I think he was in Casablanca, lights up two cigarettes at once and gives her one."

"Yes, that's right, that's the fella," I said, smiling at the thought of Paul Henreid giving Bette Davis 'one', but that was not quite what Anja meant and I don't think the censor of the day would have allowed anything as graphic as that in the movie!

"Oh yes, I like that one as well. I think we have similar tastes, but I also think there are things you can show me and introduce me to that I'm not aware of. There's a lot you can teach me."

"I doubt it."

I was pleased that my tastes in music and films, as wide and varied as they were, appealed to her. I was falling under her spell, intoxicated and beguiled not only by the scenery, but more importantly by Anja. Slowly, but surely seduced by her beauty and that of her country.

We passed by farms, small villages of wooden houses, their back-gardens the mountains and below their front-windows, the fjords. Every now and then we passed a "hytter", a small cabin the Norwegians traditionally escape to at weekends or during holidays. We seemed to be climbing higher and higher and I could feel the pressure changes in my ears as the road became steeper and steeper, hair-pinning its way up in to the mountains.

"Is this old car going to make it Anja?" I asked.

"Fuck you!" she cried and tried to grab at my leg. We were both laughing as we reached the summit. "Would you like to stop for a while?" she asked

"Yes, good idea, it's an amazing view and, being a tourist, I wish I had brought a camera."

"Sorry, didn't I tell you, no cameras allowed on this trip."

More mystery. We parked the car just off the road in a rough surfaced lay-by and I gave the bonnet a pat when I got out.

"Well done you old beast...and the same to you car," I said, but Anja either didn't hear it, or maybe she didn't get it.

We stood and marvelled at the views that had opened up all around us. Like my beloved Scotland, it was a stunning, wild country. Anja took my hand and we sat on a large boulder by the car drinking in the cool, clear, mountain air. To the north and east, snow covered mountains and their glaciers rose ever higher above us. To the west we could see the blues and greens of the North sea and to the south the highlands gradually tapered off into farmland. We watched as the sun cast the shadows of small wispy, cirrus clouds causing a dappling effect that faded the waterfall-streaked slopes to shades of grey. Anja put her arm round me and kissed me on the cheek. I didn't react and just stared at the view. It was quiet up here. I felt at peace with myself. The scenery evoked memories of my first trip up Lochnagar on the Balmoral estate, when coming over the 'saddle' below the Meikle Pap, I had seen the great corrie for the first time and had felt humbled by its dark and brooding crags.

"What are you thinking, Paul?" she whispered.

"Nothing."

It was the second time she had asked me that question and it was the second time I had lied. I looked back over a backdrop of sea, rock and sky.

We went back into the car and started to make the descent down to the valley floor. We drove on for maybe another forty minutes. Although the mountains were all around us we didn't seem to climb as much again. I had absolutely no idea where we were, and was just about to ask when Anja suddenly pulled off the road, through two unobtrusive white gate posts and onto a long, winding tarmac drive. The track we were now on was lined by fir and birch trees and just through their cover I could see the cold, grey waters of a loch. The drive turned sharply away from the loch and we came upon the house. It looked magnificent, a large whitewashed timber building of three stories, with a colonial style wrap around verandah, that supported a first floor balcony, which looked out over the tree tops to the waters of the loch and the mountains.

"Well Paul, here we are."

Anja mentioned the house by its Norwegian name, but my non-existent grasp of the language prevented me from being able to repeat it or remember it. She parked the car at the back of the building in a gravel covered courtyard area and we retrieved our cases from the boot. It was good to be here at last and if the setting was anything to go by, it would be a memorable weekend.

*****

Richardson had travelled to Bruges that morning by train and was already seated at an outside table to the left of the main entrance of the cafe when the priest arrived. Although he was shadowed by the awning from the late autumn sunshine, Richardson continued to wear the darkened pilot glasses. Somehow the priest knew Richardson's eyes were upon him and that they had been ever since he had crossed the cobbled, pedestrianised square known as the Burg. Father Cahal Byrne still wore the collar of office, but it had been at least twelve years since his actions and morals had been denounced and disowned by the Church hierarchy. Throughout his vocation he had developed a fondness for alcohol and women which shadowed his calling. He had a saying, 'If God hadn't wanted me to drink he wouldn't have given me a mouth and if he didn't want me to screw, he wouldn't have given me a cock'. He prided himself in the knowledge that in the business he was referred to as the Priest.

"Good morning, Mr Richardson," said Byrne as he adjusted the position of the bentwood chair to allow him to sit comfortably at the table.

"I'm afraid I will have to rush you this morning as I have a busy schedule. I also fear I may be taking a serious risk meeting with you."

"What happened to your hand?" asked Richardson.

"Oh, it's nothing, hazard of the job."

Richardson leant across the table.

"Please explain to me what happened to your hand."

Before Byrne had a chance to answer a waiter in starched white apron appeared at the table.

"A Ricard for me, do you want anything?"

"Coffee please, black coffee."

"And a black coffee."

The waiter turned and stepped into the cafe. Byrne began his explanation.

"Just after that assassination in Strasbourg."

"Which one?"

Byrne looked at Richardson, puzzled by his question and his apparent ignorance of such a high profile incident.

"The hit a few months ago when a countryman of mine was wiped out by a single shot in the head. You say you know not of it. Strange, I would have thought you would have heard all about it. It was all over the newspapers but perhaps you were out of the country."

"No, I'm not aware of it. Maybe I was out of the country at the time. Have the French police caught the perpetrator?"

"Not as far as I'm aware," he said slowly.

"Hmmm. Anyway, a few days afterwards I received an unexpected visit from some acquaintances from the old country. They wanted to know if I knew anything about what had happened." Richardson said nothing; Byrne continued, "I told them I knew lots of things. I told them I knew lots of people..."

"And?"

"Well, on this occasion I couldn't help them. I couldn't remember anything that might have assisted them with their enquiries."

"So that's what happened to your hand?"

"They thought it would help me remember. Each broken finger was meant to act like an aide memoire. Dirty, Godless bastards," he said nursing the memory of the pain and the bandaged hand.

"And did it?"

The priest was cautious now. "There was nothing to remember," he said abruptly.

He immediately sipped the Ricard that had just been placed on the table.

"Do you have my money?"

85

"Yes."

"Can I have it now?"

Richardson ignored the question.

"The equipment I ordered - has it all been transferred to Oslo and securely stored, ready for pick up?"

"Yes, yes, of course. Of course." Byrne was impatient now, "Here are all the details. Now please can I have my money?"

He pushed an envelope over to Richardson's side of the fake marble table.

"Please, Mr Richardson, I have another appointment. I'm going to be late."

Richardson picked up the unsealed envelope and removed the contents. His eyes, still hidden by the sunglasses, glanced over the page.

"Your money is in a child's napsack. It's in the toilets, the middle cubicle, placed behind the U-bend."

Byrne downed the remnants of the Ricard. He felt he had outstayed his welcome. He knew Richardson was an awkward bastard, but he had been a little more congenial on previous meetings.

"Thank you, Mr Richardson. As ever, it's a pleasure doing business with you. Please excuse me, but I do have another engagement. I'm a busy man you know. Like you, there seems to be an ever increasing demand for my services."

He rose from his chair and offered his hand to Richardson. Richardson remained seated, picked up the one page document and placed it in the breast pocket of his jacket. Byrne withdrew his hand, snorted indignantly and scurried into the cafe in the direction of the gents toilets.

He entered the dingy room which stank of disinfectant and urine. There was no one around. He moved quickly to the middle cubicle and leant down, his arm outstretched feeling for the bag. As Richardson had promised, a child's yellow dayglo napsack was stashed behind the U-bend. He eased himself forward and tried to remove the bag. It didn't budge. It was jammed in the piping. He moved closer and stretched further forward, struggling to remove the bag. A bead of sweat ran from his forehead down over the bridge of his nose. He cursed Richardson. This was not how a man of his position should be treated, scrabbling on his hands and knees in a Belgian shite house.

The place stank. He stretched again, adjusting his body to get a better purchase on one of the dangling straps. One sharp tug and it would be free. As he concentrated on removing his prize, he did not heed the faint creak as the unlocked cubicle door was pushed open. The priest smiled as the bag was finally released from its hiding place. The smile evaporated instantly as he felt a great chunk of hair on the top of his head being grabbed. He gasped as his head was jerked backwards then violently propelled forward, smashing his face on the cold porcelain of the WC. The attacker immediately repeated the assault. He dropped the bag.

"Take it, for God's sake take it!"

He felt the grip on his hair tighten. The priest began to panic, his hands now flailing frantically in an attempt to release the grip of his assailant. He felt his head being ripped back then pulled forward and once again his unprotected face cannoned off the toilet bowl. This time his legs buckled, but in the confined space of the cubicle, his semi-conscious body did not sprawl on the floor. It lay hunched between bowl and wall. The attacker eased the body back and carefully rested Byrne's injured head on the ground. The priest moaned. Faint traces of blood had begun to drip from wounds to his nose and forehead. The assailant's gloved hands removed a ball point pen from Byrne's jacket and placed it point first at the entrance of his ear canal. Then with one sharp, stubbing kick, the pen entered the ear piercing the brain for several inches.

The attacker calmly heaved the former priest's dead body onto the toilet seat. He then turned and bolted the door before scaling the wall and dropping down into the adjoining cubicle. He left the toilets and walked slowly through the corridor toward the busy bar, peeling off the black gloves. As he placed the gloves in his pocket, he reached further down and retrieved his sunglasses and placed them on his face. He walked through the bar and out into the bright sunshine. The train journey back to Brussels would take about an hour. He would still have plenty of time to catch the flight to Oslo.

In the cubicle, the yellow napsack lay unopened only inches from the dangling left hand of the corpse.

*****

The back door of the house opened and a striking, blonde woman with high curved cheek bones, I would guess in her early to mid forties, called out to us in English.

"Hello you two, I'm glad you have arrived safely. Anja, Bjorn is waiting for you in the study. As usual he needs your help with some notes and accessing data from his computer files. He's been quite unbearable, you know."

"Hi, Nina," called Anja and they then proceeded to jabber away in Norwegian. I put my case down as Nina walked toward us. She was dressed in a pair of ski pants, walking boots and a very colourful Norwegian jumper - you know the kind, the very colourful ones with the silver clasps on them. The kind of jumper your mum would threaten to dress you in when you were a kid and you wouldn't want to be seen dead in it - but on Nina it looked great. Apparently, the different designs represent a particular area or valley in Norway. Nina and Anja hugged and kissed.

"Nina, this is Paul."

I held my hand out and she shook it gently and kissed me on the cheek. It was a warm and friendly greeting and I immediately liked her.

"So finally, this is Anja's Paul. She hasn't stopped talking about you for days. Welcome to Manefossen!" Nina continued, "I hope Anja has been looking after you."

Before I had a chance to answer, Nina said something to Anja in Norwegian, which was incomprehensible to me, but caused her to blush and then both of them to giggle. We walked across the gravel, then through a stable-style split door and into a kind of utility room which led directly into the kitchen. There were a number of Barbour-style waxed jackets hanging up and a couple of pairs of well used walking boots were drying out on the floor, their laces slackened off and lying untidily on the coir matting. There were also some colourful golf brollys and several intricately carved walking sticks resting in a wrought iron holder and a navy coloured Duffel coat, minus a few toggies, had been slung casually over the back of an old bentwood chair. Two large porcelain sinks and a work top completely filled the back wall and I suspected the room may have doubled as a scullery in the past.

"Let's get you two settled into your rooms. Then, if he's not too engrossed in his work, I'll introduce Paul to Bjorn. He's in the study, Anja, and he wants to see you as soon as possible. He's tremendously excited about the next few days, Paul, but also a little tetchy, as he has been struggling to access his computer files. I think he has forgotten his password, but Anja knows only too well what he's like and she can handle him."

We went out through the large kitchen, which looked like it had once been the domain of a Hudson and a Mrs Bridges, then up a short flight of steps into the hall. I felt comfortable in the house. It had a warm, homely feel to it, despite its size and the quietness and remoteness of its location. It was decorated in what I imagine is a traditional Scandinavian style. The floorboards were stripped back to the bare wood, stained, sealed, varnished then covered in rich coloured rugs. There was an abundance of what appeared to my untrained eye to be expensive antique tables and dressers. Traditional oil paintings adorned the walls and dried flower arrangements in terracotta pots or hand-painted ginger jars sat on shelves in all the alcoves. Anja had obviously been there before and she disappeared. Duty called.

Nina showed me to my room.

"If you need anything, more towels, a new duvet, if that one is not warm enough for you, whatever, you only have to ask. When you have unpacked and sorted yourself out, just make your way down to the kitchen and if Bjorn is preoccupied, I'll give you a quick tour of the house, OK?"

"Yes that's fine." I wanted to say 'thank you' in Norwegian, but I didn't have the confidence.

"Good, I shall see you in a little while." She smiled, then deftly flicked her hair away from her face and left.

My room was superb. A modern central heating system had been installed and it was very warm. I dumped my cases on the giant bed, a bateau lit (which Hannah would have loved) and checked out the en suite bathroom. The bath was massive. Raised on four small brass legs, it was both long and deep and obviously part of the original fittings. I looked forward to a long relaxing soak at some stage. A modern shower cubicle had also been installed, but it was out of character with the ambience of the rest of the house, which is probably why they had tucked it away, out of sight, in a corner behind the door. I went back into the bedroom. Everywhere you looked there were pieces of furniture that were probably worth a fortune and would have been swallowed up by collectors back home. I turned my attentions away from what I could nick and looked out of the window. My room was at the front of the house and, pulling back the pale blue chambray curtains, I had an unbroken view over the trees, down to the loch and beyond to the now mist shrouded mountains. Unfortunately, the door from my room onto the balcony was locked and there was no key.

I quickly unpacked, put my pants and socks in a drawer next to the bed and hung everything else up in a magnificent carved pine wardrobe with blue stencilled flowers on the doors. I emptied my toiletries bag and neatly arranged everything on the shelves in the bathroom, then I had a wash, brushed my teeth and made my way back down through the house. I crept down the back stairs and entered the cosy warmth of the kitchen.

"Come on in Paul, don't be shy, this is Mr and Mrs Rolfson, the resident house-keepers. They will be looking after us for the next few days. As you will soon find out Mrs Rolfson is a wonderful cook and I think Anja has already told her all about your likes and dislikes...you should eat your greens you know, they're very good for you."

I shook hands with the couple and mumbled how nice it was to meet them. They both nodded and smiled. Nina poured me a cup of coffee, which I just looked at. Astutely, she realised my predicament and called to Mrs Rolfson.

"Mrs Rolfson, can you get my young Scots friend some milk and sugar, please."
The two women laughed and I felt a little embarrassed. I gratefully accepted the sugar and milk and took a sip, the first mouthful tasting awful as it reacted with the toothpaste. Nina sat down with me at the huge wooden table, and poured herself another cup of black coffee and lit a cigarette. Her smoking surprised me. She then began to tell me about the house. I sat and listened as she gave me a history lesson on the building and its former occupants.

It had been built in the late 1920's by a very wealthy ship owing family, who had originated from Haugesund and it had been donated to the Norwegian Government who had held it in trust for the last fifteen years, when the great-grandfather and founder of the business empire had died. It had been his special place, his retreat from the pressure of business life, but the family had all moved on to other things and the great family get-togethers of distant summers had long since faded and gone. There were no obvious signs of the family's sea-faring connections, other than the brass anchor-shaped door knocker on the front door and a massive ship's wheel in the drawing room above the fire place, taken from the ship that had been the first of the fleet and to which the old patriarch had fondly referred to as his 'mistress'. He had lost two sons in the War, the eldest killed on active service with the Royal Norwegian Airforce, and his youngest son killed whilst leading a raid by the Resistance against a German garrison. It had almost broken him to have his sons buried before him. The remaining offspring, notably his daughters and his grand-children and their families, had all but cashed in the old man's great legacy. The new generation did not share his great sense of tradition, nor his love of the sea.

Nina asked me about my life in Aberdeen then, after I had finished my coffee, led me out of the kitchen, back up the steps, through the hall and into the drawing room. It was an impressive place. A vast open log fire roared in the hearth and above the high mantelpiece was the ship's wheel, just as Nina had described. A grand piano dominated one corner of the room and the rest of the floor space was full of sofas, high-backed wicker and leather chairs, chaises longues, an old globe and a superb original horn gramophone which would have looked great in my flat. There was not a speck of dust, no doubt a tribute to the hard work and dedication of the Rolfsons. A set of French windows opened directly out onto the verandah. It was a magnificent room and I tried to imagine it in its heyday, with the grand old mariner presiding over his children and his grandchildren. A room full of laughter and music. I noticed an old photograph of two little boys, no older than five and eight, dressed in sailor suits, standing next to a tall man dressed in a blazer, polo-neck and light coloured slacks. Nina noticed my interest.

"It's a lovely photograph, two little boys and their father."

"He looks so proud of them."

"Yes, I'm sure he was, but the boys were the ones who were killed in the war and they say the old man never really got over it."

"That's such a sad and tragic story."

We walked on. I was in awe of the place and I wondered what the other guests would be like and how I'd fit in. I hated unknowns, but I would try and relax and enjoy the weekend with Anja.

We left the drawing room and returned to the hall and from there we entered a superb dining room, which was dominated by a great rosewood dining table set for ten and decorated by what I surmised were genuine silver candelabra and a large vase of freshly cut flowers. Nina glanced at her watch.

"We will be dining at eight, but in the meantime would you like to go for a walk outside. Bjorn and Anja must still be preparing for the other guests."

"Yes, that sounds good," I answered. Preparing what, I wondered.

We went back into the hall then out toward the front door, which I opened for Nina and allowed her to pass through. She smiled and thanked me.

The house was surrounded by a well-raked and weeded gravel path, and we walked its course around the building. I felt at ease with Nina, although I couldn't help but get the feeling she was sussing me out, gauging me for whatever lay ahead. I was desperate to ask who the other guests were and what Anja and Bjorn were preparing, but I held back. Anja could provide me with that information later. We walked another half circuit of the house before arriving at the back-door. I could see by the lengthening shadows that the light was dying and darkness was falling quickly. It had become quite chilly. Frosty even.

"Let's get freshened up before dinner. You know your way to your room?"

"Yes, I think so."

"Good, we'll see you later Paul."

"Yes."

"By the way, it's nice to have you here with us."

"Thank you."

It was only 5.45 pm I made my way back up to my room, kicked off my boots and lay on the bed. I was puzzled; the whole trip was cloaked in more than just a little mystery. I sat on the bed and read some magazines, but the time dragged. I tried to snatch a few Zs, but to no success, so to help pass the time I took a long shower, turning the controls up to full power and adjusting the shower head so that the water exploded out of the nozzle under full pressure, pummelling the skin of my neck and shoulders. At 7.50 pm Anja appeared. She knocked on the door but came straight in. Fortunately, I was already dried off and dressed. She came right over, sat on the bed next to me and kissed me.

"Has Nina been looking after you? She's very beautiful, don't you think?"

"Yes, to both questions, but it would have been nice to have spent some time with you."

"Oh, poor you!"

"Anja, what have I let myself in for this weekend?"

"I'm sorry Paul, I don't understand."

She was teasing me, so I pulled her over and pinned her down on the bed.

"Bullshit, who's coming here tomorrow?"

Anja laughed and changed the subject.

"Come on we have to eat now."

I let her up, and gave her a look that told her I wanted some more information. She smiled at me knowingly as we made our way down, not to the dining room, but into the kitchen where the table was set for four.

Chapter 4

CHAPTER 4

At precisely eight o'clock, Nina entered the kitchen. She was followed some moments later by her husband, who just breezed into the room. He was tall, athletic and very self-assured. Anja squeezed my hand, to let me know she was there.

"Professor Pederson, this is my friend Paul from Scotland."

The Professor shook my hand firmly.

"Anja, don't be so formal. I'm delighted to meet you Paul...and please call me Bjorn."

Nina and Bjorn were a very handsome couple. She was poised, sophisticated and had retained all her beauty. Then there was Bjorn. For a man who must have passed his fiftieth year he was wearing very well. I suppose his look was a little like Peter Strauss of 'Rich Man Poor Man' fame. He was tanned and healthy looking, in fact they both were, but while she was fair haired, he was darker with distinguished grey streaks in the swept back hair above his ears. He had a slight mark, probably scar tissue, on his cheek, below his left eye, which enhanced the character of his face. In fact, the scar could easily have been explained, (if I allowed my imagination some freedom) as the foil or rapier mark of a Heidelburg student. He had, however, studied at Oxford and not on the banks of the Rhine and his accent was indiscernible and as I was to find out as the weekend progressed, his command of the English language was impressive, probably better than mine.

We all sat down at the table and Mr Rolfson offered each of us a freshly baked bread roll and then proceeded to serve up a bowl of fish soup, which tasted like a cross between Cullen Skink and chowder.

We ate our first course in relative silence and as Mr Rolfson cleared away the bowls, Bjorn spoke.

"Paul, apart from the obvious attraction of spending time with Anja, you must be wondering what is going on here...yes?"

I nodded.

"Well perhaps it is time to brief you. You are no doubt an intelligent young man, Paul, a journalist Anja tells me. However, before I continue, I would respectfully ask that you do not reveal details of any of the proceedings or the identities of any of the participants of the next few days here at Manefossen."

I nodded again, "No problem."

"You are, I am sure, well aware of the recent Arab-Isreali Peace Accord...of course you are, well that came about as the result of a little 'back door' diplomacy by the Norwegian Government and a colleague of mine, and his staff, back in Oslo. Several months ago, in fact it's well over a year ago, as the Arab-Isreali discussions began to make progress, just before the media circus caught on and became involved, I was given the opportunity to try and help end a conflict here on our own doorstep in Europe. My country's Government, the Storting, have long believed that the various public political initiatives that had taken place have disguised a basic strategy of inaction by the real peace-brokers in this 'war'. This coincided entirely with my own beliefs and I was given a very delicate brief to try and effect meaningful change."

I immediately thought of the Balkans and the strife in the former Yugoslavia, but Bjorn continued.

"Tomorrow, we will be joined by six men from opposing sides of this conflict, two on opposite sides of the intellectual divide, two from opposite sides of the political divide and the final two, who have over the past twelve or so years been actively involved in the armed struggle as deadly enemies."

My pulse was racing and my mouth had gone dry. He had clearly and deliberately used the phrase 'armed struggle'. This was nothing to do with the Balkans and just as Bjorn was about to confirm my guess, Rolfson served the main course. A traditional dish called 'komle', which was a stew of smoked sausage, smoked pork and a kind of suet doughball. It was very good, but very filling.

Bjorn continued.

"For the past nine months, we have been secretly meeting here in Norway, away from the constraints of normal diplomacy, political pressures and the glare of publicity, in an effort to get some sort of agreement or at least a basis for negotiation to achieve a lasting peace on the island of Ireland and somehow end the campaigns of violence on both sides, particularly in Ulster. We are focusing in on the part played by the paramilitaries. They are the ones with the guns and bombs, and if we can persuade them to remove the weaponry from the equation and offer them a voice at the discussion table, then I believe it will be quite straightforward to bring the mainstream political parties into the fray. We have therefore worked very hard during these groundwork meetings, to establish a position that will eventually bring all parties to the table.

"These discussions are held informally and without the official blessing of the Governments of London and Dublin. They are held secretly for security reasons and of course voluntarily there is absolutely no pressure on any of the group to attend these, shall we say, 'get togethers'. I should also point out, we are not some obscure group, although as I have said we have no official sanction to proceed from any Government other than my own. I am also very aware that for years, there have been secret discussions between London and Dublin and more frequently, between the Republican paramilitaries and officials of the Dail, usually set up through the intermediary of a priest, but in all the years these 'talks' have gone on, there has never emerged a clear and genuine sign of progress. It is a delicate and complex process, as I am sure you are aware. Feelings run deep on both sides of the sectarian divide. On the other hand, we have been making great progress and we like to feel we more than played our part, no, I am convinced we were the catalyst that led to the Republican cease-fire declaration, although the process nose-dived to a worrying level soon afterwards, when the Head of the Sinn Fein delegation, on his way to meet with members of a European Parliament economic support group, was assassinated by an unknown assailant. That single violent act almost pushed the Province to the edge of civil war, but we have continued to work away behind the scenes, trying to de-fuse the situation and move forward, turning toward a progressive democratic process.

"As you are well aware, there has been never been a declaration of responsibility for that murder and the contacts I have within Loyalist paramilitaries vehemently deny any involvement, even though the media hype surrounding the incident has lain the blame firmly at their door. It's a simplistic, but not unreasonable conclusion, even though I am convinced it is incorrect and I am prepared to say that quite categorically, as I have been given firm assurances on this. I have developed an understanding of the situation in Ulster, but the sudden nature of the IRA cease-fire, so soon after the Sinn Fein rejection of the Downing Street Declaration, left Unionists and Loyalist paramilitaries alike deeply suspicious, believing that the British Government had secretly done a deal with the Republican terrorists, in return for the cease-fire, that would ultimately lead to London washing its hands of and abandoning Ulster.

"I am very keen to help the majority Protestant population to escape from the perception and paranoia of the feared 'nod and a wink' diplomacy between the so-called Pan-Nationalists and the British Government. However, even though I fully endorse and support the rights of the majority to democratically choose their future, strictly off the record, it is only sensible that cross-border institutions are eventually set up for the benefit of both North and South. It is not inconceivable that some may even take on executive powers, including the right to deal directly with Brussels on wider European issues, but the principle of consent by the Unionist majority enshrined in the Downing Street Declaration must be continually reiterated. Any other proposals for 'joint-authority' for the North by Dublin and London will alarm and panic Unionists, among whom there is extreme unease, so I hope that your Prime Minister is not foolhardy enough to exclude the Leader of the Unionists from the initial consultative process. There is no doubt that the political realities have changed beyond all recognition over the past months and any talks between all the sides in this sad conflict, have been a long time in coming...too long."

Having attended so many boring, meaningless meetings over the years, I had carefully honed my listening skills, nodding every now and then, or making the odd grunt of understanding, to show people I was still awake. I did all these, as Bjorn continued to explain, but listening skills or not, I concentrated fully on his every word. This guy was actually sitting down at the table with the Loyalists *and* the Republicans...it was hard to believe.

"We'll have coffee in the drawing room, please Nils," said Bjorn, directing the elderly caretaker with obvious affection.

Anja took my arm and we went up to the drawing room. A few minutes later Rolfson appeared with a cafetiere, four dainty china coffee cups and a selection of mints and petit fours.

"So how did all this start, Professor?"

"Well it was quite simple actually. I had met two of tomorrow's guests at various conferences and seminars over the years and, following a similar initiative for the Middle East by a colleague at the University, it was suggested by a junior member of the University staff that it may be worth getting the two of them together over dinner. So I set it up, but if the truth be told it wasn't entirely my idea. I was given the green light by friends in the Storting to proceed and see how far it could go. The three of us met, we talked about various world affairs, the situation in Ulster and I merely asked the question if it would be possible to set up an informal working party, without

Government interference to look into the 'Troubles' and perhaps seek some solution or at least a strategy for progress. I just asked them the simple question - would they both like to participate?"

"They were both quick to respond positively, but that is perhaps understandable, given their frustrations in the official talks where progress had stalled. Without boring you with all the preliminary details, the group has now grown and developed, not only in size, but in trust and understanding. Of course the timing could not have been better.

"When Sinn Fein-IRA announced their cease-fire in September 1994, we felt we had at least reached a critical juncture, as the Republican movement and their so-called 'struggle' entered a new phase. However, it failed to completely take account of the feelings of a beleaguered Protestant population, buried in generations of unease and suspicion. It also failed to convince a nervous British Government, who sought clarification of the cease-fire statement and a 'copper-bottomed' commitment, that 'complete cessation' meant a permanent end to violence.

"However, we kept prompting and we were pushing for a similar cease-fire declaration by the Loyalist paramilitaries when the Strasbourg incident had a disturbing impact on our plans. The IRA cease-fire has miraculously held, but the build up of pressure by Republican hard-liners to retaliate is enormous. The constitutional talks between London and Dublin have become increasingly strained, yet I still feel we can make a significant contribution to returning to the democratic peace process and getting all parties back on track. The media and the doom and gloom merchants predict the outbreak of civil war, but I am not so pessimistic. If you have followed the complexities of the saga so far, then you will know that the biggest stumbling blocks are caused by two key words - decommissioning and demilitarisation."

I nodded. Bjorn continued.

"The question is - is it guns before talks or talks before guns? The IRA have so far refused to entertain any suggestion of the handing over of any of their weapons. It is a highly sensitive issue. They fear a loss of credibility among rank and file Republicans, if they make any public concession and perhaps more importantly they are particularly paranoid about the possibility that any move by them will be wrongly interpreted and publicised as a surrender."

I summoned the courage to interrupt and offer an opinion,

"Personally I can't ever see the IRA handing over all or even some of their weaponry. They seem too committed to achieving their aims by continuing the violence and the terror campaign. If by some miraculous change of policy they do hand over some

Semtex and guns and the democratic process progresses to full round table talks, but goes against their particular political objectives - what is to stop them robbing a few Post Offices or even worse, plundering the coffers of misty-eyed, sentimental Irish-Americans to get cash to re-stock their arsenal? Nothing will have changed. For me, progress will only come when the IRA do not just agree to the removal of the threat to use weapons, but commit to the removal of the implied threat. Their determination to hang onto their guns and bombs during democratic talks seems incomprehensible to me."

"Ja, ja, what your are saying does not surprise me and is quite valid, but I wonder if the events of the next few days will give you reason to revisit your concerns."

I changed the subject slightly.

"Why have you allowed me to come here and join you?"

"Anja asked if she could invite you, it is as simple as that. These meetings have no timetables, no agendas, they are designed to be relaxed, informal get togethers where dialogue is free and open and if something positive comes as a result of them, then it will have all been worthwhile. Anja has been involved since the beginning, she is well known and trusted by the group. As a friend of hers you are welcome to join us, but I would stress again, you must not discuss these meetings with anyone on your return to Scotland. What you learn, see and hear can go no further than the front door of this lovely old house. Unless of course I expressly authorise you to prepare a report on our behalf."

I suddenly realised why there had been an interest in me from Special Branch back home in Aberdeen. I even began to wonder if the whole thing had been a bit of a set up.

"Did you by any chance have me vetted?" I asked Bjorn.

"Yes, I'm afraid so, there wasn't time to go into all the details, but we were more than satisfied with what was *unofficially* reported back to us. I apologise for the intrusion, I hope you are not offended. I also did some research of my own and I was intrigued and impressed by your articles on Scottish Nationalism. I particularly liked, "Independence: a Dream Too Far", and the, how should I put this, the stinging "The Power in Edinburgh?" You have been much influenced by the changes in the political situation in the UK, with the party political focus homing in on Devolution and Government de-centralisation, although I'm not quite sure if I correctly read between the lines and picked up your own personal convictions. I would say your writing is of a very high quality, your points well researched, your arguments well balanced, but the work feels detached, as if you are writing as an observer, with the words coming from the head and not the heart."

"I'm pleased you took the trouble to read those pieces. They are, as you point out, just my observations - but as to my own feelings...I avoid openly displaying them."

"He's a dark horse this one, Anja...I think you'll have to watch him," advised Nina, as she raised her cup to her mouth.

"Oh, I think I can handle it." They both laughed, as Bjorn returned the conversation to more serious topics.

"As a result of the information I was able to accumulate in such a short time, I took the liberty of calling some of the people who will be among the guests here this week-end and they all agreed you would make a welcome addition to the group and besides, it'll keep Anja happy. It would also appear to be the case that being Scottish is the acceptable face of being a 'Brit' for their more hard-line Irish consumption. They also appreciate the potential benefit of having a neutral journalist participate in our talks, should we decide to one day utilise your skills."

That was a relief, or was it! Again I felt set up.

Nina refilled everyone's cups. I was suddenly feeling out of my depth. I really was a very small player when it came to the journalistic stakes, preferring to pick and choose what articles and pieces I worked on. I had only come over to be with Anja. I hadn't expected any of this. The question now niggling at the back of my mind was - why had Anja really invited me here?

Nina entered the conversation.

"Paul, I'm sure you will enjoy your week-end here. Anja will look after you. As Bjorn said, this is a very informal gathering and our two children will be joining us tomorrow. My sister is driving them down from Bergen. When the group first met, it was difficult, very difficult, don't you agree darling?" The Professor nodded, and Nina went on, "the atmosphere as one would expect, was tense and strained, with Bjorn, Anja and myself making all the running. It was Einar, our son who helped things to relax, by getting the men to kick a ball about on the lawn. Sport and children have become useful diplomatic tools in our efforts to remove the barricades."

"The children," Nina continued "have attended at least three of our previous sessions and their presence helps bring home the raison d'être of the group...the future of the children of the Province. All the men you will meet tomorrow are fond of children, they are all either fathers, grand-fathers, uncles or brothers and let's just say Bjorn prefers to have the children here."

Bjorn interjected.

"Our guests will begin arriving, mid-morning tomorrow. Once they have settled in I have arranged for lunch to be served, then we can all go for a walk around the lake. It is normally during dinner that we do a lot of our 'serious' talking. Progress is being made, unlike the official talks which have been dogged by set back and stalemate. We tend to stay up late if our discussions or debates are, shall we say, 'lively' and you are welcome to participate and share with us any comments or observations you may have...I think it will be good to have some fresh input". He looked round the table at Anja and Nina and they smiled their agreement.

"I hope Anja reminded you to bring your walking boots. I am sure you will enjoy the countryside here; it is one of my favourite parts of Norway."

Anja remained noticeably quiet throughout the meal, as Bjorn took centre stage. He oozed self-confidence and came across as a committed, dynamic man and I felt honoured that Anja had invited me - even though there was now a doubt in my mind as to her real motives. I was anxious and intimidated by the whole show. I decided that the best course of action, as the weekend unfolded, was to remain seen and not heard.

Bjorn continued to talk about his guests and the initiative they had embarked upon. He was the star turn, but it was apparent that both Anja and Nina were more than just bit-players in the supporting cast.

"What about the Downing Street Declaration and the Framework Document, or any changes in the leadership in Dublin or Westminster. Would that affect your talks?"

"That's a good question, but the answer is a simple one: no, not at all, at least not directly. As I have explained, this is a very informal gathering, and as far as the main diplomatic players are concerned, we don't even officially exist, although they have a cynical awareness of us. The Downing Street Declaration with its draft Framework Document, is without doubt a major political initiative, but by its very nature it is fraught with difficulties and concerns from both sides, as has been evidenced by the needs of Sinn Fein to have it clarified. As far as the leadership question is concerned, no new political leader of either Britain or the Republic could afford to back away from what has been started. The move for peace is irreversible and for them to impede it would be electoral suicide. In addition, there is no item on our somewhat loose agenda for any of our 'friends' to try and grab the moral high ground or the initiative with the media. We are not involved in a political ping-pong match.

100

"Our talks are continuing in complete isolation from what is going on between London and Dublin, but...who knows what can be achieved here? There is no need for heavy security, press conferences, theatricals, there's no pressure, there's no interference from faceless civil servants, we are just able to get on with the job in hand...apart from a very select band, nobody knows we're here. I am confident we will eventually achieve something and as a result, we will be able go back and quietly, but perceptively influence the organisations we represent. I am only a facilitator, but I know people in Government, who know people in other Governments and momentum could be built up very quickly if we make a break through. I must stress, however, that we are not parleying and pandering to terrorists. In the short-term, we are seeking to achieve a genuine and established cessation of the violence and once that is done, all parties can at long last get round the table. I am striving to get tacit agreement from both sides to remove their guns and bombs, but I have no wish to engender a policy of appeasement. History has already borne grim testament to the fact that, as a peace strategy, it is doomed to failure."

"Ultimately, we must find a solution, that respects the identity and freedom of all sections of the community. Over recent months, prior to the cease-fire, there has been a noticeable deterioration in the security situation, with an ever increasing spiral of murders. As a group we believed we had helped move the process forward and our efforts had reduced tension behind the scenes, but we were collectively horrified and dismayed, when the whole process was thrown into turmoil and the cease-fire was almost abandoned, after the Strasbourg incident, and the bombing of the Sinn Fein offices in both Belfast and Dublin. Undoubtedly, tension and unease has risen again, testing the resolve of Sinn Fein-IRA to continue the cease-fire and maintain their commitment to peace. Punishment beatings and robberies allegedly continue, as do other illegal activities. I've had to recall the group several times recently to help get the momentum going again and to get everyone back on side and on track."

"We are trying to bring hope to a community, that has fostered a generation born and reared in the bleak legacy of the 'Troubles'. Of course any new peace will be an anxious, precarious peace as the paramilitaries on both sides will not just go away. I am sure however, that as long as even an imperfect peace holds, the paramilitaries will become increasingly isolated and marginalised. Real peace will only come when there is a combined will from all parties to end hostilities." It was a long speech and a bit of a lecture, but I was beginning to understand what was going on.

We chatted for a while before Nina said she felt tired and we all agreed it was time for bed. I walked Anja up to her room, which was just along from mine. I kissed her goodnight, then added,

"Thanks for inviting me back to Norway."

"That's OK. Are you angry with me for not telling you more about the group?" she asked in a soft whisper, tilting her head to the side as she spoke.

"No, of course not, I could never be angry with you."

"That's nice. I wasn't sure how you'd react, but I'm happy you decided to come over. Maybe if I'd told you more, you might not have come back."

I shook my head, "I don't think so."

I wanted her to take me in to her room, but I felt my shyness return. I didn't make a move. Anja would have to take the initiative. We kissed again. I felt her push against me and I let my leg ease gently between her thighs. I felt the push of her pelvis and the gentle pressure of her thighs, as they tightened around my leg. I felt her breath warm against my ear. I pulled her head round and kissed her, my tongue gently probing her mouth, my intentions clearly stated. Just then Nina went past.

"Good night you two, sleep well!"

Anja pulled away, embarrassed. She smiled, shrugged then retreated into her room.

I stood, my hands in my pockets, trying to give her the impression I was a lost and lonely boy who just needed some love and attention. The door continued to close slowly. Then it clicked shut. I was left alone in the hall. Fuck! I was so used to being with Claire and us always ending up in bed together that it felt strange not to be sleeping with Anja. I guess that was one of the problems in my relationship with Claire; it was too easy and I had become complacent. There was no chase, there never had been. I felt pissed off and frustrated. This was the first clear opportunity we'd had to spend the night together and it wasn't going to happen. I then had a sobering thought - perhaps Anja didn't want me. Sure, maybe she liked me, but maybe that was it, no physical, sexual attraction. I turned to walk back along the hall, pausing to adjust the stiffness in my boxers...naw, surely not.

I returned to my room and went to bed. I reached over and switched off the light. I hated the dark as a kid and had suffered more than my fair share of nightmares, but this was not a house of dark shadows. Although disappointed not to be lying with Anja, I quickly fell asleep. I felt warm and safe. It was such a peaceful place.

Bjorn and Anja were already at work when I eventually came down for breakfast and only Nina and Mrs Rolfson were in the kitchen.

"Good morning Paul. Did you sleep well?"

"Yes, thank you. I'm sorry for over sleeping, but it was such a warm and comfy, I mean comfortable bed, that I was out in no time."

"Was that your own bed, Paul?" Nina asked. "You can have whatever you want for breakfast, there is some smoked salmon, some cold meats, cheese, bread or yoghurt, just let Mrs Rolfson know what you want, there may even be some cornflakes. You can have coffee or even some tea, I know how much you English love your tea." I raised my eyebrows, "Oh, I'm sorry Paul, I did not mean to insult you by calling you English, please forgive me."

"I think I can forgive you this time," I said. Nina looked at me, took a long, slow draw on her cigarette, then she blew out a long thin stream of blue-white smoke.

I would have preferred a traditional breakfast of sausages, bacon and mushrooms, but when in Norway...I settled for some smoked salmon, some fresh bread, a yoghurt and a cup of coffee. I could certainly get used to eating smoked salmon on a daily basis.

By the time I finished breakfast, I was alone in the kitchen, I cleared my dishes from the table and went outside for some fresh air. In some ways it was good to be alone and take stock. A couple of issues puzzled me - why had I, a stranger and journalistic lightweight, been so easily accepted by Pedersen for such a landmark meeting? Surely the explanation wasn't as simple as he put it. Then there was this situation with Anja. In some ways it was a relief to think that she wasn't an easy screw, but on the other hand, this chastity thing was doing my head in. The doubts this created just niggled away at me and I really wondered if I had been *selected* to attend.

The morning was cold but dry and hung heavy with the scent of pine. As I walked down the well-worn path through the trees to the loch, I soon realised I should have taken a jacket. I watched the cold waters lap gently on the pebble shore. I crouched down and selected a few smooth, flat stones and began skimming them across the water, disturbing the calm surface of the lochan into irregular, wavy patterns.

I had been doing this for a few minutes and had become quite engrossed in my task, when I became instinctively aware that I was not alone. I felt the hair on the back of my neck stand up with that uncomfortable tingling sensation, but tried to stay calm. Maybe it was Anja sneaking up on me. I carefully picked out a perfect skimmer from among the shingle and pebbles and gave it my best shot. It bounced about six or seven times before sinking in to the icy depths of the loch, the ripples reaching out in ever increasing circles to the shore, before disappearing.

"Nice shot!"

I turned round, and a man in his late 30's early 40's stepped out from the trees. He had a head of closely cropped, wiry, red hair, a full beard, and he was wearing a pair of old brown cords and a baggy Aran sweater which had seen in a few winters and a boil wash too many.

"Hello there! I hope I didn't startle you...I'm Seamus Coyle," he announced, as he stepped onto the shingle and walked toward me.

"You must be Paul."

His name sounded familiar and I racked my brains to remember how I knew it. I normally prided myself on my memory for names and faces. He obviously knew who I was. He walked down onto the shingle and we shook hands. His grip was firm and his eyes revealed a friendly but alert man.

"Yes you're right, I'm Paul Robertson, a friend of Anja's. How you doin'?"

"I'm fine thank you and it's a pleasure to meet you," he said in the faintest of Irish brogues, that seemed to carry a trace of scouse, but I couldn't be sure.

He walked further down over the pebbles, picked up a stone and hurled it into the lake, it bounced two or three times, then sank without trace.

"Christ, I've lost my touch!"

We each threw a few more stones, then we made our way back toward the house.

"Have you just arrived?" I asked.

"Yes, I flew into Bergen from Oslo this morning and picked up the hired car Anja had organised for me and drove down. It was a glorious trip, the sun shining, no traffic. Lovely. I originally came from Amsterdam by a round about route...let's just say some of us have to be careful! But should I be telling you this?" he laughed, then his tone changed. "How long have you known Anja?"

"Not long."

Seamus continued to politely question me all the way back to the house and once again I got the feeling I was being checked out. Yet another informal vetting. We walked round to the back of the house and I noticed that the Saab and Anja's Volvo had been joined by several other cars.

Anja was standing waiting at the back door. She brushed a hand along my waist, kissed me on the cheek, then greeted Seamus.

"Hei! It's good to see you again Seamus."

"Hello there darlin', I just met yer man there down at the lough, all on his own. Are you not looking after him?"

"He's a big boy."

The Irishman embraced her and I felt a little awkward - not jealous, just awkward.

"Everyone is here now Paul. Come and I will introduce you. The children are here too," she said excitedly.

We left Seamus by the back door and walked round to the side of the house, where a boy of 12 or 13 was playing with a football on the lawn. We walked over to him and he kicked the ball to me. I controlled it with my right foot, flicked it up on to my thigh, then my head before letting it drop and firing a half-volley straight back at him. The lad was obviously impressed and his face just beamed.

"Einar, this is my friend Paul, from Aberdeen in Scotland. He used to play a lot of football, but he had to give up because he was too old!"

"Hey, there's no need for that!"

Einar and I shook hands and we started passing the ball between us.

Anja called out, "Bloody men" and began to walk away back to the house.

"What team do you like?" he asked, believing he had found a new friend and a fellow football fan.

I thought for a moment, but seeing as he was wearing a Man United away strip, I told him that I was a fan of Ryan Giggs and, when it revealed itself, the footballing side of Eric Cantona. I kicked the ball back to him and jogged after Anja.

"Will you play football with me later Paul?" he shouted after me.

"Sure, no problem!" I called back.

We went in to the kitchen, which was already full of people and chatter. Anja took my hand and began to take me round the assembled throng. She introduced me to Professor Michael Docherty, of Dublin University; Kieran Ryan, a Derry councillor; Dr John Renfrew, Queen's University, Belfast; Chris Nicholl, a Belfast councillor, a Tom McCreery and finally Seamus, whom I had already met.

All had given me a firm handshake and a warm greeting except McCreery and I felt an instinctive unease with him. He was a bit older than me, about 36 and he looked fit and hard. He had a thick neck, deep, broad shoulders, short greying hair and a distinctive scar on his upper lip. His face appeared to carry a permanent scowl, as if he was a man with a chip on his shoulder and nothing would ever please him. My prejudices suggested that he must be the IRA man. I made a mental note to get Anja to fill me in on the backgrounds of all the guests, particularly Tom McCreery. He looked as if he could be a right *coorse* bastard. He was certainly not a man I would want to cross in the shadows of a darkened Belfast alleyway away from the watchful eyes of a security patrol. He was danger personified and radiated menace.

Mrs Rolfson had prepared a smorgasbord of smoked fish, prawns, cured meats, bread and cheeses and Bjorn and Nina walked round the kitchen fussing over everyone, making sure they had either a glass of wine, a beer or a mineral water.

We finished lunch and Bjorn asked us to rendezvous at the back of the house for the next item of his loose weekend itinerary, the afternoon stroll. Everyone disappeared off to their rooms and reappeared suitably attired in walking boots, warm jackets and an assortment of headgear. I put on my new Red Wing boots, and my Patagonia jacket. I didn't feel out of place - well not so far.

The afternoon air was cold and fresh and the breeze blew through the tall pines, causing the upper branches to lurch and sway, and ruffling the once still waters of the loch to form little waves. Dark clouds had begun to amass away to the north and I wondered if it would snow. It was certainly cold enough. Before we began our walk towards the loch, Anja appeared hand in hand with Bjorn and Nina's eight year old daughter, Mette. I said hello and we began to walk along the gravel path. I had Anja on one hand and little Mette on the other. The group walked slowly and there was much talk and a fair smattering of laughter. I noticed that Nina walked with Coyle and Bjorn with McCreery, and I wondered if that was significant.

Doctor Renfrew held back and walked along with me. We talked about Aberdeen and it became clear that he had a strong affinity for the city he had studied in during the 1950s. He spoke fondly of the Chanonry, his digs in Old Aberdeen and several pubs, one or two of which had long since gone, the victims of over-zealous and unimaginative city planners. I suggested that he should visit us again soon; quite a lot had changed...not always for the better.

So far, the mood had been light and I found it difficult to believe that this forum could possibly make progress or have any bearing in solving the problems of Northern Ireland. My first impressions were of a group of friends on a weekend jolly at a country house. However, Pederson was a very astute man and the Norwegians had already shown the world what they could do with their back door diplomacy for the

Middle East. Even though that process had become a little unstuck, hopes still remained high of a peaceful resolution to the bottle-neck in Gaza and the West Bank. At least the ball was rolling. People were talking.

We must have walked for about six kilometres, when Bjorn suggested we return; the dark clouds that had gathered to the North were now over us and a low grumble of thunder startled Mette who was holding my hand as it resonated round the mountains. Poor Mette, she was trying desperately hard to understand my accent and, with her limited English, conversation was difficult. She was a cute wee girl, destined to break a few hearts when she was older.

Anja was obviously well skilled in this form of diplomacy and she moved among her guests, breaking the ice and generally relaxing the group. She obviously knew a great deal about their personal and domestic circumstances, as she asked how their respective families were doing, referring to individual names of wives and children. The walk was a very effective ploy and Pederson, Nina and Anja were taking full advantage.

We had just stepped back onto the gravel path, when McCreery appeared alongside me.

"I recognise your name, I've read some of your stuff."

I cracked a smile, encouraged by his willingness to engage in conversation. Maybe I had been wrong about him.

"You did a piece for the Herald a couple of years ago about Loyalist fund-raising connections in Scotland. If I remember correctly your sources were pretty good, and you succeeded in doing us a little bit of harm. For a few weeks afterwards the coffers were empty as donations dried up. If my memory serves me well."

"Well you know what it's like, we journalists are licensed information gatherers and we never disclose our sources," I joked. Unfortunately there was no softening in his look and I changed my tack.

"It was an impartial piece. It was intended to question and condemn the Scottish connection on both sides. If my memory serves me well," I added defensively.

"So you didn't get a visit then?" he grinned and walked on. Bastard! What was that little aside all about?

When we arrived back at the house, the sky above us was thunderously overcast. Bjorn asked Dr Renfrew and Professor Docherty to join him in his study; the rest of us had some time on our own before dinner at 7:30. I stayed in the kitchen with Nina, Anja and the children and chatted to Einar about football. The young lad sat open mouthed as I told him about my own footballing heroes, Best ,Cruyff, Beckenbauer, Pele, Platini, Krol, Hansen, Dalglish and all the others.

Mette asked me if I was in love with Anja. I said that I had thought I was, until I met her, and now I wasn't so sure. The women laughed and Anja told Mette that she was becoming very jealous and that she should stop flirting with me. Then Nina took the children upstairs and left Anja and I alone in the kitchen. Anja was wearing her glasses again and she excited me so much, I wanted to hold her. I bent forward and kissed her. She kissed me back and pulled my head close to hers, I let my hands drop and they gently brushed her breasts before coming to rest on her thighs. Anja sighed and we continued in our embrace. I wanted to take her to my room but just then Kieran Ryan appeared, looking for a glass of cold milk, as he was suffering from indigestion. I gave him the benefit of my experiences with stomach problems and ulcers.

"Anja, you need to tell me about your friends. I don't want to come down for dinner tonight and make a fool of myself," I whispered as Kieran returned to the fridge for a re-fill.

"OK, I do that, let's go up to my room."

We said we'd see Kieran at dinner and crept upstairs to Anja's room, which was larger than mine and had an old writing bureau in the corner. A lap-top lay on the desk, attached to a printer which had been discreetly positioned in a corner behind the dressing table. Anja pulled in a chair and set to work. She keyed in her password and asked me what I wanted to know.

"I just want some background on these guys, just enough to work out who's who and who's done what."

"OK, what I'll do is print off some of the notes Bjorn has made about the group and if you want to ask me any questions, I'll try and answer them as best as I can."

She typed in the name Michael Docherty, hit Return and waited. The lap-top whirred and clicked, then the screen responded, and she pressed print. Within seconds, the screen bleeped as the report spooled to the laser jet. I ripped the report from the roll of continuous paper.

I scanned the details held on his personal file:

Born 1936, Co. Cork, graduated first class honours History, Trinity College, Dublin

University 1957, with a further degree in Political Sciences. He had written several papers on Irish Nationalism and Eire's future place in a Federal Europe.

Anja added that he had been the first person Bjorn had approached, and that he had become the driving force in helping to get the group to gel and in developing an atmosphere of trust. I read on summarising the details in my mind. He was well connected socially and an extremely effective operator who had excellent contacts among Nationalist politicians at Westminster, in the Dail and in the Irish-American lobby of the US Congress and Senate.

"He's so enthusiastic, he always sees the good side."

"An optimist."

"Yes, an optimist."

She concluded that he was a very emotional man and, like many an Irishman, he could be persuaded to sing when the mood took him and he'd had a few. Even-tempered, with a great sense of fun, it was sometimes difficult to get him to stop talking when he did get going.

The next name she typed in was Kieran Ryan:

Born in 1962, he had left school at 16 to become an apprentice joiner, serving his time with a local Derry builder. Politics had always interested him and he had considered joining the SDLP, but joined Sinn Fein in 1985 after his brother in law had been randomly murdered by Loyalist paramilitaries, simply picked out because he was Catholic. He was a dedicated party worker and a rising star within the organisation, with frequent contributions to 'An Phoblach'. More importantly from Bjorn's point of view, he had the ear of the leadership in Belfast and Dublin and was tipped in some places as a future leader.

"Bjorn says Kieran is a weevil, if you feed him the right lines he can carry all the right messages and signals up through Sinn Fein and he has also maintained links with the SDLP. As far as we're aware his only connection with the Nationalist movement is political, he's never served with the Provisional IRA. He is the youngest of the group, but he's well liked and has kept the momentum going when things looked like they were stagnating or about to break down. The Strasbourg murder did affect him and we did worry he'd revise his views, but we should have known better. He's very persistent and committed to finding peace. He urged restraint among Republicans after the killing. He's definitely more of a, I think you say a Dove than an Eagle. Like the others he has some concerns about the Downing Street Declaration, the delays in publishing the Framework Document."

She had said Eagle, but meant Hawk, but I didn't correct her.

"OK, who's next?"

Dr John Renfrew, born Belfast 1938. His father was killed in the war, dying as a prisoner of war in Burma and he was brought up by his mother. He studied Divinity at Queen's, Belfast and worked for the Church of Ireland Synod for many years, before returning to academia as a lecturer. Bjorn had added some comments at the bottom of Renfrew's report, 'John is a staunch Loyalist with impeccable links with the Orange Order. He is the very personification of Unionism and Protestantism'.

"He was a very disruptive influence when the meetings began and claimed he'd never allow his party or his people to, as he said, 'dance to the Pan-Nationalist tune'. He was very reluctant to sit at the same table as Kieran and Seamus, but gradually Bjorn and Professor Docherty have worked on him and have won him round and he is now as committed as anyone to bringing peace to Ulster through a political settlement, although he remains loyal to his Church and the majority Protestant population and would never support a deal that would be detrimental to them. We no longer worry that he will advocate or support the use of the, I think they call it, the 'Orange Card'. He moves in the same social and political circles as what Bjorn refers to as 'the Fire and Brimstone boys'."

I knew exactly who she meant, with all their posturing, dramatic rhetoric, histrionics and verbal belligerence.

She continued, "and he has dismissed the Taoiseach's forum for Peace and Reconciliation, as a soapbox and platform for terrorists."

"OK, what about Chris Nicholl?" I asked, fascinated by all the information I was being given.

Chris Nicholl, born Belfast 1943. He inherited his father's struggling printing and packaging business and went on to build it up into a multi-million pound success story. He sold out to a German based consortium in 1989 and has been living in semi-retirement since then. He has close links with moderate and the more extreme Unionist politicians and access to the leadership of various Loyalist paramilitary groups and like Dr Renfrew he is an active member of the Orange Order.

The Orange Order, I mused: the most enduring symbol of Ulster Protestantism.

Once again Anja added a finishing piece to the information that appeared on the screen and on the report.

"Chris is not only a very wealthy and powerful man, but he is also a very influential figure among Loyalist and Unionist Ulster men. By winning over people like him we can hopefully develop a ground swell of support for our efforts among the Protestant working and middle classes, Unionist politicians and the Commanders of the key loyalist paramilitaries. Money is power, whether it's in Northern Ireland or anywhere else in the world and he has plenty of both."

"That leaves us with our two friends, Seamus Coyle and Tom McCreery...I think Bjorn described them as being on 'active service'?"

Anja seemed to sense that it was these two I was fascinated by.

Her fingers once again eased over the keyboard and the system responded.

Tom McCreery, born Belfast, aged 35. Was sentenced to five years for firearms offences in 1985, he was released after four years but immediately rejoined his colleagues in the UDA and its affiliate, the UVF, of which his uncle was a founder member.

"He also spent some time, two years I think, living and working in Glasgow in the late 1980s. From there it was easy for him to move in and out of Belfast. He happily embraced the Loyalist cause from a very early age and although we don't know for sure, we believe that over the years he may have been responsible for planning several attacks on Catholic businesses or known Republican sympathisers and Nationalist politicians. If this initiative is to succeed, then we need to win over people like Tom who are in the front line or sharp end of the terror campaign. He is a deep, sullen man and he can be a bit non-communicative at times, but when he opens up and wants to make a point, it's invariably valid and well thought out. He was at first deeply suspicious of the IRA cease-fire and has as yet been unable to commit his own organisation to a back to back cessation of violence, but we are working on him...and finally that leaves Seamus."

"Yes, tell me about Coyle." I must admit, I had thought that McCreery was the IRA man.

Anja let me read directly from the screen, adding her own anecdotes as before. For some reason she didn't send the report to the printer.

Born in Co Kildare 1953, his parents were killed in a car crash when he was eleven. He was sent to Liverpool where he was brought up by his elder sister. He did well at school and studied Economics at Liverpool University, where as a student he joined a small Republican Support group who would hold various fund raising events for 'the Cause' back home. He joined the Provisional IRA in 1974 and was a 'sleeper' for a number of years before he became one of their most effective operatives throughout the late seventies and eighties. A self-professed opponent of the State, we believe he has been on the British government's ' most wanted list' for years and because of the pressure he fled to Boston for several years, during which time he liaised closely with those influential Republicans interned in the Maze, before things settled down and he returned to Eire. He now moves between the Republic and Europe, switching his identity all the time and never stays too long in any one place. He alleges he is no longer on 'active service', but he has access to the heart of the IRA command structure and because of his past exploits, he's regarded as a bit of a hero among the 'rank and file' and is revered by the higher echelons of the organisation, both in the Provisional IRA and Sinn Fein and the Dublin based Republican Sinn Fein. He seldom ventures across the border into the North, as there is an Exclusion Order on him, as well as an outstanding warrant for his arrest. Anja spoke as the screen changed.

"Seamus is a very intelligent man. He understands the political cause, its history, as well as having been actively involved in 'the violent struggle'. Since being invited to join the group, he has personally renounced violence and has fought hard to convince other IRA Chieftains, Brigade Commanders and those in Active Service Units of the need to end the shootings and bombings. In some ways he is Bjorn's personal favourite and we have pinned much of our hopes on him. Not that we condone his past, but we firmly believe he is a changed man. He supported the Sinn Fein leadership in persuading the key Commanders in the Provisional IRA. to give the political process a chance and was closely involved in the formulation of the IRA statement that signalled their cease-fire. He is one of the most influential figures in the Republican movement."

"Yes, I met him earlier today and I couldn't help but like him. I can just imagine him researching the Republican cause and being influenced by the words and deeds of Collins, De Valera and Tone and the rebel songs and stories about 'lorry loads of volunteers' planning raids on border garrisons. Tom McCreery on the other hand, well there's something about him I just don't like. He's likely been brought up on a diet of loyalty to the Union flag, the legend of the Red Hand of Ulster, the Apprentice boys, King Billy and the Boyne. You know, he looks like a villain, he's much quieter and more sinister than Coyle. Coyle seems to be a more gentle man, it's hard for me to believe he could be a killer. He doesn't come across as a wild colonial boy. I guess it must say something for the people who advise the Sinn Fein hierarchy as well, because on camera at least, they come across as reasoned politicians and not terrorist bully boys, but that's what makes it all the more frightening, because just what the reality is behind the public facade, no one but them really knows."

Anja responded to my final comment with a hint of warning in her voice.

"What did you expect? Some sort of terrorist stereotype, wearing a beret, black gloves, a face mask and toting an AK47 or an Armalite...Don't be fooled by the public image, Seamus Coyle is no angel. You must have seen him in newsreel film, attending Republican funerals, walking a few steps behind Adams and McGuinness, his hands behind his back, his eyes lowered, his head bowed. Yes, he is charming, he is amusing, but I have spent time with him, I have done some research on him...he is not a man to be crossed. Both he and McCreery are deeply devoted to the cause they serve, they both have beliefs that are so deep rooted, they are almost part of their DNA. As participants in the war, both have blood on their hands and we shouldn't ever forget that. To some they are heroic volunteers, freedom fighters or defenders of a faith and a way of life and yet to others, they are murderers. So there you have it, Paul, I hope you're not angry with me for not telling you what to expect this weekend, but as you can see this is no ordinary get together."

"You're absolutely right there! I hope that there's a successful conclusion to all your efforts. The statistics, over 3000 deaths, are a grim reminder of the suffering of the population. I've always thought of myself as a wishy-washy liberal, but the extremists in any conflict bring out the worst in me and if I had the power, I would sanction the, I would sanction the..." I paused and amended my intended statement, "let's just say I would happily sanction the arrest of known ring-leaders from both sides."

"I know what you mean. It is very frustrating for us as well, but even as we talk of peace and the British and Irish Governments talk of peace, the murders and the punishment beatings go on. Rounding up the ring leaders, or sanctioning any other 'action', as you seemed to suggest, would only cause more problems and could lead to a new batch of 'hard-liners' taking their place."

"How do events in between your 'meetings' affect things?"

"What do you mean?"

"What happens if there has been a spate of killings or bombings, or for example the Strasbourg incident, or that robbery when the innocent postal worker was killed?"

"Oh, I understand. At one of the meetings, I think it was to be the fourth, things had been progressing well and everything was set up, but on the eve of the meeting there was a number of attacks and sectarian murders in the Province. A car bomb killed a former soldier in the UDR, leaving a young widow and two fatherless children. An eighteen year old Protestant youth was also found shot dead. The Provisionals claimed responsibility for both attacks. Of course the Loyalists retaliated and machine gunned a betting shop in a Catholic area of Belfast, killing three innocent people and injuring several others. Bjorn was very worried that both Seamus and Tom would not appear because of what had happened, but to our relief they both turned up. As you can imagine things were very tense and strained. I think there was a lot of guilt. I was given the job of looking after the others and I took them on a trip up to a waterfall, the one the house is named after, whilst Bjorn and Nina spent time with Tom and Seamus. It is easy to forget how important Nina is in all this, but she really is Bjorn's partner in all senses. By the time the rest of us had returned, they were all chatting quite amicably over coffee in the kitchen."

"Yes, that kitchen is the best room in the house, everything tends to gravitate to there," I observed, as Anja finished her story.

"It was the same after the Strasbourg assassination. Bjorn and Nina really earned the credit for averting a possible catastrophe. When I spoke to Bjorn afterwards, he freely admitted that without Nina, her help, influence and sensitivity, the whole thing could have halted and collapsed there and then."

"Yes, they are a very impressive couple."

"As you suggested earlier, we've had to face the challenges created by the Strasbourg murder and they were serious problems, after all Cahal Ryan was an important member of Sinn Fein, behind only Adams, McGuinness and McLaughlin in terms of seniority and influence. Fortunately the cease-fire has held. Bjorn was so concerned by what had happened, he called Tom McCreery in Belfast. McCreery assured him that Loyalist groups had not carried out or sanctioned the 'hit', nor were they aware through their own intelligence sources of any rogue elements who had carried out the shooting and the bombings in Dublin. We suspect it was the work of a professional, or some unknown dissident faction, working for some outside Agency. Since then we have had three meetings in close succession and while the Press would claim the threat of Civil War is a real one, I don't think it is quite as serious as that and maybe, just maybe we're back on track. Are you looking forward to dinner then?"

"Yes, I am now, but first things first."

"What's that?"

"Aw, nothing. It doesn't matter"

"Come on, what were you going to say?"

"I was just going to ask if I can kiss you. You're the reason I'm in Norway and I don't think we've had any time together since the journey up here."

"Oh, poor you, very well you may kiss me, but just a peck!"

We started to kiss while she was still sat at the desk, I led her over to the bed, and it was obvious she wanted me although this was not exactly the seduction scene I had planned.

"Would you like to have a shower with me?" she asked.

The blunt directness of the question took me by surprise and I hadn't even begun to answer when Mette burst into the room.

"Shit!" I heard Anja say under her breath. Mette asked Anja if she could sleep with her. It appeared that Einar had frightened her with stories of ghosts and trolls. Anja sat up on the bed, gave Mette a hug and looked up at me.

"Of course you can sleep with me and don't you worry about what Einar said. There are no ghosts in this house, you're perfectly safe here. I'll have a word with your big brother and if he doesn't behave I'll ask Paul to sort him out."

"Oh will you Paul?"

"Sure Mette, just say the word and I'll fix him," I winked to Anja

I returned to my room and showered alone. Sleeping with Anja was I hoped only a matter of time. I dressed in navy Polo shirt, chinos, splashed on some JHL and went downstairs. This was the part I had been dreading; crowds and strangers in close social proximity to me could be daunting and it was an effort for me to walk confidently into a room full of people I hardly knew, which seems hard to believe for someone who is a journalist. I always worried what they would think of me. Sometimes I was able to put on an act and hide the shyness, but it was a double edged sword and sometimes the shyness or the bravado were mistakenly interpreted as arrogance and conceit.

Everyone was in the dining room, standing chatting and once again it was evident that Bjorn and Nina were fussing around everyone, making sure they all had a drink. They were the perfect hosts and Anja was a very able assistant. It was plain to see Bjorn relied on her. I helped myself to a mineral water with ice and lemon and observed once again that neither McCreery or Coyle were drinking. Unusual, two tee-total Irishmen in the same room: I wondered what odds I'd have got for that.

Bjorn called everyone to the table and I found myself sitting opposite Anja and next to Professor Docherty. Bjorn and Nina sat at the respective heads of the table, with Nina being on my right. Mr Rolfson served the first course, a light, flaky pastry vol au vent filled with prawns and scallops in a cream sauce. This was followed by a beef consommé and then a main course of roast lamb which was carved at the table. The meal was washed down with copious amounts of Australian wine and Aquavit, for those who wanted it, or in the case of myself and the two terrorists, mineral water. The conversation was light, probably because the children were still present although they had been given a small table of their own to sit at. They behaved perfectly and spoke only when spoken to. I remained on the periphery and was a bit of a spectator, as Professor Docherty chatted to Nina and Anja engaged in conversation with Kieran Ryan. When coffee was ready to be served, Nina asked the children to say goodnight. Mette went round the table and gave everyone, including Tom McCreery, a kiss and a hug, then Nina ushered them up to their bedrooms. Rolfson filled each of our cups and Nina returned to her place at the table. Bjorn rose up out of his chair and began to speak.

"Ladies and Gentlemen, first of all let me welcome you all back to Norway and can I just add a special welcome to our new guest Paul whom you have all now met and who, for some reason, Anja keeps referring to as her 'friend' from Scotland, whatever that means."

Anja blushed, as Bjorn looked directly at me and added.

"Welcome, I hope you enjoy our company."

I smiled and mouthed a nervous thank you and nervously brushed the embroidered horseman on my shirt.

Apart from McCreery, everyone nodded and smiled. Bjorn continued.

"Over the past twelve months, our group has met and discussed the situation in Northern Ireland. We have debated, argued and at times torn our hair out as we have sought to arrive at some consensus that can eventually be taken back to our own respective organisations and from there to the governments of the UK and Eire so that collectively we can begin a process towards a genuine and lasting peace and a new partnership between two traditions. At the end of our last meeting several weeks ago, I asked each of you to take upon yourselves the task of winning support for our efforts with those whom you most closely associate...those that have influence. There is much talk of Civil War, but knowing this group as I do, I cannot subscribe to that view. I am sure it will never now come to that, but I would admit, it may have been perilously close at one time."

Bjorn paused.

"But before you each brief us, I would like somewhat unfairly to ask Paul to give us an outsider's view of the situation. As a Scot, living in Aberdeen, he is sufficiently divorced from the Irish question, so hopefully he can give us a personal, unbiased and objective view of the 'Troubles' and recent events."

116

I looked across at Anja, but it was obvious that she was not aware of Bjorn's plan. I looked at Nina and she smiled and squeezed my hand.

"Paul, would you like to say a few words?" Bjorn's question was as unexpected, as it was rhetorical.

My stomach was immediately beginning to knot, my mouth felt dry, I felt the first tingles of perspiration break out along my scalp line, but I felt bound, as Bjorn had suggested, 'to say a few words', even though I was completely unprepared. I didn't want to refuse and have them think I was a fool. I sipped from my glass of water, gave a slight cough, as if to clear my throat and stood up, desperately trying to recall the techniques of a Presentation Skills course I had attended in my oil days - good strong voice, plenty of eye contact, don't fiddle with your balls! With the edge that you are sometimes given by a combination of nervous tension and adrenaline, I started to speak.

"Ever since I was a little boy I have been fascinated by certain historical and current events. From a historical point of view the First World War and its hellish and futile loss of life has fascinated, appalled and saddened me and over the past twenty five years the media, TV and newspapers, have brought two events into my living room, into my life and they were the Vietnam War and the so called 'Troubles' in Northern Ireland. The Vietnam War is over, or at least the American involvement is, but I can still vividly remember the newsreel footage of the Rolling Thunder and Linebacker bombing campaigns, the napalm, My Lai, Tet, the Cu Chi tunnels, the panic to leave Saigon, the devastation of Agent Orange, the war photography of McCullin.

"With regard to Ulster, it has been a case whereby the daily scenes of violence have become sickeningly familiar. I remember the coverage of the killings in the Bogside during Bloody Sunday, Internment, CS Gas, Rubber Bullets, the Hunger Strikers and their 'dirty protests', the H-Blocks, the B-Specials, the riots, the barricades, the grey armoured Land Rovers of the RUC patrolling the streets, the various Civil Rights marches, the infamy of the Falls Road, the grenade attack at the IRA funeral at Milltown cemetery and for me, worst of all, the horrendous scenes that led to the barbaric murder of the two off duty soldiers, as they mistakenly drove into a Republican funeral. It was terrifying to watch as their car was surrounded by black cabs to prevent their escape, before they were set upon by the mob, taken away, stripped and beaten, then summarily and cold-bloodedly executed. It is a scene I will always remember and for millions of people who watched, it is damning and shocking evidence of 'man's inhumanity to man'. All in all it seemed to sum up and encapsulate all the suspicion, the hatred and brutality of Northern Ireland. Under the unrelenting eye of the media, Ulster has become a place where murder and violence has a stranglehold on the impressionable minds and opinions of people, not only in the UK, but all around the world."

I took a deep breath, had another mouthful of water and continued. The room had gone quiet, the silence only broken by the crackling of the log fire. I looked over to Anja, trying to draw inspiration and went on,

"I vividly remember the Harrods, Birmingham, Guildford, Hyde Park bombings, as well as the Grand Hotel at Brighton; the deaths, sorry the murders of Neave, Gow, Ewart-Biggs and Mountbatten. The carnage at Warren Point and more recently Enniskillen, Warrington, Shankhill and Graysteel, the alleged, 'shoot to kill' policy, Gibraltar, Stormont, the Anglo-Irish Agreement and all the retaliatory, 'tit for tat' murders. I am essentially a non-violent man, I have no strong political affiliations, but I have been once again fascinated, sickened and saddened by what I have seen and read. I have also had cause to cringe at a British legal system which has sentenced allegedly innocent people to terms of imprisonment, taking away parts of their lives they can never ever have again and reducing the credibility of the English and I would emphasise, the English Justice system to a sham, in the eyes of the rest of the world.

"These images, whether they are of the Somme, Verdun, Passchendale, Saigon, Hanoi, Londonderry, Belfast, wear you down. On a personal level I can't stand extremism, no matter what side it is on, and I'm not just speaking about Ireland, I would say the same about South Africa, the Balkans and the Middle East. If real peace is to be found in any of these areas of conflict, people on both sides need to set aside their weapons, they need to talk, to compromise and to take steps to peacefully co-exist. It can only be done if a climate is created where there is no coercion and people consent to change. You build peace by talking and open dialogue will resolve so many perceived and real problems."

My audience remained silent and impassive. I sipped again from my glass and continued.

"I hope I'm not boring you all, I must admit I'm pretty much out of my depth as far as political comment on this subject is concerned. The history of Scotland is more my forte. Mind you, I have always meant to read up on some of the books on the subject, like Callaghan's, 'A House Divided: The dilemma of Northern Ireland', the works of Conor Cruise O'Brien, but I've never got round to it."

"You're doing fine, Paul, please continue." It was Kieran Ryan.

I looked around the table. All eyes were on me. I fired the occasional furtive glance at Anja who was still sitting opposite.

"As a journalist, and I use the term loosely, I obviously believe in Press freedom, freedom of speech and democracy. People must live and work under the rule of law and should not be terrorised and confronted by armed revolutionary or reactionary

organisations who seek to attain their objectives by terror and violence."
I paused. I felt I was now straying into what was for me uncharted, even forbidden territory.

"Apart from a one off piece I produced on paramilitary fund-raising in Scotland, I know little or nothing of the hidden world of the terrorist paramilitaries in Northern Ireland and I am certainly not an expert by any means on the goals of the Republican movement, but I have read in the papers about political initiatives that assume there is no answer until there is an end to the violence and I would agree with that. What worries me is this question, what kind of political initiatives, be it the Downing Street Declaration or any other, could disarm a dedicated group whose minds are, I assume, set on achieving objectives that are not necessarily desired by the people they claim to represent and apart from a cessation of violence, what else can they offer? My belief is that they should not be allowed to hold a veto on democracy. You must forgive me if I overstep the mark here, I don't mean to offend, but even though it forms only part of the Irish peace story, some sort of commitment toward the destruction of stockpiles of terrorist weaponry must be a prerequisite for any serious and substantive talks with Government. A move in this direction should not be seen by either side of the paramilitary divide as a humiliating climb down, or the loss of a major bargaining chip. It should be regarded as the removal of a major stumbling block in a finely balanced bargaining process. I also fully realise that the question of decommissioning conjures up the complex issue of the psychology of surrender and it is something I believe both sides have to face up to and overcome.

"As I've said, I don't know enough about the situation to make any comment that you may think is valid or worthwhile, but what I will say is this - if, by these meetings, the people who are here can bring about peace and an end to the loss of life, I would urge that you pursue it with all your power, or the innocent people, that is, the children of all Ireland, North and South, children just like Mette, like Einar, will have nothing to look forward to but a future of hopelessness, another generation denied their childhood. If progress is not forthcoming, then no doubt the governments of Britain and Eire will continue their unrelenting pressure on the extremists on both sides and the cycle of terror will escalate and continue and more people will die.

"You all have my utmost respect and admiration for the courage you have obviously shown just by sitting round this table. I hope you can go all the way and ultimately produce an agreement that is reasonable, sensible and workable. From what I have clearly seen so far, you are not here to discuss who's right or who's wrong and with over 3000 deaths there can be no winners, only losers. In my opinion, the time has come to abandon your prejudices; you cannot continue to wrap yourselves so tightly in either the Union Flag or the Irish Tri-colour and real peace will come with consensus and compromise and from within the youth of the country; after all it's their future you are playing with. Politicians are a notorious impediment to progress and you should not be deviated or discouraged by their blinkered dogmas.

"What I'm trying to say is that maybe peace, real peace can be achieved and progress can be made in an atmosphere where there is an existence of peace and not just a prospect of peace. Both sides must then be willing to compromise. The Nationalists should accept the right of self-determination of the majority of Ulster people and conversely the Unionists should yield some ground and recognise the need and benefit of the creation of some All-Ireland institutions, perhaps harmonising a range of common policy areas like,...like education, agriculture, health, even tourism on a joint basis.

"Like Scotland, Ireland, North and South, has suffered from the emigration of large sections of its talented youth, so for what it's worth, I would suggest that a referendum is held for the under 25s. They are the generation conceived and reared in a lifetime of the 'Troubles', let them choose for themselves, without party political influence, the path to the future. Let them reap the benefit of the millions of pounds and dollars of investment that awaits them, if a lasting peace is found. Once again I salute your courage, your perseverance, your boldness and determination in leading this initiative. I think it is great that you can all meet here and talk in an atmosphere where the threat of violence is absent. Can I just say, you can't afford to gamble with peace: too much is at stake.

"Finally, I would also like to thank you for allowing me to join you this weekend. When Anja invited me over, I had absolutely no idea what to expect. I sincerely hope you succeed in your quest. It certainly won't be easy, but we live in interesting times. Thank you."

I bit my lip, raised my eyebrows, bowed my head and sat down. I felt only slightly better than hellish. I hoped I'd not embarrassed Anja, Bjorn, Nina and their other guests. I hoped I'd made some sense and not just whittered on. It was McCreery who spoke first.

"Well done, son, that can't have been easy for you. You even managed to come across as, what was it you said to me earlier today, 'unbiased and impartial'," he said. "Don't look so worried - you're among 'enemies'!" he continued with a dead-pan delivery.

Every one laughed and Bjorn thanked me for my contribution and apologised for asking me to speak without any warning and preparation. My stomach was still churning but gradually I calmed down and relaxed. I looked across at Anja and she smiled reassuringly and raised her eye-brows in mock admiration. Nina stretched over and touched my hand without looking at me, her touch lingering a few seconds.

For the next two and a half hours, I listened to the group as they spoke individually and collectively about the progress that had been made and what still required to be done. There was an inevitable tension, but I detected that a climate of trust was emerging. There was a noticeable degree of concern and frustration, almost as if they needed now to see some tangible results from their efforts. It was obvious that Bjorn's request from their last meeting had been productive. Each of the six reported that they were able to say on behalf of the people they represented that they would support any agreed statement or initiative from the meeting that led to the peace process being re-started and progressed. Quite intentionally, I remained slightly peripheral to the discussion that was underway, not really 100% confident in my acceptance as part of the group or in their reaction to my speech. I was intrigued by a comment made by Chris Nicholl, who claimed that he'd had discussions with both Catholic and Protestant businessmen from the North and almost to a man, they expressed no wish to be under the thumb of Dublin.

I kept a prudent silence, as I listened absorbed by proceedings, as Bjorn skilfully facilitated the debate, pushing, probing, cajoling, coaxing the group down the same path, bringing them back into line, as and when necessary. I wanted to interrupt, offering my ten bobs worth and asking them questions about the 'Troubles', a subject that did genuinely fascinate me. Questions like, do British Military Intelligence really know who the terrorist leaders are on both sides; are the rumours true that, at certain levels within their respective organisations, the terrorist 'god-fathers' actually talk to each other and carve up the 'black economy pie', with recent departures into drug dealing, CD piracy, Post Office and bank hold-ups; are people living in constant fear because of the violence or does it only effect isolated working class areas; are there 'fat-cats' somewhere getting rich out of the misery of others, by controlling the finance, the Government and Euro grants available for the much needed and often neglected Urban re-generation of the Province. I had read somewhere that, in the past three years, more than £600 million to figures of £3 billion of Government money alone, had been pumped into Northern Ireland. To me, the whole problem had always seemed more than just groups of Catholic and Protestant working class thugs, wandering the 'ghettos' killing and maiming each other, whatever their cause. There seemed to be other interests at work, but for as long as the paramilitary gangs remain intact, there will always be problems in Northern Ireland. Fairly recently I had heard that a new dilemma had been created by the IRA cease-fire, as they had turned their attentions to the policing of their own areas. There had allegedly been a marked increase in punishment beatings and an apparent dichotomy had developed whereby small-time drug dealers were being 'dealt with' to protect the community, but some of the big time players were being left alone to ply their trade, having paid off their paramilitary protectors.

At approximately 2 am, as we all began to tire and wilt, a direct result no doubt of the combination of travel, good food, alcohol and the day's physical and mental exercise, Bjorn offered everyone a final night-cap. As the crystal glasses were drained for the last time, Bjorn spoke again.

"I suggest we call it a night and we all retire to bed. Tomorrow will be a day for walking and talking. For achieving and agreeing. Yes?"

The Rolfsons appeared and began to clear the table, as the company said goodnight and went to their rooms. Nina insisted they should leave it and clear up in the morning, but they would have none of it. Anja and I left the warmth of the dining room and sat in the coolness of the staircase, as everyone trooped past us, heading for their beds. She slipped her arm around me and rested her head on my shoulder.

"You did very well tonight. I'm sure Bjorn will be pleased. You helped get the evening off to an interesting start."

"Thanks. It was bloody nerve-racking and at times I'm not even sure if I made any sense, but I tried to express myself as honestly as possible, even though I felt I rambled on a bit."

"You seemed quite knowledgeable about all the subjects you mentioned. I think you gave Bjorn a pleasant surprise, he really likes you...so does Nina."

"I wouldn't say I was knowledgeable. I just have a general awareness and a genuine interest."

I clasped my hands and bowed my head. For the first time in days, I felt weary. Anja pulled me close to her again, and whispered.

"I think I go to bed now. We have a busy day ahead tomorrow."

I pushed my hand through my hair. The dark locks, with the first flecks of grey now creeping through, fell naturally back into place. We kissed and went upstairs. I saw her safely to the door of her room. Anja opened the door and taking my hand she led me into the darkness.

"Anja?" It was a child's voice.

Anja grabbed me and hugged me tightly.

"I'm sorry, I forgot about Mette."

She held my face in her hands and kissed me. It was a passionate, probing kiss. It seemed to carry with it a promise.

"Good night, sleep well," she said.

I placed my finger on her mouth then dropped it down over her neck, over her hardened nipples, down to her waist. I felt for the button at the back of her skirt and undid it. I eased the zip down and her skirt dropped to the floor. My hand drew an invisible line round her belly button. I felt the muscles of her abdomen tighten as I moved my hand down to the top of her knickers, gently tugging the elastic. She offered no resistance. I eased my hand between the soft cotton of her Sloggis and the softness of her skin, until I felt the touch of her thatch. I moved my hand lower. Her head pushed against mine. Her breathing was warm by my ear. My hand slipped down again, getting closer and closer. Then I stopped. Slowly I withdrew my hand.

"Good night," I whispered.

I walked back to my room. I knew she was still standing there, her eyes following me, but I didn't look back.

In my own room, I undressed and lay in bed with my eyes wide open, my senses aware of the darkness, the silence, my isolation, my need to be with Anja and I touched her perfect body in my mind.

Chapter 5

CHAPTER 5

Next morning, I was woken by the sound of rain and sleet peppering the window in intermittent blasts. Winter had howled down early from the mountains. I lay awake, put my hands behind my head and stared at the ceiling, trying to unscramble the events of the past couple of days. I flashed back to my meeting with Anja at Sola and the journey here. I closed my eyes, reviving thoughts of the dream-like view from the top of the mountains and my first sight of the house emerging through the trees as we came up the drive. Now here I was amidst a collection of men who between them had the potential to push and coax Ireland down a road to peace. I thought of Hannah; I always did that when I was confused and a little unsure of myself. My little speech of the previous evening still upset me slightly, and with typical Paul Robertson insecurity, I wondered what they all thought of me. I finally got out of bed, quickly rattled off a hundred odd press ups (but missed out the sit ups!) showered and dressed. I put on my jeans, a Scotland rugby shirt, a navy Devold jumper and went along to Anja's room. I knocked on the door but there was no answer. Mette and Einar appeared behind me and said that everyone was in the kitchen, so I went downstairs to join them.

"Good morning, Paul," said Dr Renfrew, as he shook my hand.

"Morning," I replied to the various greetings. There was no sign of Anja or Bjorn.

"Paul, help yourself to some breakfast," Dr Renfrew added, "The Prof. has cancelled this morning's walk because of the weather, but he is hoping to hold a session with everyone in the drawing room: You'd be most welcome to join in."

"Thank you, I'd like that."

Everyone stood or sat around drinking coffee and eating freshly baked croissants, relieved no doubt that Bjorn had wisely chosen to scrap our planned sojourn up the mountain, given the prevailing weather conditions. I helped myself to coffee, then watched McCreery slip into the adjoining utility room, where he put on a Barbour-style waxed coat and a cap, before stepping out into the heavy sheeting rain and sleet and disappearing out of sight. Maybe he needed some fresh air.

"Well, Paul, are you a good journalist then? Do you tell it the way it is, or do you package it all up neatly and tell people the things they want to hear?" It was Chris Nicholl. He had joined me without invitation and I turned to face him, my concern about McCreery broken by his interruption. I wasn't sure what he meant but I answered him.

"I'm just a talentless hack who has bills to pay and who can't be too fussy what assignments he takes on, but I do have certain standards." Nicholl just grunted.

"I'm going over to Scotland in the New Year, Edinburgh in fact, for the rugby at Murrayfield. I think we'll stuff you!"

"I've got a tenner that says you won't!"

"Done."

We shook hands, then Nicholl grinned, lit a cigarette and we both stood at the window and watched the weather. He was a big, solidly built man, of the anthropoidal, hairy shoulders and knuckles variety, a former front-row forward, his splintered nose a lasting testament to one ruck or collapsed scrum too many. Judging by his performance at dinner the previous evening, he was a loud, boorish, confident man, a bully who was used to getting his own way. His wealth, if not necessarily his good taste, was evidenced by the thick gold chain round his neck, the gold bracelet, the garish rings on his fingers and what appeared to be a Rolex, more than likely an original, on his wrist. I had heard that to the lay-man the only difference between the real McCoy and a cheap South-East Asian imitation was that the second hand on the genuine article swept round the face, but the second hand on the fake had an obvious ticking movement. I tried, but failed to ascertain if the second hand swept round.

Mrs Rolfson removed another batch of hot croissants from the oven of the black, Aga style range. Nina came over to me; she was smoking again and I remember Steve telling me that it was not uncommon to see Norwegian women smoking. It seemed to contradict the impression I had built up of the classy, health conscious, outdoor Scandinavian.

"Good morning Paul, did you sleep well? Anja is with Bjorn; you'll see her soon. They're preparing some notes as a result of last night's discussions. I'll have to have a word with Bjorn about all his demands on Anja's time; it means she ends up neglecting you. I realise it is her job, but she has a guest to look after."

"It's not a problem, we'll have plenty of time to be together," I said, then in a slightly nervous outburst, I commented on the weather, with a statement of the glaringly obvious, "It's not very nice out."

Nina just grinned and nodded her head in agreement, then was called away by Rolfson. I poured myself another cup of coffee and walked back over to the window just in time to see McCreery walking across the car park, his head bowed against the driving, lashing sleet. I wondered what he'd been up to. It was a bloody awful day.

Bjorn eventually appeared in the kitchen and asked us all to go up and join him in the drawing room. When everyone was there (we had to wait for McCreery to appear), the Professor stood up and began to speak.

"I'm sorry our Norwegian weather prevents us from going for a scramble on the mountain, but with your agreement I would like to spend the morning building on the good work of last night. I want now to raise the stakes and breathe some much needed energy and urgency into the process and if..." he paused and looked around.

"And if we are all in agreement, I would like us to prepare a statement that I can take back with me to Oslo, where I will pass it to the Storting, who in turn will take it to London and Dublin at the highest levels. I confess I share with you the feeling of frustration at the speed and direction of Government policy, but I believe we are about to pass a crucial milestone in our historic mission to bring peace to Northern Ireland. I am confident, gentlemen and ladies, that the weeks and months of effort are now beginning to come to fruition and I believe we are about to square the circle. I want us all now to help finally remove the gun from Irish politics."

Bjorn was obviously excited and was quite animated in his address as he paced the room, making as much eye contact with his group as he could. I'm sure it wasn't intentional, but I just didn't feel part of what was going on.

"Are we agreed? Yes?" he said, with widespread arms.

There was no answer to another of his rhetorical questions. Anja passed around a short two-page document to each of the six, which they all quickly read. I felt a little left out

126

and I assumed it contained a brief synopsis of their past meetings and the progress that had been made so far. Bjorn spoke again.

"Gentlemen, I would now like to push you into agreeing a statement, a few words that will signal to the world that Ireland is again ready to take a further step on the long, difficult and sometimes tortuous road to peace. We must help remove the fear and despair, that has prevailed in Northern Ireland for the past two and a half decades and on the island in general for centuries. Let us harness the optimism and willingness of the people and accept this opportunity to break the impasse that has dogged the official discussions. You must now find the safe path to lead your people down and help banish the tears of the past."

I wondered what effect, if any, the outcome of this meeting would have on the current 'official peace initiatives', with its intense media profile, its diplomatic rhetoric and the ping-pong war of words between the British Government and Sinn Fein. Instinctively I felt more progress was being made here and noticeably there were no calls for clarification or allegations of a 'sell-out'. I looked round the room; the relaxed and happy faces of breakfast time had become tight lipped and serious. Renfrew, Docherty, Nicholl and Ryan exchanged nervous glances.

In a corner of the room, Seamus Coyle had been biding his time and he chose this opportunity to strike. He stood up and everyone in the room focused in on him, everyone that is except McCreery. The sleet continued to batter and thrash against the glass of the French windows and the burning logs crackled and hissed in the hearth. Suddenly the door burst open and Mette came running in. She and Einar had been quarrelling and she was crying for her mother. Nina hugged her daughter and sat her on her knee. The bearded Irishman asked if she was alright and then spoke, his soft, lilting voice filling the room.

"For many months I have observed the development of our little tryst, having arrived at my first meeting, I have to say, something of a sceptic and a military and political fugitive. Whilst I still remain a fugitive in the eyes of the British Government, I too have become wearied of the damage and suffering that has been inflicted on my country and its people. My initial scepticism, however, has wained, as I have eaten, drank, debated and laughed with men I had always thought of as my enemy. Men I would have previously been happy to draw arms against. I have envied and admired the way Professor Pederson and his team, Nina, Anja and the children, have nurtured and developed our group. Anyway, as a direct result of the efforts and progress that has been made here, I am again prepared to throw my cap into the ring, on behalf of the people I represent as our struggle enters a new phase."

I glanced around the room. Only McCreery was not looking at Coyle. Instead, he stood alone at the French windows, as if hypnotised by the sight and sound of the sleet on the glass, his flint like features and unblinking eyes peering through the rippling waves of water running down the panes, gazing out over the loch to the cloud and mist-cloaked mountains and beyond. He looked older and wearier in the natural light of the morning.

Coyle continued.

"If this group will commit its support, my people, the Army Convention of the Provisional Irish Republican Army, are willing to continue their unconditional cessation of military activity in the Province and on mainland Britain. This command group meet only rarely for obvious reasons and it is in recognition of the measure of importance they have attached to the talks of this group that they have seen it as appropriate to meet again and to support my presence here. This declaration should therefore be regarded as both unambiguous and emphatic. The British Government and their Army of Occupation should have no doubts of our intentions. It is certainly a high risk strategy for the Republican movement, as for years we have believed that force was the only thing that the British Government would respect or respond to, but we have come to the pragmatic recognition that it's been a long war, our people are weary..." Coyle paused, then continued, "It's a war we know we cannot lose, but equally we know we cannot win. All we can do is prolong the conflict and watch the casualty statistics mount up. We must also accept that we as Republicans or Nationalists do not have a monopoly on suffering and we too have had to bury our people. This realisation has been fundamental in the shift in the strategic thinking of the 'Falls Road think-tank'. Our commitment to a permanent cease-fire represents a huge tactical shift by the IRA and we believe it will eventually be rewarded by progress in the fundamental, political, democratic and constitutional situation."

I remembered previous cease-fires in 1972 and 1975 and I was aware that they resulted in a reduction and loss of Republican support. Times were different now and I detected that the Republican mood was different too even though their objectives had not changed. Coyle continued.

"All our Units have been instructed that our cease-fire statement is clear and definitive and will hold no matter what pressures and provocation's are mounted against us. It is true that the devastation caused by the bombing of our Party offices and the 'hit' in Strasbourg, so soon after our initial declaration, plunged the whole peace process into stormy waters, as my organisation feared that it was the beginning of the much prophesied Loyalist back-lash, which has destroyed previous peace initiatives. It was a chilling reminder and indeed, we worried about a new kind of conflict, bloodier than in the past, as Loyalists fearing there had been secret deals, secret concessions, vented their frustrations, their scepticism, their fears. Fortunately, there has been a lull in the Loyalist killings and although there is talk of war in the streets, I am sure that the people here will do their utmost to see that it never happens."

Coyle went on to vent his organisation's frustration with the perceived prevarication and ambiguity of the British Government, and the distinction between what they call, 'exploratory talks' and full 'democratic talks'.

"In order to speed up the mechanisms of peace, we are willing to handover or destroy, under controlled conditions, and witnessed by independent, neutral observers, a substantial inventory of our stockpiles of Semtex and make harmless a considerable stockholding of our arms cache, if and I repeat, if, there is acceptable progress on interim arrangements and our political representatives are involved in inclusive negotiations. Of course, the fundamental issue for us is the principle of self-determination for the Irish people, but had we known that the British Government would make decommissioning a pre-condition for talks, then you would have found that there would have been no cease-fire. It is our rational and logical belief that unilateral decommissioning of weapons is an unreasonable and bogus request by the British Government, unprecedented in peace negotiations anywhere in the world, but they have developed this mind-set and they have backed themselves into a policy cul-de-sac which is holding up political negotiations. It is as if they are trying to achieve a victory through politics. It is also very important that the public image of the peace process is not distracted by the question of the decommissioning of arms. It is time for our Movement to receive parity with all other political parties and equal access to talks. We want to see at long last an end to this endless war of words over Ministerial talks. This is a defining moment in our history, an unprecedented and heroic step by the volunteers of the Provisional IRA."

Coyle left none of the parties present under any illusion that his announcement must in no way be made public. He made it clear that it should be known to only this group and the respective governments of Norway, Eire and the UK, at Prime Ministerial, Foreign Secretary and Secretary of State level, absolutely no-one else. He went on.

"All our official public announcements will continue the rhetoric of defiance and we will not publicly display any obvious signs of compromise on the question of handing in our arms, until there is an agreed solution to the key political questions. We propose that, as a measure of our commitment and as a gesture of goodwill, our cease-fire should continue to last a minimum of two further months, after which time we should all meet here again in Norway and this time we must have in attendance the British, Irish and Norwegian Foreign Secretaries and for the sake of correct diplomatic protocol, Mayhew. If that meeting is held and the discussions prove positive and fruitful, there is no reason why we cannot set a timetable for full round-table talks with all political parties, be they DUP, SDLP, the Official Unionists, Sinn Fein, the Alliance Party, the Progressive Unionists, the Ulster Democratic Party, whoever has a democratic mandate of representation."

He displayed an obvious distrust of the media, whom he suspected would be scrabbling around, trying to get their grubby little mitts, on what was being fed to them through 'official channels' about 'talks about talks', the creeping progress of the Downing Street Declaration and the much talked about 'Draft Framework Document'. I tended to agree with him that hysterical tabloid coverage was good 'box office' and no doubt helped sell papers. He also voiced a vague compliment about the dubious abilities of servants of the British Government and the part they could play in respect of their fogging and dis-information techniques.

"I briefly mentioned that we are willing to allow the disarming process to proceed under neutral observation and control and to this end we have been approached by several Senior US officials who have offered their services. They are prepared to act as independent arbiters, honest brokers you might say, in the witnessing of the first stage of the destruction or removal of weaponry. These people are Senators, Congressmen and Military men with political ambition, but I feel I must stress they are not in any way agents of some Boston based pro-Republican, Irish-American lobby. Again, I must make it perfectly clear that if for any reason these discussions and our agreement to remove some of our weapons from this war is made public, my movement will vehemently denounce it, if there is any military or para-military action taken against our people during this time, we reserve the right to defend ourselves and we will immediately consider resuming all covert military operations."

Bjorn interrupted. "Seamus, you and your people have my country's unconditional support," he beamed, but Coyle grinned, held up his hand, as if harnessing and controlling Pederson's unabashed enthusiasm.

"Thank you Bjorn, but I haven't quite finished yet..."

He paused, as if to remember the well rehearsed lines of a speech, but somehow I knew he wasn't speaking from notes, although there was no doubt that the delivery was from a man completely immersed in the well rehearsed and often cited clichés of Irish Nationalist propaganda.

"Should this meeting with Senior Government Ministers take place, then I would repeat, *all* issues must at least be open to debate and discussion. Subjects like self-determination, that is to say, a democratic referendum of all Ireland on the future of the North, an amnesty of all political prisoners, from both sides, which is, I must insist, an issue of paramount importance, the lifting of the absurd Exclusion Orders, although I suspect this may happen sooner, rather than later, the repeal of the British Government's Anti-Terrorism laws, the eventual disbandment of the RUC and in particular the demilitarisation of the weaponry in circulation on all sides of the conflict and by this we not only mean the destruction of Loyalist weapons, but the scaling down of the British presence on the streets and their eventual withdrawal back to barracks in England. In particular we wish to see an end to the siege of

Crossmaglen and the occupation of South Armagh.

"If we do meet, it cannot be to only discuss a single issue agenda and we would propose that no topic should be excluded from our talks, which we would prefer to be free and completely open. The British Government must engage in common sense dialogue, as any cosmetic and limited concessions by them will not be enough. Any attempt to prevent my organisation or more accurately our political wing attending full round-table talks with Government - and we'll be represented by our most influential people, Kieran, you'll have a major part to play in briefing your President - will be seen as a signal to continue the war. Of course, there is no doubt there are people who will want us to fail, but together, through the efforts of this group we are opening the door. Do we now all have the courage to walk through it?

"Just before I return the floor to Bjorn, a word of warning. Our movement is in general disciplined and well organised, but sadly, there are elements, more accurately, there are younger, hot headed men and women who have infiltrated our movement recently. Whilst we cannot doubt their commitment to the cause, the word peace has not entered their vocabulary. They have not yet progressed from the now redundant policy of the 'Armalite and Ballot Box' to our current 'Unarmed' strategy. They are a new breed of idealistic or revenge Republicans, who not only want to take up arms to protect their communities but, more worryingly, are not convinced that the road to victory will be achieved by talking. Unfortunately, it is not inconceivable that they may engage in certain maverick acts. Their 'enthusiasm' shall we say, presents us with a potential problem, which in the short-term we can subdue and control. The same can be said of INLA, although they have not yet declared a cease-fire, we are monitoring their movements, along with, I have to say, certain elements of the British armed forces."

Coyle made it clear that within the command structure of the Provisional IRA, they had concluded that the time was right to make their move, both politically and militarily. The normally soft voice hardened when he emphasised that this was not a surrender and that they weren't continuing their cease-fire from a position of weakness. They firmly believed they had the political strength to make their commitment with confidence, but there was a sting.

"If we wait, or the process is, what do the politicians say, 'de-railed', it will allow this small group, who are not surprisingly mostly based in South Armagh, time to expand and exert their influence. They have already intimated that they will fiercely resist any moves on the disposal of arms and our concern is, if the delays in progressing to full round table talks are long enough and the problems serious enough, then as Republican tradition dictates, eventually the current leadership will be replaced, or in the worst case scenario, there could be a 'split' in our organisation and in my opinion, if that does happen, we will not see peace in my country, in our lifetimes, as the war

131

flares up again and drags on indefinitely."

Coyle's voice almost broke as he delivered the warning and this last line.

"Please believe me when I say what we are proposing is no hollow gesture and we will need to have the confidence that there will be some reciprocal offer. The British and Irish Governments should not underestimate the generosity of our actions and I must emphasise that if they do not take reasonable steps to break the stalemate, then we are on a slippery slope back to the dark days from which we have just emerged. We would say to all Unionists, we understand your fears, but now is the time to bring your hopes and dreams to the negotiating table."

After a few seconds, McCreery emerged from his trance and what had been a distant, faraway look in his eyes had now become a sharply focused stare. He turned to face Coyle. The hair on the back of my neck stood up. Anja, who had been sitting on a soft seat by the fire place, edged over and sat on the floor at my feet. This was it. The watershed. McCreery approached Coyle, slowly and deliberately, fully aware that they were now both very much centre stage. It was not a time for great oratory, a delivery from the heart would do. He began to speak, his voice clear and slow, as if he was deliberating over every word.

"People talk of the British presence in Northern Ireland and refer to the British military, but it should never be forgotten that the Loyalist population is the British presence and peace in Ulster is an illusion without our consent. I, for one, would have never believed that the day would come when I would say that it is now time for all Loyalists, Unionists, Protestants, whatever categorisation you want to give us or associate us with, to think the unthinkable. The time has come for us to help break the deadlock and take decisive action that may lead to peace.

"Ulstermen have been fighting a rear guard action for nearly one hundred years ever since the introduction of the first Home Rule Bill. It has therefore taken much skill and patience behind the scenes for us to come to terms with the possibility that the IRA cease fire may indeed be permanent, even though they still stockpile tons of Gadaffi weaponry. In our minds there can be no retreat by the British Government - no concessions until we are convinced the Sein Fein - IRA commitment is genuine and not just a ruse. We have to believe they are committed exclusively to peaceful political means and that there have been no secret deals between them and Westminster."

McCreery made it clear circumstances had changed and it maybe was time for the Loyalists to move away from their rallying cry, 'No Surrender!' He explained that if the IRA did commit to the partial destruction of their arsenal then his people would prefer the involvement of the Norwegian authorities in the decommissioning process, as they deeply mistrusted the motivation of the US and their universally unpopular

President, whose administration would be massively boosted by the support of 40 million Catholic Irish-Americans if he claimed the Irish peace process as his own Foreign Policy triumph. Where, asked McCreery, do his loyalties lie? Is he committed to the people of Northern Ireland or is he driven by his personal ambitions to secure a second term of office in the White House? There was no doubt from McCreery's words that they were against any internationalisation of the process. He did however concede that, whether they liked it or not, the United States would have a major influence on the situation. He also made it evident that they would block any attempts by the US to hi-jack the peace process and any decommissioning phase for their own purely selfish political ends.

"On behalf of the, shall I say the 'opposition', the Combined Loyalist Military Command, we will match the Republican cease-fire under the same pre-conditions they have set down, and we will also commit to the destruction of a proportion of our own arms under the auspices of the Norwegians. A form of progressive decommissioning you might say. I would remind you all that normally we would have only agreed to give up our arms as part of a final political settlement - not before, but we want to play our part in breaking the stalemate."

McCreery outlined the concerns his organisation had about the legality of the decommissioning process. He stressed that a formula or system would have to be set up so that some of their key operatives would not be arrested whilst in the act of destroying or whilst being in the possession of arms on their way to be destroyed. It seemed a reasonable point.

Like Coyle, he called for a wide ranging political agenda to be covered during any round table talks. His objectives, however obviously prejudiced to those of the Loyalists, covered items such as the right to negotiate the principle of the South relinquishing their constitutional territorial claim on the North. He also expected not to have to deal with a Sinn Fein, SDLP, Dublin Government contingent who speak with one voice. McCreery's response continued.

"There is no doubt that in two months time, if the cease-fire holds, there are many imaginative and realistic ideas to be debated, constructive suggestions from both sides in the so called democratic market place of ideas, to be kicked around the table. Let there be no doubt, in anyone's minds, we want to be at that table. Perhaps the days of saying 'no' are behind us. Our people, the Protestant majority of Ulster, want their leaders involved in talks. We are therefore developing a team of leaders, made up of our most capable intellectual, political and academic talents, who can sit at that table with all interested parties and clearly and articulately formulate a case for Union. The world, particularly the US, must be sympathetic to our fears; the legend of betrayal is deeply ingrained."

The Protestant population had, according to McCreery, become cynical, believing history may be about to repeat itself. How could Ulstermen have any faith in Ministers who said repeatedly that there had been no talks with the IRA, only weeks before their secret dialogue was confirmed, or how could they believe in a Government that now claimed that it had no political or strategic interest in Ulster. However, McCreery too added some words of caution...

"The Unionist population will not accept any 'sell-out' by the British Government of their constitutional situation which results in a green, one way ticket to a united Ireland. We will never allow the Protestant people to be disenfranchised but, if this cease-fire leads to a permanent cessation of violence, then all things are possible by discussion. Finally, on that note of caution, if there is a breakdown in the peace or any under-hand attempts to do back-door deals between Sinn Fein, London and Dublin, the consequences will be catastrophic and will, I fear, lead to civil war on the streets of Ulster, perhaps escalating to the streets of London, Dublin and Glasgow, with the IRA cease-fire having been no more than a cruel hoax.

"To some it would appear that the prospect of a united Ireland is closer now than at any time since partition in 1920. The British Government must act honourably and without treachery, but if deals are taking place in little ante rooms in the gossipy corridors of Westminster between junior Ministers, following some Nationalist agenda, then to our mind negotiations will not take place and the Loyalist veto will be used and any subsequent attempt at full round-table talks will meet the barren wilderness of the politics of the empty chair. Personally, I hope it never comes to that and that the work done here over the past months has helped pave a way to a just and lasting peace.

"Based on our analysis of the opinions of grass-roots Loyalism, our meetings with some of our key people still incarcerated in the Maze, public feeling and recent political developments, we will, as I have said, shortly announce at a press conference in Belfast a universal and permanent cessation of Loyalist violence. It will remain in place as long as the Republican cease-fire holds and they commit to the removal of their weaponry. We will also make clear our intention to become more publicly proactive in the peace process to counter the Sinn Fein propaganda barrage and their virtual monopoly of the media coverage. We will also highlight our organisation's sincere remorse and deep regret for the deaths of all innocent people throughout the 'Troubles' of the last twenty five years. For far too long we have stood among the wreckage of broken lives. Like Coyle, I sincerely hope that round-table talks begin as soon as possible. If they don't, then the British Government is in danger of becoming a victim of its own complacency, in that it evidently fails to appreciate that solutions to the problems of Ulster will be resolved out of the practicalities of political horse-trading and not polite, rational discussion and argument."

In a departure from character, McCreery continued.

"I love coming here to Norway. It is a relief to be away from the constant fear of a knock on the door in the dead of night; it is a relief to be away from check-points, sand-bags, barbed wire and the pressures of just being involved. This house is a great place, it's been an inspired choice and I believe it is fair to say that in any other country or location, what we have tried to do here might never have happened.

"Finally, I would just like to say that we want to play our part in shaping the future of Ulster and we want to come to the negotiating table armed only with our mandates. Right now, everything is perilously balanced on a knife's edge, our people are slightly bewildered by peace on the streets, but it wouldn't take much for the situation to get out of hand, with all the old fears and hatreds re-emerging in bloody war. What we don't want is a phoney peace, where guns and bombs are just mothballed ready to be dusted down and used again at a moments notice. We want to see an end to the 'Troubles' for all time and a sincere and genuine attempt to democratically achieve long term stability that has the consent of the people of Ulster. The Protestant majority of my country relish the prospect of peace, but we have a responsibility to bear and we cannot accept any proposal that is just a prototype for a united Ireland, or a shot-gun marriage between North and South. It's easy to call a cease-fire; what happens next is the hard part and the true test."

In a scene that had a touch of pure poetic drama, the like of which only Irish and Celtic people have, the Loyalist gunman held out his hand and it was gripped and shaken firmly by the Republican, the glare in his eyes softening. The sentiments and fears of the two sides had been articulately expressed and the tension and anxiety which had built up over the past half an hour seemed to subside and evaporate, giving way to spontaneous applause. Anja hugged and kissed me, there were tears streaming down her face. She went over to Bjorn and Nina and they embraced, everyone else was shaking hands and laughing. The crack was very good. The two 'volunteers' (and I apologise for glamorising them), the two terrorists had turned again toward the French windows and they stood side by side, gazing back out across the loch, staring back out over some great distance of time and memory. I wondered what must have been going through their minds. What weight had been lifted from their shoulders? What even greater weight had replaced it? Could a cease-fire ever hold and permanent peace ever be achieved? Interesting times.

Bjorn sent Anja down to the kitchen to involve the Rolfsons and she returned with the two elderly retainers, bringing with them two bottles of chilled, Perrier Jouet La Belle Époque, the champagne with the painted flower on the bottle, and a tray of crystal flutes. Dr Renfrew immediately proposed a toast.

"To all my new and old friends in the room and to the children of Ireland, may they grow up in an atmosphere of peace and mutual co-existence. You know, for years our culture has hurt and alienated sections of the community, inflicting a terrible misery on our people, it will be incumbent on all of us to ensure the pendulum does not swing back to the days of terror and murder on our streets. We must slam shut the gates of violence. A new generation must be given the chance to succeed, but they will need the investment that only political stability can bring."

Bjorn spoke again, this time lowering his voice in a way that only served to increase the solemn gravity of the message in his words.

"The burden of history lies heavy on your island and its people. For months I have been aware of the difficulties you have all faced by joining me here. Now there is a chance for peace in Northern Ireland, even though for a long time it has been unlikely and unrealistic. We must take heart from what has happened in black South Africa and in the setting up of a Palestinian state in Gaza, although that process has not yet ended and I believe that there are a few more chapters to be written before that story is complete. Our optimism will be tempered by the caution, suspicion and the inbred fear of the population, as we embark on a journey that is fraught with innumerable hazards and which must have, if it is to stand any chance of success, the confidence and consent of all the people of Northern Ireland, who for years have been frozen in a feeling of hopelessness. We have made a significant step forward on the road to permanent peace. Let us celebrate an end to violence and the instability that has plagued the country for decades. Hopefully, we have provided the catalyst that will ultimately trigger Governmental support and further negotiations. Let us tear down the physical barriers to peace, as well as the numerous barriers of mistrust in our minds. Let the guns fall silent, let us all strive for the prize that awaits us. Soon it will be up to the politicians to pick up the torch and lead us to a lasting peace."

We all cheered and sipped from our glasses the perfectly chilled, dry champagne. Then Docherty called for silence. He had a toast to make (more a case of no show without Punch!), and would not allow the chance to demonstrate his eloquence to pass.

"The realisation that change can no longer be affected by the sword is a remarkable and honest conclusion and I salute both of you. We must also be aware that in a land as troubled and divided as ours, reconciliation is easy to preach but, when there has been so much grief, so much fear, suspicion and hatred, it will take a long, long time for life to return to normal, or hopefully to a normality that is experienced on the mainland of Britain. It would be quite wrong to wish for a return to the status quo of twenty five years ago, as it was the very fabric of life in those days that led directly to a quarter century of desolation and darkness. Let us not dwell on the grim reminders of the past, let us give thanks for the gifts and opportunities we now have."

Whilst he had the floor Docherty looked forward to the impact the novelty of peace would have on the two communities in the run up to Christmas with the promise of a threat-free festive season. It would, he feared, take years for the psychological imprint of what they had suffered to lessen.

"The people have developed an appetite for peace. I can only pray that this temporary respite from violence becomes a strong and lasting peace. To get back to the job in hand, I would like us all to charge our glasses and toast our most delightful guides and mentors on this journey, Bjorn and Nina Pederson, their children and of course the lovely Anja. Without your enthusiasm, pragmatism, your sympathetic understanding of the situation, as well as your boldness and determination, we would not I fear be here, and peace, true peace would still be beyond our grasp. I give you the Norwegian connection, Professor Bjorn Pederson, Nina, Anja and the children, God bless you!"

We all repeated the names in unison as we raised our glasses. The room resounded to the sounds of glasses chinking and people saying cheers, skol and I chipped in with slange.

Bjorn then raised his hand.

"My friends, please, my wife would like to say something."

Nina demurely flicked the hair from her face and raised her glass.

"You must never become deflected in your quest for peace, even though I fear each year will bring its own flash points as once opposing groups find it hard to ignore the traditions of their past. You must remain single-minded and committed and lasting peace, the ultimate prize, will surely be yours. Now please, let us drink to the children of Northern Ireland and their future."

It was then unanimously agreed that the Rolfsons should prepare a lunch of sandwiches and other finger snacks and that this would just be eaten in the drawing room. No one was interested in a formal sit down lunch. There was too much excitement. Outside, as if on some divine cue, the dark clouds moved out to the south-east and the rain and sleet eased off and traces of blue sky began to break through.

Bjorn and Nina had gone over to the piano and Nina had sat down and began to play, her husband standing by her. I recognised the first melody, the love theme from the television series the 'Thorn Birds'. This was followed by "Serenade for Klara" from the movie 'Klara'. The room was brimming with the sound of her playing and the excited chatter of a very happy and contented group of people. I was sitting in a well-worn, high-backed leather chair, with Anja again sitting at my feet, her head resting on my lap. I ran my fingers through her hair and watched, trying to take it all in.

Nina stopped playing. She eased herself over to the side and was joined on the piano seat by her husband and they began to play a duet. I recognised it instantly, it was a melody by Grieg and had been used in the fifties and sixties as the theme tune to the children's radio programme 'Listen with Mother'. It was a personal favourite of mine and the one I had previously tried to describe to Anja. I felt a lump in my throat as I recalled childhood memories of times spent with mum and dad, my brother and sister.

By now Einar had come down from his room to join us and the Rolfsons were serving coffee. There was an amazing mood in the room and I felt I was a spectator at an old family reunion. I wondered what the old ship owner would have made of the scene. Surely we had re-awakened and rekindled the true spirit of the house. It was all a bit unreal considering we had two terrorists in attendance. I shared McCreery's feelings for the house and the surroundings. It was a most wonderful, near perfect place, even under the morning's leaden skies. I imagined the place under a mantle of mid-winter snow, or below the sky of high Scandinavian summer. It was the kind of place I would have wanted to return to again and again. I think I understood why the old guy had built the house here.

It seemed appropriate that this truce was being agreed in Norway, with the paramilitaries on both sides giving up the gun and the bullet and Bjorn committing to organise and facilitate round table discussions with Government. I thought of Steve's story of the Three Swords at the Harfsfjord.

Meanwhile, Anja had left my lap and was working again, chatting and joking with her guests. I got up off my seat and walked round the room shaking hands with everyone. I walked over to Seamus and shook his hand. He greeted me warmly.

"You know son, for the last twenty five years, there has been a very selective approach to the coverage of the Troubles by British journalists, as you well know," and he added, "Do you still think we're all bad bastards!" perhaps hinting at my latent or implied prejudices. I didn't realise they were so evident, but he had obviously spotted them.

"The jury's still out, but time will tell."

I looked around for McCreery, but he was not in the room. He was, undoubtedly, along with Coyle, a key player in this group but he was also a man of mystery and latent menace. He was the lone representative of the self-proclaimed Combined Loyalist Military Command and their role was crucial in any future peace process.

The chilled champagne had taken effect on my plumbing and I left the drawing room and made my way to one of the toilets that were scattered around the house. I was moving quietly along the corridor on the first floor when I heard McCreery's distinctive voice coming from the study. I was making my way for the bathroom just beyond the entrance to the study, and as I walked past, McCreery caught my eye, glowered at me and slammed down the phone. As I eased the bathroom door shut, I watched him leave the study. He worried me and I debated whether or not I should tell Anja but instead I did what I had to do and returned to the room and congratulated Bjorn on his achievement.

"Congratulations Professor, I hope you can go on to persuade and encourage the Governments of the UK and the Republic to support your work and to meet here in two months time."

"I'm sure I can Paul, but the key will now be the paramilitaries decommissioning their weapons. What was announced here today was what I have been working toward all along and I'm sure progress can now be made on all fronts. Can I just thank you for your contribution last night; it was well received."

"Professor."

"Paul, please, I am more comfortable if you call me Bjorn."

"Yeah, OK...I hope you don't mind me making the suggestion, but if the cease-fire continues and the peace becomes more and more entrenched, I was thinking that perhaps someone could organise a sporting festival, with the proceeds going to some all-Ireland charities"

"What do you have in mind exactly?"

"Well, I'm shooting from the hip, and I haven't given it too much thought, but maybe a soccer match, a British/Norwegian select against an all-Ireland select. You could do the same with rugby, mind you I don't know if there is much rugby played over here. To avoid trouble, tickets would only be available to family groups. I've just had another idea you could even have a massive rock concert, with the top UK, Irish and Scandinavian acts, a sort of Band-Aid revisited, with all proceeds going once again to children's charities in the North and South."

"An excellent idea, but one that will have to wait some time before it could be fulfilled. Thank you once again, I'll note your suggestions and talk to some people. Now if you can excuse me, I must talk to Nina."

By 2 pm on Saturday afternoon several of the guests indicated that they would prefer to leave early and return and report to their organisations, such was the excitement that had been generated by Coyle's words and, equally, those of McCreery. Bjorn understood and respected their wishes and by 3 pm that afternoon we were wishing Kieran, Chris Nicholl and Professor Docherty a safe journey home. Nina was also leaving, having decided at the last minute to drive up to Bergen with the children to visit her sister. She had played her part. Staying up in Bergen for a few days would make a welcome change, as she knew Bjorn would be involved in some frenetic diplomatic and political activity when he returned to Oslo. The next priority would be to build up the momentum of the political process and arrange the meeting that would see the paramilitaries engaging in positive dialogue with Ministers from the two Governments.

I helped load up the car with their cases and Mette gave me a kiss and a hug and asked Anja if she would see me again. Anja told her she would and promised her she would take me to Oslo to see them all. I said good-bye to Einar and advised him to stick in at his football. I glanced across at Anja and Nina, who were now standing together. The obvious gap in ages did nothing to alter the fact that they were both exceptionally beautiful. Before getting into the car, Nina took my arm and walked with me a few steps, leading me away from the car and the others. She whispered to me.

"Paul, look after Anja. Bjorn and I are very fond of her and it is very obvious to us that, together, the two of you are a beautiful and well-matched couple. You are very good for her."

"How can you tell?"

"Just call it feminine intuition! Please come and see us in Oslo. Bjorn, Einar and Mette would very much like that."

"What about you Nina, would you like me to come?"

"Of course." With that she kissed me on the lips and tenderly, almost seductively, touched the side of my cheek. We walked the few steps back to the car and she was embraced by her husband. He then kissed her, shouting good-bye to the kids as she climbed into the car.

The weather had improved, but there was only an hour or so of good daylight left as the last of the four cars made their way down the drive on their way to their various destinations. We stood together like a close-knit family group and waved until they were out of sight. Apart from Anja and I, only the Rolfsons, Bjorn, Dr Renfrew, Coyle and McCreery were left.

Weather wise it had been a dreary day, but now as the shades of night came down, the sky had become much clearer and as darkness fell the temperature dropped and the moon rose over the dark mass of the mountains. Darkness came early to this part of Norway and without the interference of the artificial light of the city, it seemed that the sky had introduced thousands of new stars into the heavens. Anja and I decided to get our warm clothes on and go for a walk. We asked if anyone would like to join us, but were quite relieved when there were no takers. At last we could be alone. Before getting ready, we went back into the kitchen and had a coffee with the Rolfsons. I had got to like the old couple and Mrs R. was forever fussing over me. Her English was not as good as her husband's and the two of us had the odd interpretation problem, which was usually solved by her offering me more food. Half an hour later, we togged up in our boots, fleecys and jackets and walked down to the loch. Anja wanted to show me the waterfall that the house took its name from - Manefossen, the waterfall of the moon.

It was cold, and our breath steamed and formed little clouds in the clear, evening air that settled in the low ground at the water's edge. So much had happened. There was so much to say, so much to talk about, but we didn't utter a word. We were happy to be alone and together for more or less the first time this weekend. We followed a track that took us along by the loch and through a copse of pines before it veered off and we found ourselves on a path partially hidden from the main road by large shrubs and conifers. We walked slowly along the path heading for the waterfall, away from the white gate posts signalling the entrance to the private grounds of the house. It all seemed perfect: the night was still, order had returned to the world and everything was in its rightful place. The path to the top of the waterfall grew steeper and more slippery and at one stage we had to pull ourselves up the bare rock using a length of chain that had been bolted into the stone to aid access. The scene at the waterfall was unspeakably beautiful, magical, made even better by the bright moonlight and the company. Anja would not let me stand too near the edge of the gorge, as it was wet and slippery and quite treacherous underfoot. The cataract roared as thousands of gallons of water poured over the precipice into the dark pools over one hundred feet below. The sound of the tumult was both terrifying and wondrous. Once again I felt humbled by the powerful elements of nature that surrounded me as I stared, mesmerised, into the water. Anja slipped her arms round my waist, her head snuggling against my back. She broke my trance and returned me to the chill of the evening.

"It's great up here, but I think it is time to go back, yes?"

"Yes," I said and added, "Anja, thank you for asking me back to Norway, it means a lot."

"That's OK, I would never have asked anyone else."

The descent back down the path was even more difficult than the climb up and I was grateful for the grip and support of my boots.

We had only been away for about an hour and a quarter and were only fifty or so metres from the gate when two dark coloured four-wheel drive, Land Rover type vehicles roared past us and skidded through the gate posts and up the driveway. We were hidden from the road by bushes and as they hadn't acknowledged our presence we assumed they hadn't seen us.

"That's strange," said Anja, "I don't think Bjorn is expecting anyone this evening."

"Who knows we're here?" I asked.

"No one really. Only the members of the group and some selected colleagues of Bjorn's at the University and the Government buildings in Oslo."

"Could it be the police or the military?"

"No, I don't think so. Bjorn arranges for the house to be swept and screened for bugs and any other devices a few days before we all arrive for any meetings. Security is never a problem, these are not official meetings; we are all very careful, no one knows we're here...Paul, you're scaring me!"

There was a hint of panic in her voice, as her mind sifted and weaved through the options.

"Come on, let's get back," I suggested.

We started to jog along the path, back toward the house, the evening's cold frosty air gripping at our lungs, causing our breath to rasp and purr.

As we came within sight of the house, we could see the vehicles parked there, their headlights still on, their doors open and their engines idling, sending a faint plume of fumes into the cold night air.

"Oh God! What's happening?" Anja began to run toward the house, but I pulled her back roughly and she struggled to free herself from my grip.

"Let me go! Let me go! Something is wrong, I can feel it."

I pulled her to me and whispered.

"Anja, be quiet, we have to be careful. Come on, this way."

I relaxed my grip on her wrist and led her round to the front of the house. Our eyes had more or less adjusted to the darkness, but I was still fearful we would fall or collide with an unseen object and cause a disturbance that would bring the uninvited attentions of our visitors. My stomach was knotted and instinctively I knew all was not well. We edged along the wall of the house, ignorant of the fact that the Rolfsons lay dead in the kitchen, each killed by a single gunshot through the head.

In the drawing room and, like the fate of the Rolfsons, unknown to us, Bjorn, Coyle, McCreery and Dr Renfrew had been forced to lie face down on the floor. Bjorn was almost hysterical with shock and outrage. He pushed himself up onto his hands and knees and was demanding to know what was going on and who the hell were these people who had the gall to violate his hospitality.

There were four gunmen in the room, each armed with semi-automatic machine pistols, fitted with silencers. It was obvious that these were trained men, who knew how to use the sinister black metal objects that were slung from narrow leather straps on their shoulders. They didn't wear masks - a distressing indication that even if they were recognised, they would be taking a course of action that would mean their captives would never live to finger them. They stood over their prisoners, their weapons pointing at the stricken men.

Outside, Anja and I had crept along the verandah, inching our way slowly through the shadows. My mind was racing; we were either the victims of our own over-fertile imaginations and we were about to make fools of ourselves, or we were going to be part of a scenario too frightening to contemplate. The lights of the drawing room shone out onto the verandah and, being extremely cautious, I ushered Anja onto the lawn and we crouched down behind some trees and bushes several feet from the edge of the gravel path that circled the house. It was pure luck we had made that move because, as we took cover, I became aware of a silent, dark figure padding along the verandah from the other side of the house. He was carrying a pistol and when Anja saw his shadowy figure, she gasped.

I held Anja by the arms and whispered to her.

"Be still, be very still."

It was an unreasonable request. We were both shaking out of fear and because of the cold. The figure moved past us. Having almost completed his reconnaissance of the outside of the house, he then stopped and turned and stood at the glass-panelled doors of the drawing room. Years of training and his instincts were combining, suggesting something might be out there. He stood, his face leeward of the light, hiding the detail of his features, but I could sense his eyes darting and flashing, straining as they peered into the darkness. I muttered the most silent of prayers, 'please God, don't let him see us'. Our cover was good and after what seemed like hour-long seconds, he satisfied himself all was well and entered the room through the French windows, leaving them open. I nearly peed myself with relief. Through the open windows, just a few feet above us we could now see and hear nearly all that was going on. The Doctor was sobbing and Bjorn, still outraged, was screaming at his captors to stop. One of the men asked McCreery to stand up, but McCreery didn't move; he lay motionless on the floor. Two of the men stepped forward and pulled him to his feet.

"That's it, up you get. What's wrong? You're looking rather worried, what happened to all that, 'Heart and hand, sword and shield' stuff, eh?" The words were not spoken with an Irish accent, more West country English.

"Where are the others Professor?" The question was direct but delivered in a controlled, polite tone.

Bjorn ignored it. He had not completely recovered his composure and was now lying defiantly prostrate on a rug, watching his captors' every move in mute rage, his mutterings no more than indistinguishable sounds coming from the back of his throat.

"I shall ask you once more Professor, where are your wife and your other guests?"

The Norwegian paid no heed to the question.

"They've gone, they're on their way home," interrupted Renfrew, "looks like you're too late, you sad despicable bastards, whoever you are...you're too damn late!"

Thankfully he didn't mention Anja or me. Maybe he had forgotten we had stayed on, but he had provided us with a chance of making a safe exit. The assassins were obviously not expecting a reduced roll-call, their intelligence had failed them and they looked at each other and then their leader. Renfrew's outburst was confirmed by a sixth gunman, who entered the room from the hall and stated that there was no one else in the house, other than the housekeepers, who were now dead.

Piers Richardson rubbed his hand against his forehead, deep in thought, considering his options. Dressed entirely in black, his presence dominated the room, his face illuminated eerily by the flickering light of the fire. Watching him reminded me of the Ring Trilogy's 'Lord of the Nazgul'. He was Death. He made his decision - he walked over toward Bjorn, stood over him and fired two shots into the back of his head. The body jerked a few times then lay motionless on the floor. Anja gasped and pushed back into me as her legs buckled with the shock and she began to hyperventilate. I held onto her and whispered, "Anja, be quiet, we can't let them find us. Just take it easy. Please." Her hand gripped mine.

144

In the drawing room, Richardson gave an order, "Take Mr McCreery out to the jeep."

The order was instantly obeyed and Tom McCreery was led away by two of the gunmen. He looked back over his shoulder at Coyle as he left the room. By now Dr Renfrew had lost the place and was gibbering hysterically. He had risen to his knees and appeared to be praying. He didn't even hear his executioner step up behind him and take half of his skull off with a single point blank shot. He died instantly.

Seamus Coyle took a lung-filling breath rose to his feet and stood before the killer band. He looked at each one of them, but it was plain to see that he did not seem to recognise any of them. Piers Richardson stared back at the Irishman and silently acknowledged his barefaced defiance, his bravery. Even terrorists, it would appear, have a code of courage.

"Kneel, you Mick bastard," demanded one of Richardson's cohorts.

"Who are you? Regiment, SIS, MI6?" Coyle demanded.

"Shut up, you thick Paddy fuck!"

"Enough!" snapped Burgoyne, angered by the lack of professionalism in the presence of his CO.

Coyle continued to stand, but a pistol barrel smashing into his temple caused him to reel back and blood flowed freely into his thick, red beard. Even before his trembling left hand had reached his brow, fumbling for the area of smashed tissue and bone, a second blow to the neck caused him to collapse forwards. McCreery was already on his way to the jeep as two bullets entered Seamus Coyle's legs at the knees. His body convulsed with shock and pain. Some moments later he was relieved of the agony by a single shot to the head. The Irishman's limp form slumped full length on the floor. The gunmen then left the room, their work done for the time being.
We both sat back, squatting on the damp grass, trying to control our breathing, struggling to come to terms with what we had just witnessed.

"I don't believe it, I don't believe it. This is Norway, this isn't Belfast..." I croaked. "They just executed them in cold blood. This is unreal, just fuckin' unreal. This isn't happening."

Anja shook me, "Paul, stop it, what do we do now?"

"Eh," I took a deep breath. "Right, come on, let's go round to the back of the house and see if they've gone," I said, my voice returning to normal.

We rose to our feet and cautiously made our way back to the side of the house, staying out of the light, hugging the cover of the trees and shrubs, terrified of being seen. We looked round from the shelter of an outhouse toward the car park. Richardson was engaged in a heated discussion with one of his subordinates who suddenly turned and sprinted back toward the house. Anja and I had to dive for cover. He returned soon afterwards, his mission, whatever it was, completed, and he jumped into the passenger seat of the first vehicle. The two vehicles began to accelerate away when suddenly the back door of the second 4WD burst open and Tom McCreery jumped out. He started to run toward the house but he stumbled, trying desperately to scramble along on his hands and knees, grit ripping into his palms. The first vehicle, unaware of the problem behind them, had disappeared down the drive.

The remaining jeep skidded to a halt before being slammed into reverse. It careered backwards and it struck McCreery sending him pirouetting and sprawling onto the gravel. He tried to stand up. He staggered and fell forward drunkenly. He was shocked and shaken. Two occupants of the jeep leapt out and pulled the winded Loyalist back into the car and slammed the door behind them. We both thought we saw flashes and heard two muffled shots and I assumed that McCreery's struggle for life ended as the 4WD vanished into the frosty night, its tail-lights diminishing into the darkness.

I deliberately etched the murder scene and the faces of the perpetrators on my memory for future use. I just didn't know what was going on; surely they wouldn't have killed one of their own. We carefully made our way back to the house and entered the kitchen through the back door. Anja moaned softly to herself, unable to speak. I had never seen a dead body before and I was amazed how still and unmarked the Rolfsons looked - there was very little blood. Anja motioned toward the dead caretakers but I pulled her away and on through the kitchen. There was no time for tending to the dead. We staggered upstairs to the hall. I sat her down on the floor, propping her back against a wall and went into the drawing room alone. The room smelled like a butcher's shop. Blood, almost black in colour, gurgled onto the floor from the three men's horrific wounds, spreading freely and evenly over the polished wooden surface, before being absorbed into the rugs, the expanding stain glistening in the firelight. The room was quiet now. The laughter and music of the morning had gone. There was only the sound of the fire and it was rapidly losing its battle to heat a room that had been invaded by the frosty evening air creeping in through the still open French windows. I was surprisingly calm. I turned my attentions to more immediate and practical matters.

"Anja, where are the phones?" I called, but she didn't hear me.

I went back out to the hall, bent down and hugged her. She was sobbing unashamedly.

"Anja, you have to help me, where are the phones, we must get some help?"

146

"Are they all dead?" she asked, her face pale with anxiety and fear.

"Yes, there's nothing we can do for them."

When Anja regained her composure she led me to the study. This was where I had heard McCreery make his call. The phone and the fax were dead, they had ripped out the lines, surprise, surprise.

"Did Bjorn have a mobile? A mobile phone?"

"No, he didn't allow them. There was only one phone. He didn't want any unwanted distractions or outside interference. Paul, who did this? Nobody knew we were here."

"Somebody knew. Are you able to drive?" I asked.

"Yes, I think so."

"Good, let's go and get some help. Let's get out of here."

"What about the others? What about Nina, Mette and Einar?" Anja cried.

"I don't know, Anja. They left hours ago. My guess is they should be safe." I couldn't be sure, but from what we had heard, the assassins' plans had obviously been upset.

I too thought of Nina and the children, as Anja began to choke back the tears. Poor Nina. I remembered her touch against my face. Bjorn's loss would surely devastate her. What is there to be gained from murdering people like him? I suppose history provided the answer there, where people like Pederson are seen as threats by certain elements in the establishment or the lunatic fringes and they have to be eliminated. I thought of Martin Luther King, the Kennedys, the South American guy who was demanding peasant worker's rights, Biko, the Polish priest with the unpronounceable name who supported Solidarity - all murdered because they had the balls and the bottle to stand up and say they wanted to change things for the better.

I grabbed the bags that we had already packed and we rushed out to Anja's car. I threw everything in the back, while Anja struggled to start the engine. The engine turned over, then died with a groan.

"It's alright, just take your time," I said, trying to calm her.

After three attempts, the old Volvo roared into life. Before she eased it down the drive, she sat silently for a moment, contemplating her grief, her shock.

147

"Can we make it to Stavanger?"

"Yes, I think so."

"Come on then, let's go, but if you see a telephone anywhere on the way back, we must stop and don't worry, we'll be alright."

Anja was much calmer now. I put my hand on her thigh and left it there. I didn't know what to say. I didn't know how to comfort her. It was late evening and there were no other cars on the road. It was a clear night - the moon was full but the magic of the journey up had gone. I drifted from feelings of panic and disbelief to a near state of euphoria and relief that we were still alive. I decided I wanted to stay that way; I had to get Anja to safety - after all I had promised Nina I would look after her. I thought that the police station in Stavanger would be our best bet and that we should probably make for there.

We drove back over the mountain pass that had given me so much pleasure only a few days before, but as we drove by I hardly paid any attention to the place. A few kilometres down the road, Anja - who seemed to be driving on auto-pilot, staring straight ahead not seeing much of anything - suddenly braked as she spotted a telephone kiosk as we passed through a tiny hamlet. I asked her if Bjorn had ever given her an emergency contact number to call in the unlikely event of something like this happening. She shook her head, there was no number.

"Give me a break, Paul, this is Scandinavia, murders and assassination attempts just don't happen here."

I thought of Olof Palme and Rushdie's publisher, but I didn't contradict her. Her innocence was more than likely founded in Scandinavia's relative isolation from the traumas and stresses of the rest of the world, but it still surprised me none the less.

"I guess you'd better call the police."

"Yes, I do that right now."

I watched as she barged out of the phone box. I was surprised by the speed of her call.

"Well, what's the story?"

"Those assholes think I'm drunk. They told me not to waste police time. God I feel so angry."

"Shit! There must be someone we can call." Anja said nothing. "Come on Anja, think."

"I'm sorry, Paul, I'm sorry I can't think, I can't think. I'm scared. Besides no-one really knew we were there, Bjorn was always so careful."

I held her and kissed her. Her eyes were soft and moist with sadness. I tasted her tears on my tongue.

"I only have a telephone number for Bjorn's colleague, Professor Per Aldquist. Maybe he will know what to do."

Anja called the number she was given and this time she looked visibly relieved when she came out of the kiosk and returned to the car.

"Was he in? What did he say?" I asked.

"He told me not to worry, to take care and to drive to Stavanger. He would get his assistant to contact the authorities and he would arrange for someone to meet me there."

"Where, at the police station?"

"No, outside the Stavanger Domkirke."

"Why there? What the hell's he playing at - does he think you are alone?"

"I think so, I'm not sure."

"Did you say or did he say anything else?"

"No, eh, yes, he asked me what kind of car I was driving."

"Is he a stupid bastard, what's that got to do with it?"

We got back into Anja's Volvo and continued to head back to Stavanger which was now about forty minutes' drive away.

I wondered why he wanted to meet her at the cathedral and not the police station and why he wanted to know what kind of car she was driving. It was strange, bloody strange...

Anja didn't say much. She had stopped crying just after we had left the house, but I had no idea what was going through her head. If she wanted to talk, I was happy to respond, but only if she wanted me to. She had pretty much controlled her grief, but a time would inevitably come when the dam would burst. I dreaded trying to cope when it happened - I wasn't good with stuff like that. We were both in shock, but it was far worse for her, she was much closer to it than me. She knew the victims well and in the case of Pederson, very well. I just wanted to get to safety, I wanted us both to come out of this physically and mentally intact.

*****

The phone rang in the small, cramped office on the Oslo University campus. It was unusual for anyone to be in at such a time and it was not uncommon for the phone just to ring out. Sorry, no one home. Today was different. A lone figure sat slumped in a chair, the thick ski jacket still zipped up to the neck, gloves still on and the coffee he had made earlier lay cold and untouched on the cluttered desk. The phone continued to ring. He wished he had the courage not to answer it. He knew who would be calling, just as he knew the reason for the call, just as he correctly anticipated the tone and abrupt manner of the caller. He had met with him face to face only once, at the Annen Etage and had instantly been unnerved by him.

It had all moved on so quickly since the University hierarchy had chosen not to include him in their Irish initiative and he had decided to exact some revenge. It had after all been his idea, his initiative, even though right from the start, that arrogant bastard Pederson claimed it as his own and the bitterness of being excluded burned like a toxin in his body. The only cure, the only antidote in his mind was sabotage, revanche. Of course, the bitterest pill was that should it all go perfectly, Pederson would become very famous, he would receive international accolades and plaudits, possibly even a Nobel Peace Prize nomination, on the back of what had been his idea. Meanwhile, he would be left to fester in an academic no-man's land, bowing and scraping to officialdom. Still he hadn't quite realised things would go this far and the situation had left his control a long time ago. He had been paid and paid well for the information he had passed on, foolishly thinking all he had done was to throw a spanner in the works, but it hadn't stopped there and he had been drawn in. Then he imagined Pederson's face splashed over the front pages of the world's press and he felt the heat of anger and bitterness return, as he reconvinced himself he had been correct to choose this route and betray an Institution that he believed had held him back for so long. The phone continued to ring. It was therefore an incoming call from an outside line and not the buzz of an internal call. His mouth felt dry. He took a mouthful of cold coffee, the skin that had formed on the surface sticking to his lips and the stubble below his nose. His hand trembled slightly as he picked up the receiver.

"Yes."

"This is Richardson. Your information was incorrect. There were only four men in the house, six including the cook and the caretaker. You do realise that the success of my operation was based entirely on the provision of accurate, quality intelligence and you have failed to provide me with this. You must also realise that you have not only jeopardised this assignment, but you may have compromised the safety and identity of my men."

"I'm sorry Mr Richardson, I don't know what went wrong. They were all scheduled to be there until late Sunday evening. However, I am relieved you have contacted me. There has been a call, Pederson's PA has reported that she witnessed your visit. She's seen everything. She was still at the house when you arrived. Your men must have missed her during your raid."

His last remark was an attempt to deflect some of the blame back on Richardson's men. He wasn't going to take all the responsibility if the mission was aborted in failure.

"Damn!" Richardson cursed, under his breath.

"I'm sorry, Mr Richardson, what did you say?"

"Nothing, please continue."

"She's on her way to Stavanger, very frightened and probably in shock. On my suggestion, we are arranging for someone, a business acquaintance, to meet her and take her to a safe house and from there he'll contact us for further instructions."

"It's his PA, you say, and what about the others?"

"They have all left, Mr Richardson. I believe they left quite unexpectedly in the afternoon. I don't know where they are."

"This 'safe house', give me the address."

"I'm sorry, I do not have that information."

He was lying, but giving that out would have been tantamount to advertising to the world his complicity in the affair and that would not have been a very smart move.

"The authorities, have they been alerted?"

"Not as far as I'm aware. If we're lucky, I think there may be another few hours before they're involved: it all depends on what happens when the girl is picked up. I will certainly try and keep things quiet for as long as I can, but I can't do it indefinitely, or I'll draw suspicion on myself."

Richardson asked for some more details, warned that he would 'be in touch', then returned to the waiting group.

"Quickly get back to Stavanger, we might just be able to solve this little problem."

The powerful, off-road vehicle accelerated south-west in the direction of Stavanger. Richardson did not carry out an internal enquiry into the failure of his men to locate the girl and thereby eliminate everyone at the house. Something had obviously happened, some unforeseen factor that had allowed her not only to avoid them, but to see them and witness the executions. He did not believe in fate, and still felt confident he could alter any pre-ordained course of events. His attentions turned to his men, recriminations were unnecessary. They were being given a chance to redress the situation and salvage the operation. He was confident that this time there would be no mistakes and when he reported to London, it would be to say that his mission had been a success, all objectives had been achieved, albeit following certain deviations and improvisations on the original plan. For a man who's face never betrayed emotion, he permitted himself the barest crease of a smile.

In Oslo, the angle-poise desk light was clicked off, plunging the room into darkness. The figure closed the office door behind him and then walked briskly down the corridor toward the main entrance of the faculty building, the fingers of his right hand fumbling inside his breast pocket, making sure his passport was still there. He decided to remain in Oslo for a further forty-eight hours at the most then, depending on the content of Richardson's next call, he would consider his next move. If the situation deteriorated, there were options. He could drive over the border to Sweden; he had a friend in Stockholm, or he could catch the ferry to Denmark and drive down into mainland Europe. Whichever choice he made was irrelevant, he just knew that if Richardson failed to eliminate the girl, it would not be wise for him to remain in Oslo.

Chapter 6

CHAPTER 6

Soon the lights of Stavanger appeared and I sensed Anja was about to start crying, but she fought away the tears.

"Don't worry, we'll be safe soon," I whispered.

We drove into the centre of the city and made our way toward the Domkirke. We had just turned right past the Atlantic Hotel and were only a hundred or so yards from the meeting place.

"We're just about there, I'll park just on the hill," said Anja.

She appeared to relax at the thought of seeing Aldquist's contact and being helped to safety. We looked across to the Domkirke and spotted a middle aged man in a long raincoat, standing at the top of the steps by the main entrance doors.

"That must be him," she said, "thank God."

"Anja, drive, drive!" I screamed at her. "Drive, put the foot down and keep going!"

"What's up? What's up, Paul? You're scaring me again!"

I had noticed, quite by chance, one of the dark coloured jeeps lurking almost out of sight in the shadows below the trees by the Breiavatnet pond. Anja put her foot down and the Volvo accelerated up the hill. A bus pulled out not expecting to meet a car driving against the one way system. The Volvo swerved, narrowly missing a sign post. The bus driver flashed his lights, but Anja had gone, bumping over a grass verge and back onto the main road that skirted the lake.

"Anja, I don't want you to panic but I think our friends from the house are here."

"What do you want me to do?"

I twisted round in my seat to see if we were being followed and I could see the headlights of their 4WD come on, as it pulled away from the verge. I looked across and I could see Aldquist's man standing at the corner of the Domkirke, his eyes appeared to be following Anja's car and I wondered where he fitted into all of this.

"Anja, drive back around the lake and head for the Vagen. We'll park there and go into a pub or something, somewhere busy. Your car won't outrun them if we try to escape."

The traffic lights went in our favour and we easily pulled away from our pursuers. Anja drove toward the Vagen as instructed and pulled up outside the Fun Pub, cutting across the flow of traffic, who honked their horns in protest.

"Paul, this is the busiest place, maybe we should go in here."

This was the place I had been in when I had been out with Steve on my first trip over. I agreed with her logic. It was certainly the nosiest, if not the busiest place in town. Anja locked the car as I took our bags out of the back. We stood on the pavement outside the pub. There was a queue of about twenty people waiting to get in and my heart sank. Shit! We needed to get inside and quick. I felt Anja grab my arm and pull me toward the entrance which was guarded by a massive doorman. This guy must have been in his early twenties, with fair hair styled in a crew-cut and a Fun Pub cap-sleeved T-shirt that displayed a pair of very powerful, muscular arms. He was the archetypal Nordmann, the kind of pure Aryan specimen the Nazis tried to recruit into their ranks during the Occupation. There didn't seem to be any way past him. So what the hell was Anja up to?

"Hi, Anja," the massive Viking called out and he began speaking to her.

She kissed him on the cheek before turning to introduce him to me.

"Hi, Paul, nice to meet you." His voice was soft for such a big man.

I let my case drop to the ground and shook his shovel-like mitt.

"You guys want to come in?"

Anja answered for us both and he opened the door to let us in, amidst howls of abuse from the queue. Jens, the door-man, just grinned. Looking round as we entered the Fun Pub, I saw a dark coloured 4WD cruise past the door, but it didn't stop.

We pushed our way through the crowd and found a place at the bar. I ordered a 'lite' beer for myself (which I couldn't drink; I was too wound up) and a cognac for Anja, which I made her sip immediately. I'd seen them do this in old movies. It was meant to help, but fuck knows if it did any good.

"Anja, we've got a problem. For as long as we're in here, we're relatively safe. There's too many people, they won't try anything...I think, but once this place closes and we're turfed out on the street, we're really struggling."

Anja bowed her head and brought her hands up to her face. My mind was flashing through our limited options. The obvious thing to do was to go to the Police and report the incident. The downside was that we had to get there and even then they would take a lot of convincing as to the truth and credibility of our story. They would have to check us out with senior officials in the Storting who may not be contactable on a Saturday and they would have to check out the house. It would all take time and I didn't know if we had time. Even more worrying was my doubt that, in the short-term, if they did take us into safe, protective custody - did they have the facilities to keep heavily armed killers at bay. I was so unsure. I even doubted whether or not we should call Aldquist again, after all we had made one call and we had just about walked into an ambush. I decided to call Steve.

"Stay here," I said. As if Anja was about to go anywhere. "I'll be back in a minute."

I fought my way through the crowd to the public phone and dialled Steve's number. I prayed that he'd be in. The phone rang and rang. I was just about to replace the receiver, deflated by my lack of success, when...

"Hello."

"Steve, it's Paul. Christ, I thought you were out, the phone's been ringing for ages and I was just about to hang up."

"Sorry about that, I was just trying out the speakers on my new hi-fi and didn't hear the phone."

My brother then began to fire a volley of questions at me.

"I can hardly hear you. I was expecting you to call me yesterday. Where are you? What's up? What's happened?"

Maybe we were connecting telepathically, because I'm sure I could detect some anxiety in my brother's voice and I chose not to volunteer an explanation.

"Steve, I need your help, just listen to what I have to say and don't ask any questions."

There was silence at the other end of the phone.

"Right, I need you to do two things. The first is I need to borrow your car. The second is I need you to get hold of Andy in London and tell him I'll be calling him with first hand news of a quite unbelievable story. I'd call him from here, but I've lost his number - do you understand?"

"Paul, what the fuck's going on?" His anxiety level was beginning to rise even further. "Where are you?" he asked. "What unbelievable story?"

"Never mind that for now, I'll fill you in on the details later. Just bring your car into Stavanger and leave it in the street outside Harry Peppers. Leave it unlocked, with the keys under the driving seat. Get a taxi and go home. Do not under any circumstances hang about. Can you also leave a note of Andy's number. Do you understand?."

"For fuck's sake Paul, I'm your brother, tell me what's going on!"

"It's because you are my brother that I can't involve you. Just trust me and I'll phone you later."

"You're worrying the shit out of me you know, but I'll do it, I'll be there in fifteen - twenty minutes, is that OK?"

"Yes, that's great."

*****

Steve replaced the receiver. His face had gone ashen grey and he felt strange inside, his legs felt weak.

"Stephen, what's wrong, what's happened?" Jane had got up off the settee and walked over to him.

"Stephen, what's wrong? Is it bad news? Is it my father?"

"No, it's not your dad, but I'm not sure what's up. That was Paul, sounds like he's in some sort of trouble."

"What do you mean trouble? A fight or something, over here in Stavanger?"

"*I* don't bloody know," he snapped.

"Hey! There's no need to take whatever's wrong out on me," she retorted.

"I'm sorry, I'm just worried about him. He's in Stavanger - he wouldn't say where - and he just asked to borrow the car and for me to call Andy in London for him."

"Why Andy?"

"I told you I don't know. It's worrying the fuck out of me though, you know how introverted and secretive he is at times, but I've promised I'll help. Can you get Andy's number for me, it's in my case. I'm just going to get my shoes on, then I'll phone Andy and go into Stavanger."

"Where are you meeting Paul?"

"I'm not, all I have to do is leave the keys in the car and a note of Andy's number. He's definitely playing it long this time and not giving anything away."

"Something's definitely up. This isn't like Paul. I admit he can be a moody sod, but he's not usually like that with you. Something's wrong, I'm coming with you."

"OK," Steve said, pleased by her support. He didn't really want to go on his own.

*****

I put the phone down and started to make my way back toward Anja. I pushed through the mob and dodged a waving hand which was armed with a lit cigarette. I looked over toward the bar and I felt my heart go into free fall. Jesus! Anja was no longer alone.

While I'd been away, one of the assassins had entered the bar and was standing beside her. He appeared to be speaking to her and I noticed she was trying to prise open the grip he had on her upper arm. As far as I was aware, they (whoever they were) thought Anja was alone, so I slipped past behind them and caught Anja's eye as I moved toward the door. She looked at me in dismay. Her eyes were red and swollen but she didn't give me away. I pushed my way through to the door. The place was packed. It was Saturday night, the music was blaring and people were out having a good time, unaware of the danger that Anja and I were in. The guy was in all probability armed and I would have been a fool to take him on, but I knew a man who could. I finally shoved my way through to the door and Jens motioned as if to open it for me.

157

"Hey, Paul, what's up, you had enough?"

The living Troll Wall held out his hand and I shook it again, pulling him down to me so that he could hear above the noise.

"Jens, I've got a problem. There's a guy in there at the bar giving Anja a hard time. I don't want to start any trouble by giving him a slap, can you help?"

The big Scandinavian didn't have to be asked twice. He nodded in understanding, signalled to one of the DJs to watch the door, then he burst through the crowd and I followed in his wake. When Jens arrived where Anja was sitting, she was still being held by the arm.

"Anja, this guy giving you a problem?" Jens growled.

Anja answered in Norwegian and Jens' massive hands began to tear open the grip on her.

"Look, friend, this doesn't concern you, it's just a lovers' tiff, there's no problem, so just BACK OFF!" growled the killer in English, but with a thick Dutch accent. He thought he had been completely unobtrusive in making his move on Anja and there was no doubt he was surprised by Jens' intrusion.

Jens was unimpressed.

"Don't fuck with me, man! Anja, do you know this guy?" Anja shook her head.

In one swift, flowing movement, Jens had ripped away the hand that gripped Anja and had jerked it up her molester's back and he began pushing him out toward the front door of the pub. He met with little resistance. The guy knew we weren't going anywhere. I watched as Jens crashed the door open and threw his troublemaker out into the street. The crowd who were queuing outside laughed and jeered.

Wim Claessen picked himself up from the gutter, turned and gave Jens an unnerving, icy stare, then crossed the road to join his accomplices who were sitting in the off-road 4WD. He was embarrassed, but the other two men did not increase his discomfort by mocking him.

"Are you alright?" asked Richardson with genuine concern.

Claessen just looked at him.

"Is she in there?"

"Yes."

"Is she alone?"

"Yes, I think so, apart from that overgrown cretin at the door."

"How was she when you saw her?"

"Upset, frightened. She'd been crying. I had her, but I still don't know how she managed to get help from Noggin the Nog, that poxy oaf of a doorman. I'm going to slot that big bastard before the night's out."

"You will do no such thing. His elimination is not part of my strategy. Did she try and scare you off by saying she had called the police?"

"No."

The three men watched the door of the Fun Pub for the next twenty minutes as the crowds poured in and out.

"Is there another exit?"

"No."

"Are you sure?"

Claessen knew that his next answer would determine his future on the Richardson payroll.

"I'll check."

"Yes, I think you'd better."

Claessen crossed the road and disappeared up a side street. He returned several minutes later to report.

"As far as I am aware, there is no back door, but I'd prefer to stay round there and keep watch, just in case."

"We'll wait here. Get back round and take a position to cover any possible exits. If she's still in there we'll just wait for her."

Claessen left.

*****

I turned to Anja and put my arm around her. She had buried her head on my shoulder, then she looked up at me. I don't know what questions she was silently asking me, but I managed to smile at her, trying to reassure her.

"They're going to kill me, aren't they?"

"No, no they won't, not if we can keep away from them."

"But they know I'm in here, they'll just sit out there and wait for us."

"That's where you're wrong. I've arranged for Steve to leave his car for us and I've told him to contact a friend of mine in London who might be able to help."

"That's great. What are we supposed to do, just walk out of here, jump into your brother's car, drive away into the sunset and live happily ever after?"

I wiped her tears away and whispered, "Trust me, Anja, I won't let anything happen to you."

"I know, I'm sorry, I'm just so scared. I really believed that it was the end and that the guy was going to take me outside, drive me away somewhere quiet and kill me. Can you trust this friend in London?"

"Yes."

I told here to finish her drink and wait for me. I battled and pushed my way through to the front door and looked out across the road. Their vehicle was still there with its three occupants, but there was no sign of Aldquist's man. In fact we never saw him again.

"Is Anja alright?" asked Jens.

The big man had come over to see how we were.

"Yes, she's fine now. I owe you one."

"No problem, the guy was a jerk! What happened anyway?"

"It's a long story. I'll buy you a beer sometime and tell you."

"Sure, let's do that."

I patted the big fellow on the back, then asked him to make sure the three blokes in the truck did not gain entry into the bar. As far as Jens was concerned, that was not a problem either. However, what he didn't know was that they were all armed and if they had wanted to take him out they could have. I went back to Anja and she smiled weakly at me on my return. I felt a little bit guilty about asking Jens to keep them out, but he was safe enough for as long as the crowds flocked to the shore of the Vagen and by closing time we would be long gone. He wasn't really in any danger.

"OK, let's go, it's time to make our move."

A slightly puzzled look replaced the smile, but she dutifully followed me as we squeezed and jostled our way with our bags to the fire exit at the back of the bar.

"Where are we going?"

"Just follow me...just using some local knowledge."

She laughed and it felt good to hear laugh again. I pushed the fire exit door open with my case and we were out in the yard among the kegs and the empty crates, although the container from my previous visit had gone. I turned to Anja.

"Come on, we've got to make tracks. Close the door behind you."

We walked through the yard, opened another door and we were in the downstairs bar of Newsman. Our sudden appearance was met with a few surprised looks but apart from that everything else seemed fine. We struggled upstairs with our bags and cautiously left through the front door, which the bouncer courteously held open for us,

"Have a nice evening," he said, as we cautiously made our exit. I had to smile at the completely unintentional irony of his words.

The street outside Newsman was mobbed with young, drunk Norwegians, crawling from pub to pub to club. We made our way along the road, dodging everyone, furtively looking back to make sure we hadn't been followed. If Anja recognised any of her friends, she didn't let on. She knew there was no time for hanging about, distracted by schoolday reminiscences. As we got further away from Newsman, the crowds died out and we were alone in the cobbled street behind the Skaggen Brygge Hotel. It wasn't far to Harry Peppers and, hopefully, Steve's car. We moved quickly. I turned to look round again, checking for anyone following us, when I was startled by Anja's shrill, heart-piercing scream. Fuckin' hell! I dropped the case and bag and spun round ready to confront our pursuers.

Instead of looking into the muzzle of a silencer, I was face to face with a pissed

161

teenager, a member of the Stavanger white sock and grey 'slip-on' brigade, who in drunken oafishness had jumped out at Anja, as a jape. I grabbed him roughly by the neck and shoved him unceremoniously against a wall, as the release of adrenaline surged through my body. I felt like punching his lights out, but Anja's hands were pulling at my shoulders.

"No, Paul, he's just a kid, he doesn't mean any harm. Leave him alone, it's OK, I'm alright."

I slowly released my grip on his jacket and backed off, passing up the overwhelming temptation to give him a right slap. He muttered something to the effect that I was some kind of psycho and that I should be locked up, before he staggered down the street toward the city centre.

I picked up our cases. My heart was racing, my legs were like jelly. I felt suddenly weary, but we pressed on toward our getaway car. I kept glancing round apprehensively.

We turned into the side street where Harry Peppers Tex-Mex restaurant was located and I scanned the street for Steve's car. A group of five or six spilled out of Harry's and made their way down toward the Victoria Hotel. Further up the narrow cobbled lane, several teenagers hung about outside a youth club disco. I looked back along the street and then I saw it.

"Quick, over there."

We hurried over to the other side of the street where Steve had left the green Audi. The door was unlocked as requested, the keys under the driver's seat. I opened the back door and threw our cases and bags into the back .

"I guess it makes sense if you drive. Is that OK?"

"Sure."

I had no experience of driving in Norway, on the 'wrong' side of the road, with all the idiosyncrasies at roundabouts and junctions. It was better for Anja to drive.
At best I thought we had until closing-time, maybe a couple of hours start and hopefully, as long as they hadn't realised we had gone, it should be enough. Anja handed me a note that was on the front seat. It was from Steve. He had left a message with Andy in London to await my call as well as scribbling down a note of his direct number at the office.

"Where are we going, Paul?"

162

"I'm not sure. We need to find somewhere safe to spend the night, so we can gather our thoughts and make our plans. In the meantime, I need to find a telephone to call London."

Anja pulled away from the kerb and drove in the opposite direction, away from the Fun Pub.

"Paul, I think I know where we can go tonight."

"OK, this is your territory, you decide."

Anja handled the powerful Audi easily and made her way to a nearby ferry terminal.

*****

Richardson and his lieutenant waited patiently and impassively for their other three colleagues to rendezvous with them. Eventually a second vehicle drew up along side and the tinted electric window was lowered.

"Where's the girl? Where's Claessen?"

"We believe she's still in there." Richardson's lieutenant pointed across at the Fun Pub and continued, "Wim went in for her, but was forcibly removed from the premises by Erik the Viking over there on the door. He's now gone round to cover any rear entrances although we're not certain there is one."

Burgoyne snorted his disapproval at Claessen's bungled attempt to snare Anja.

"Simon, you know what she looks like, you've seen her picture, go check it out and make sure she's still in there, but take no action and do not on any account draw attention to yourself. Is that clear?"

"Yes, sir!"

The former Sandhurst man responded immediately to Richardson's instruction. He climbed out of the vehicle and walked some way along the Vagen, before he crossed the road and doubled back to join the queue at the door. He looked like any of the hundreds of revellers out on the town. As he approached the entrance, he was viewed suspiciously by Jens, but the Viking sentinel allowed him to pass. Simon Burgoyne entered the Fun Pub and pushed his way through the heaving bar. He smirked when he thought he had Anja in his sights, but was disappointed to see that when the blonde girl turned to face him, she was not his prey. He moved round by the pool table and

163

watched the door of the female toilets for over ten minutes, but Anja Andresen did not emerge. He checked out the 'gents', just in case, but as he expected she had not sought refuge in there. Burgoyne had an intense dislike for the noise level in the bar and, the indiscipline of the bar's patrons, but he had a job to do and an order to follow, personal opinion was of little or no consequence. He moved to the back of the bar and stood by the fire exit. He pushed the panic bar and the door opened easily. Burgoyne stepped out into the yard and listened to the sounds coming from the fire exit at Newsman, only a few feet away, which had been opened to let some fresh air in.

He closed his eyes and cursed Claessen' slackness. Anja Andresen had gone. They 'd had her cornered. Now they had lost her. Even worse, they had no idea when she had left or where she had headed, or who she had contacted. Burgoyne walked through the yard and into the lower Newsman bar. He found his way upstairs and then out into the street where he was approached by Claessen.

"Where the hell have you come from?" queried the Dutchman.

"In there!" he snapped pointing to the bar entrance, "The girl has gone, let's get back to Richardson. Double time."

Claessen looked shocked. He had performed badly. Richardson would be displeased, but would never show it openly. Claessen knew this would be his last assignment with the team. The two mercenaries jogged quickly back to the Vagen and reported in.

*****

"My parents have a hytter on an island outside of Stavanger, near Lauvik, if we can get on the last ferry, we can spend the night there."

"Will we be safe there?"

"Safer than here."

"OK, you're the boss."

Anja parked the car at the ferry terminal, went into the office, bought a ticket and came back. I watched her every move. She opened the driver's door.

"The ferry leaves in ten minutes, we've just made it. Hopefully we'll get away without being followed."

"That's good, but I need to make that call. Is there a phone here?"

164

"Try the office."

I walked across to the office and searched in my pocket for Steve's note. I turned and scanned the surrounding streets and buildings to see if anyone was watching me. It was all clear. I entered the waiting room and found the public phone which was screwed to a wall beside a coffee vending machine. I laid out the change I had on a table and called Andy in London.

"Yes, McIntosh, Foreign Desk."

"Andy, it's me."

"I've been waiting for your call. Steve says something's happened and you need some help."

Andy was a school friend of Steve's who had followed a classic and indeed a very successful journalistic career. He had started straight from school, working in local papers, before moving onto local television and now he was currently starring with an international news agency in London as their global trouble-shooter. Compared to me, Andy was a proper 'journo', he had done the Foreign and War Correspondent bit and had seen front-line action in nearly every international flash-point over the past ten years. He had great contacts and for want of a better cliché, if he didn't know them, they weren't worth knowing. In some ways he was like Steve and I and his tolerance threshold of self important people or 'big mouthed, odious bastards', as he called them, was as low as ours. He was dry, but witty and very sharp, and if people were pissing him off with tales of daring-do and their self-proclaimed, wonderful achievements, he could savage them with real life stories of what he had seen and experienced first hand throughout the world. He could cut them down with a double fingered shot of verbal napalm and a sharp twist of vitriol. He was also a habitual name-dropper and was on first name terms with scores of 'celebs', be they royalty, politicians, sportsmen and women, business whizz-kids, he knew them all.

His CV and passport made impressive reading. He also knew the Irish scene very well. Over the years, he had interviewed key players on all sides, political leaders, civilians, victims, clergy and terrorists. He had even been in the Europa one night when it was blown up, but his worst and most frightening experience was when he had to flee Belfast just hours after the IRA funeral which ended in the murder of the two off duty soldiers. His unit's live coverage of the dreadful scenes was beamed live around the world, but he also knew his crew were in great danger, because they had in their possession film of the mob that would incriminate and condemn the perpetrators. Their footage was akin to an IRA death warrant for as long as they remained in the Province. That evening he took the decision to charter an aircraft and secreted his crew back to the comparative safety of mainland Britain.

"Andy, what I'm about to tell you is only a very brief summary of what has happened to me today, I don't have time to give you the full monty. Suffice to say, the shit has really hit the fan big time over here and I urgently need your help."

Andy listened as I recounted the story. I tried to be concise, yet describe as accurately as I could the events of the day and what we had witnessed. Trying to condense it all into a few minutes was not easy. I finished off by saying where we were and what our plan for the night was. I also asked him to assure me of his utmost discretion and complete confidentiality. I wasn't sure who we could trust.

"The people you mentioned, the two terrorists Coyle and McCreery, I've heard of them before. They're definitely first team players. This is going to blow a huge fuckin' hole in the Peace Process!"

"No, this is worse than that!" I stated dismissively, fully aware of the greater implications.

"Yeah, you're right." There was a slight pause, as Andy considered his options. "Look, Paul, by the sound of it, the two of you are in some really serious shit. I know someone at the ATB, who might be able to give me some advice and help."

"Who the hell are the ATB? An exhaust-pipe repair company?"

"The ATB? They're the Anti-Terrorist Branch and although my man is a bit difficult to track down, I'll get a hold of him. How can I get back in touch with you?"

"You can't, I'll call you."

Just then Anja rushed in.

"Quick, Paul, the ferry's just about to leave."

"Andy, I've got to go, I'll call you tomorrow, stay by the phone."

"Be careful, OK!"

"Yeah, yeah, I'll call you tomorrow."

*****

McIntosh was interested by the story his friend had recounted. Very interested. The timing of the call was remarkable, coming as it did at the suspiciously coincidental

166

time as several rumours ripping through the lobbies and corridors of Westminster about a leaked document about to be published in the British Press, that had Unionist MPs battening down the hatches for a show-down with the Tory Government. He pushed himself away from his desk, his chair gliding easily over the anti-static mat. He put his hands behind his head and lifted his feet up onto the desk and for a few moments he ignored the ringing telephones, the chattering telex machines, the faxes, the TV monitors and the hectic activity going on all around him in the newsroom. His face was sombre. He knew Paul Robertson well, although it was Steve he had been closer to as kids. He knew Paul had a talent for writing and more importantly he knew he didn't bull-shit. If the story was true and he had no reason to believe otherwise, his friend and this girl were in serious trouble. As he sat in his temporary island of calm, he debated in his mind what he should do. On the one hand, here was a friend who urgently needed help, but as a good journalist he also sensed there was a terrific story here, a scoop, an exclusive and he wondered how he could play it. He was a professional journo and just maybe, Paul Robertson had become his 'Ace in the Hole'.

First things first - no Paul Robertson, no story. He had to get help, someone who could advise them how to stay alive. Someone who could help bring them in. He reached into his jacket, which was slung over the back of the chair and pulled out a pocket sized personal organiser. He flicked through the pages and found the coded, private contact numbers for George Colefax.

*****

I hung up the phone and followed Anja onto the boat. The ferry journey to the island would take about thirty minutes, then maybe another ten by car. We stood on deck and Anja held the handrail. I stood behind her, my arms around her. We watched as the lights of Stavanger faded and dropped into the distance as the ferry eased its way through the inky black waters between the islands and the mainland. The night was cold. Inland it would snow, but here on the coast it threatened to rain. Anja shivered. We stood as if in a daze, the low, resonant throb of the ship's engines and the rush of the waves along the hull lulling us into a hypnotic trance. We were like that for ten minutes before Anja broke the spell.

"I still don't understand what happened today, Paul. I just can't believe it and I know it sounds silly, but it just feels like some terrible nightmare that will go away when I wake up. Maybe if I just close my eyes and open them, all this fear and sadness will disappear."

"I know exactly what you mean, but whatever happened, happened. People, I know they were your friends, are dead and the killers know you were there and that you saw everything, but most disturbingly for us, we saw them, we've seen their faces. Andy's going to try and get some help. He'll make some calls tonight and I've to get back to him in the morning."

"Paul, do you think Aldquist or McCreery had anything to do with what happened?" she asked, her hair blown over her face.

"I don't know, but one thing's for sure, the people who killed Bjorn and the others were waiting for us at the Cathedral. If you think about it, it was a very simple operation, had we all been there. No security, no witnesses, no other evidence, only dead bodies, except for that of McCreery. Everyone would have jumped to the same conclusion and would have landed the blame at the door of the Loyalist paramilitaries. Of course, when word of that got out, it would rip apart any tenuous hopes of peace. We've already had the Strasbourg assassination, which everyone thinks was the work of the UFF or the UVF and now here is a situation where those who've always argued against peace can come to the fore and it's not inconceivable that if the wrong story gets out, there could be civil war, or at the very least a return to violence, with each side accusing the other of treachery. Right now, I don't think it would take much to tip the balance and for the vendettas to begin again. It seems that as soon as someone tries to build a bridge between the sides, there is a bad bastard out there who'll try and blow them up. The plan was very simple, very neat and in theory should have been very effective, but with Nina and the others leaving early and us, just by sheer luck, being out when the hit-squad arrived, it's turned everything on its arse! Whoever planned it hadn't allowed for that."

"I'm sorry Paul, on its what?"

"It's butt! Its backside! It's turned their plans upside down."

Still, Aldquist's part was a completely unknown factor as far as I was concerned. Was there a connection? I had my suspicions. And McCreery? Well again I wasn't 100% sure. but I was almost certain he was now dead, his body dumped somewhere, his removal from the house just part of some overall game plan.

The ferry continued unhindered on its way toward our island destination, the engine note deepening as the speed increased. Every now and again the dark clouds would clear and the moon would come out and we could make out the rugged silhouettes of the surrounding mountains, as they rose steeply from the dark, icy waters of the fjords. Sometimes we could see the pinpoints of lights of some small community, where people were safely locked up in their homes, the curtains in the rooms left wide open and a welcoming lamp placed in each window, their occupants blissfully unaware of the danger we were in.

I was still trying to come to terms with the day's events, cross-examining the thoughts that flashed in and out of my weary mind. Witnessing the murders had been bad enough, but now we were, or at least Anja was, the focus of their attention. They could not allow us to live. We were the only ones who could tell the world that the assassinations had been made to look like the work of a Loyalist splinter group, whereas they were actually a professional contract hit. Had the intended story got out, it would have completely *derailed*, as Coyle had said, any possibility for peace in Ulster, official or unofficial. The cautious progress of the Downing Street Declaration and all the great pioneering work done by the group and their deaths at the house would all be in vain. I was wondering what a part-time journalist from Aberdeen was doing tied up in the whole affair when the soft voice of my companion reminded me.

"We're nearly at the island; we'll have to go down to the car now. Are you OK?"

"Yes, I'm fine thanks...you?"

"Ja, I'm OK."

We sat patiently in the car and prepared to disembark. The ferry had been quiet, there were only four other cars and soon we were on dry land heading for Anja's family hytter. Sometimes I would glance round and check if we were being followed but there appeared to be no obvious problem. For tonight, at least, we would be safe. I put my hand reassuringly on Anja's knee.

"What did you say, Paul?"

"Sorry, what?" I hadn't been listening.

"I thought you said something about the day."

"Did I?...Oh, I think I was day dreaming, trying to remember an old Gaelic saying. I don't know the Gaelic, but I think it translates to 'this day, this day has gone against us'. Anja said nothing.

We soon arrived on the other side of the island, at a cluster of about five chalet type buildings trapped between a steep sided rocky hill and the water's edge. Anja turned off the road and parked in the short driveway of the chalet nearest the shore. A few yards away a red light flashed off and on at the end of a small, wooden mooring jetty.

"I hope the key is where we normally leave it," she joked, "otherwise we're sleeping in the car."

With her words fading in the breezy island air, Anja stepped out of the car and disappeared round the back of the timber and brick house. I stood in the cold darkness beside the car and waited. The darkness was never absolute, the wind torn clouds not thick enough to completely obscure the moon. Looking around the other chalets, I noticed the lights were on in one, but there were no signs of life. I wasn't sure whether or not I was happy to be in the apparent safety of the island, or a bit insecure that, if we had been followed, we were now trapped on a piece of rock, surrounded by water, with no where to run. The lights of Anja's chalet went on and the front door clicked open.

"Mr Robertson, would you like to come in?" my hostess asked politely.

I smiled at Anja and stepped inside. I found myself in a large open-plan living area that was separated from the kitchen by a pine breakfast bar. There were four high stools along the bar, some cast iron pots and pans hanging up on hooks and an abundance of dried flowers. There were three two-seater settees covered in an assortment of coloured patch-work cushions, an old wicker chair and a low coffee table in front of a brick fireplace. There were some ethnic, Peruvian-style rugs scattered on the floor, but there was no TV and no phone. A steep flight of steps led up to the loft area which had been converted into two large bedrooms. The place had the clean, fresh smell of pine and the fading remnants of a pot-pourri. I walked through to the back of the kitchen and out to a utility room and a bathroom. I bolted the back door. I shivered, the place was freezing.

"Anja, can I light a fire or something?" I shouted.

"Yes, of course you can, there should be some matches in the utility room and some wood just by the back door."

I adjusted the combination, then opened up my pilot's case and pulled out a lined A4 pad and began to rip some pages out. I crumpled them up and placed them in the grate of the stone fireplace. I put some dry kindling on the top and lit the paper. I watched mesmerised as the flames took hold and the fire crackled into life. I satisfied myself that it wasn't going to go out and went to the back door to get some cut logs. When I returned to the front room I noticed that Anja had pulled a settee directly in front of the fire and she ran her fingers gently over my neck as I placed more kindling and the logs in the flames. The fire crackled and sparked as it took hold and began burning and charring the dry wood.

"That's better, just like home," I said, pleased with my efforts.

Anja gave a half-hearted laugh, slipped down off the settee and knelt in front of me. She looked pained, her eyes a mixture of grief and bewilderment. I pulled her close to me and I kissed her. She held me very tightly and returned my kisses. I pulled away and our heads rested against each other.

"Are you OK?"

My voice was no more than a whisper.

"I think so. I'm still in a bit of shock but I think I'm slowly coming to terms with what happened and if I don't think about it too much, then I'm OK. Sometimes I see Bjorn's face and I want to cry, but tonight I feel safe with you and when you think about it, we're lucky to be alive. If we hadn't gone for that walk..."

"I know, I know."

She moved towards me and we kissed again. My hands dropped down onto her breasts and she didn't resist. There was a loud knock at the door and we both jumped...our pulses racing, our breathing shallow and rapid.

"Oh my God, Paul." Anja gripped my hand.

"Quiet, Anja, sshhhh," I whispered, my right index finger over my mouth, signalling her to be silent.

There was another knock. Loud. Impatient.

"Go to the door and ask who it is." I felt as if I was going to pass out. Oh fuck!

We edged towards the front door. I grabbed a heavy Le Creuset pan and stood and waited.

"Who is it?" Anja asked in Norwegian.

The answer that came back was enough to satisfy Anja that there was no threat and she opened the door. I put down the cast iron pan, but stayed out of sight. It was Captain Peder Gunnarsson. He had heard the car and had seen the lights go on in the chalet. He was a retired mariner in his late sixties and had served on bulk carriers and tankers on all the oceans of the world. He had come up for a week with his wife for the solitude and the fishing. Anja had met him many times before and she asked him in. I stepped out from behind the door.

"Captain Gunnarsson, this is my friend Paul, he's from Scotland."

He shook my hand, bowed his head slightly, mumbled something in Norwegian to Anja and left.

"I like Gunnarsson. He's an ex-Sea Captain, a charming old man. His wife is disabled, but she's so kind and friendly, Gunnarsson worships her. They never had any children and they have always taken an interest in me and my brothers. He said he heard the car and saw the headlights. He's just gone back to get a flask of coffee for us."

"That's very nice of him - do you know him well?"

"When I was younger, we were always coming up here with Mum and Dad and it was Gunnarsson who taught me and my two brothers to fish. We would swim in the sea, have picnics or barbecues, go scrambling on the hill behind the hytter. Sometimes I would take Mrs Gunnarsson down to the water's edge in her wheelchair and she would sit and read while we played. They were great holidays. Happy times."

She seemed to drift back in to the safety of her memories, obviously comforted by Gunnarsson's appearance. Five or ten minutes later, he reappeared and handed Anja a flask of coffee and an earthenware casserole pot containing two warm poached salmon steaks and some potatoes. She thanked him for the food and the coffee and he left. Anja poured the coffee and served the two huge pieces of salmon. I watched from the window and made sure the old man got safely back to Mrs Gunnarsson, then I moved back through to be beside Anja.

"I'm sorry we don't have any fresh milk or sugar for you, but I wasn't expecting guests, at least not from Scotland and I haven't done a shopping, so you'll have to take your coffee the Norwegian way," joked Anja.

"No problem."

We drank our coffee and ate the salmon. It tasted as good if not better than anything I'd had before. By now the room was beginning to warm up and I could see in her eyes that Anja was feeling better. I excused myself and went to the toilet. When I came back I noticed a ghetto blaster sitting on the window sill in the kitchen area.

"Does that thing work?" I asked pointing toward the window.

"Yes, I think so, why?"

"No reason," I replied

I went over to my pilot's case and pulled out a small package and handed it to Anja.

"What's this?" she asked.

"It's just a little something for you. It was during the weekend we met - I think we danced to a couple of slow records in that night club?"

"Yes, I remember."

"Well, I didn't expect to see you again, so I told you I'd send you a tape of some of my favourite songs. Here it is."

"I didn't think you'd remember."

She got up off the stool and went to the kitchen, picked up the cassette recorder and plugged it into a socket below one of the front windows. She tore the wrapping paper off the cassette and placed it into the machine and pressed play. She crouched by the speakers as the unmistakable intro of Dusty Springfield's "The Look of Love" began. Anja stood up and switched off the main light, leaving only a small table lamp and the warm glow of the fire to illuminate the room. She held out her hand to me and I walked over to her.

"Hello, Scots boy, would you like to dance with me?"

I took her hand and we began to move slowly round the room. "The Look of Love" ended and Noel Harrison's "Windmills of Your Mind" from the Thomas Crown Affair began. Even after all that had happened, I felt happy. It was almost perfect, a cabin in the mountains, the sea, the fire, the music, just Anja and I, but although I tried to, I couldn't get today's events completely out of my mind. We danced as song after song played on the cassette. With more than a liberal dose of dramatic irony, we listened to Lou Reed's "Perfect Day" and then some sadder songs. Songs about lost love and songs about lovers who could never be together, destined to be apart.

"I love these songs, Paul, but they are a little sad, they make me feel sad. Were you trying to tell me something?"

"Yes and no, but when I made up the tape, all I could think about was that I would never see you again and I'm ashamed to admit it, but...it hurt so much."

"I always knew we'd meet again, I think we were meant to be together. You see, I liked you from the moment we were introduced, you looked so cute, yet you seemed so shy and you had such gentle, caring eyes, something inside just felt right."

The Walker Brothers "Make it Easy on Yourself" was followed by Frank and Nancy singing "Something Stupid", then Frank singing "Strangers in the Night", then Louis Armstrong's "We Have All the Time in the World". I was aware that tears were running down Anja's face as we sang and danced along to the music. The tape eventually finished off with Crowded House "Don't Dream It's Over", "Missing You" by John Waite and my personal favourite Herb Alpert singing "This Guy's in Love with You". We kept dancing even after the music had stopped and we began to kiss.

173

Anja eventually pulled away.

"I wish we could stay up here for ever," she whispered and started the tape again. "It's too cold to sleep up in the loft. Do you want to share a duvet down here?" she asked.

I nodded. Anja quickly climbed the steep flight of stairs to the bedrooms above and returned with a large, thick duvet. I threw a couple of logs on the fire, which registered its annoyance by sparking and spitting on the slate fireplace and we settled down on the settee and pulled the duvet up over us. I wanted to make love to her so badly, but it wasn't the right time and for now I was happy just being with her. I kicked off my shoes, held her tightly and, exhausted, she soon fell asleep in my arms. I looked out of the window as the first large snow flakes began to fall, a draught from somewhere caused the fire to flicker and dance, casting long eerie shadows on the walls. I didn't want the night to end and I shared her thoughts; I too wished we could stay up here for ever. It wasn't long before my eyes grew heavy and I began to doze, then I drifted into a light sleep, as the tape played on.

Then it was morning. I woke early and eased myself away from the still sleeping Anja. I rubbed the frost pattern off the glass and looked out of the window. There was a light covering of snow and the wind had got up. Away in the distance, I could vaguely distinguish the outlines of the mountains across the water, as the darkness receded and the dawn spread palely from the East. The snow and the setting made the morning bleakly atmospheric. I went through to the bathroom and freshened up, then searched for some warm, clean clothes in my case. I pulled out a Gant, Black Watch tartan shirt and a navy Pringle sweater. The fire had burnt itself out and the room was cold. The nip in the air and the coldness of the hytter reminded me of a story from college about some of the guys who were on the same course as me. They were a right bunch of tossers and there was a story doing the rounds that they were so mean, they refused to ever use the electric fire in their flat, instead they would sit and study, or watch telly wrapped up in layers of jumpers, with their duffle coats and anoraks on. Grippy bastards! I didn't like any of them and always suspected that the truth was that they kept warm by indulging in a spot of communal chugging! The same lot, when they were on a night out up in the Union, bought individual drinks and never ever put their hands in their pockets to pay for a round. I could never have been like that.

"Paul, are you there?"

"Yes, Anja, I'm here. Did you sleep OK?"

"Yes, I did. What's the time?" she smiled, stifled a yawn and rubbed the sleep from her eyes.

"It's about 8.30 am. It's been snowing. Just a light covering though."

Anja told me that the first ferry would probably not leave until about 10 am because it was Sunday. That gave us a chance to tidy up before leaving. I made sure that all the doors were locked and that the fire was completely out, while Anja wrote a brief thank you note for the Gunnarssons. Satisfied everything was as we had found it, we left the hytter. Anja quickly crossed over to the Gunnarssons and slipped the note under their door. She quickly returned from her errand. We stood together and looked out over the fjord to the mountains. The snow had made everything look peaceful and dream-like, but the strong breeze that was blowing had began to whip up the waves, making uneven patterns with the white crests on the deep, dark waters of the sea. We walked a few yards down the path, then onto the uneven planking of the jetty, as the waves lopped and slapped against the barnacle and seaweed covered supports. All around us was nature's wonderfully unique creation of snow and rock and water, the fusion of its shades and tones enhancing the strength of the image.

"I love being up here," she confessed.

I knew exactly what she meant and I longed to return.

"Maybe we'll come back again."

"Yes, I'd like that," she said.

She seemed distant, as if she was retreating into herself and was remembering happier times. I let her drift in the warmth and comfort of her mind for a few seconds, then I reeled her back into the coldness of reality.

"Come on, let's go. I need to get hold of Andy in London and find out what he's done."

Anja drove carefully back to the ferry terminal. The Audi easily handled the road conditions, but I got the impression she didn't want to be responsible for damaging Steve's car by carelessly spinning off the road. Although we were taking a chance going back to Stavanger, I believed it probably the smartest thing to do. From there we could either head north to Bergen, or west to Oslo, the capital. At least we had options, it would just be a case of choosing the right one. The ferry journey back was slow, as the boat dipped and rose in the choppy sea. We felt the light sea spray on our faces as we stood on the open deck. Purists would have described doing what we were doing as 'bracing'. The few passengers onboard, who all sat huddled together inside, probably thought we were mad!

When we drove off the ferry at Stavanger, the tension and unease of the previous day came back in a great deluge. The night in the hytter was now long gone.

"Drive past the Fun Pub please," I instructed.

"Why we doing that?" Anja asked puzzled by my request.

"I just want to see if their car is there, and they won't recognise the Audi."

Anja dutifully did as I asked. Her car was still there. It seemed to sadden her to leave it there, abandoned. The streets around the Vagen were completely deserted. There was no-one else around, only the bitterly cold wind prowled the empty narrow lanes. The city, normally so quaint and picturesque in the sunlight, seemed cold and melancholic under the dark grey clouds and in the morning's pale wash of light. We didn't hang about, but drove on to Sandnes, a town just outside Stavanger, where we stopped at a public telephone and I phoned London.

"Paul, where the fuck have you been? We've been waiting for hours, worried shitless that something had happened and that you'd both been hit."

"Yeah, sorry, but we had to spend the night in a safe house. Unfortunately, it didn't have a phone."

I looked out at the car and surrounding roads, but fortunately there was no activity.

"I've spoken to George at the ATB and he's been in touch with his sources in Norway and they're at this very moment checking out the house. If your story stacks up and I don't doubt that it does, they'll arrange to bring you in."

"What the hell do you mean if the story 'stacks up'," I responded, insulted at the inference that I could have made it all up.

"No, that's not what we were saying, we just want to find out how serious this thing is."

"Take my word, it's fucking serious!"

"George is a bit concerned that your security for the meeting was breached, someone knew you were up there and there's Anja's call to Aldquist and the fact that your friends were waiting for you in Stavanger."

"OK, I hear what you're saying. Look, I don't know if it'll work or not but I cooked up a bit of a plan and we'll need to get going, so I'll check in with you later, maybe in a couple of hours."

"You'll call in a couple of hours? OK, I'll hear from you then. Em, Paul, by the way and look, I know this sounds a bit mercenary, but the Agency wants an exclusive on your story."

176

"You help us out of this shit and it's all yours, no problem."

"Good, I'm glad that's out of the way. I think I'd better tell you that there are problems this side of the water. There are rumours circulating round Westminster that an official Government document will be leaked in tomorrow's papers. It's alleged that a few selected excerpts from this document, which was being developed between the Dublin and London Governments as a framework for discussion among all interested parties will be published any day now. Unfortunately it isn't likely to be published in its fullest form, but that just adds to the confusion that has been generated. There will be statements in the House tomorrow and we reckon the PM will use his prerogative to go on TV to address the nation in a damage limitation exercise, by appealing directly to the people of Northern Ireland. It really has caused uproar. The Unionist MPs are going berserk! They really believe they've been shafted and are threatening to end their support of the Government and have demanded a meeting for clarification and reassurance. Once all your stuff gets out, 'ooch ya fucker'! I've already ordered a new Keflar jacket, because I know where I'll end up being sent. This is by far and away the most serious accumulation of events in years and I don't believe they're coincidental."

"So who's behind the leak?" I asked.

"Right now we don't know whose fingerprints are on it, it's all unconfirmed rumour, but its having an unstabilising effect on the already fragile relations between the Unionists and the PM. As you can imagine, he doesn't want to piss them off any more than is necessary and he's only too aware of how the Unionist contingent at Westminster can affect the parliamentary arithmetic and his ability to govern effectively."

"Christ, it almost sounds as if the hit at the house and the leak were planned to coincide. I wish I knew what the fuck was going on - anyway, I'd better go."

"Oh, just before you go, George told me to tell you trust no-one, always use public call boxes, as you never know who's listening and don't take any chances. Remember you're not Richard fucking Hannay! I'll hear from you in a couple of hours, yes?"

I put the phone back in its place and beckoned Anja out of the car.

"Did you get through to Andy?" she asked hopefully.
"Yes, things are happening, they're sending some people up to the house, to corroborate our story, but we're not out of the woods yet."

"I'm sorry, I don't understand, out of what woods?"

I couldn't be bothered explaining so I updated her on the furore back in UK.

"Why don't I call Aldquist?"

"Why?"

"I'll tell him we're going to Bergen. I'll tell him I have friends there and you think that this is the safest thing to do. I'll also tell him about the reception at the Kirke and see if I can work out his reaction."

"You think he's mixed up in this?"

"I don't know."

Anja made the call to Oslo. I didn't have to persuade her to do it - she just wasn't sure about Aldquist any more. She stepped out of the kiosk and looked at me.

"Well, what about Aldquist, what did he say, how did he react?"

"He still appears very upset about Bjorn, he's even offered to fly up to Bergen to meet me himself...he seems very concerned about me."

"Yes, I bet! What about the meeting at the Kirke, what about his man?"

"It seems that his associate has disappeared. Aldquist hasn't heard from him. He also said he's meeting with his assistant this morning to discuss the situation further and to decide on their next move. Throughout the call he sounded genuinely shocked and upset."

"Yeah, maybe he's just a very good liar," I mumbled. "Has he called the police or the authorities yet?"

"I'm not sure. He didn't say, but surely he would have been in touch with someone by now don't you think?"

"Anja I don't know what to think about this guy. You know him better than me."

I couldn't help feeling cynical. We got back into the car, left Sandnes and headed for Oslo. The plan I had developed was so simple an infant could have thought of it, but what the fuck, we were in dire straits and if Aldquist was the leak then maybe we would make some time for ourselves. We had been lucky so far. We had avoided them at the house and we had managed to elude them again at the Fun Pub. No doubt they would be desperately keen to pick up our trail and end the chase. We drove on through scenery I would have normally gaped open-mouthed at, but I paid no attention to it. I couldn't get my mind to focus in on anything other than the darkest and blackest of thoughts. It was all so different to the excitement and wonder I had experienced a few days ago on the way up to the house.

The Audi sped on and Norway flashed past the windscreen.

Chapter 7

CHAPTER 7

"Why don't we fly to Oslo or Bergen or even Aberdeen, Paul?" she asked, her face tight with concern.

"They'll probably be watching the airport. I don't know, but if I was them, that's what I'd do. I just feel that, maybe if we can keep them guessing, if we don't do anything too predictable, we can stay alive. It's up to you Anja, if you want to go to Sola, we'll go to Sola. I'm a complete amateur in all this, but all I know is, they're mercenaries, professionally trained killers and they're after you...I mean us, and I'm going to do whatever I have to do to stay away from them until we can get brought in."

Anja she just nodded in reluctant agreement and kept driving.

"Which way do you want me to go?"

"Is there a choice?"

"Yes, we can keep to the coast road or we can try going over the mountains, only at this time of year it may not be a good idea because of snow. It's a good drive in summer, but it's not a route that is recommended in winter. The coast road is longer but a lot easier."

"OK, let's take the mountain road."

"Why? We don't know what the weather will be like up there. I hope you know what you're doing."

"I don't."

Even though she doubted the wisdom of my instructions, she drove on. I thought back to our night on the island, the music, the firelight, the peace, the safety and the time we shared.

"Are you OK, Paul?"

I looked across at her and touched her face.

"Sure, just a little tired."

She shrugged and smiled.

"Why don't you have a sleep? I'll be alright."

"No, I'm fine."

We had driven for about an hour and a half when I remembered we needed to call Andy.

"How are you for petrol?"

"Less than half full."

"OK, let's get some petrol and I'll call Andy."

Several kilometres further on we came upon a picturesque village that clung to the side of a mountain and was bordered by a river in spate, its coffee coloured waters foaming and frothing as they rushed over the rocks and boulders hidden in its depths. Anja drew into a small garage/filling station and stopped the car by one of the pumps.

"Can you find out if they have a phone?" I asked naively.

Anja laughed.

"Of course they'll have a phone, where do you think this is, Pakistan?"

"Yeah, yeah, yeah, smart ass!"

Anja organised the petrol and left me to call Andy. I dialled the London number and was a wee bit surprised by the speed the call was answered.

"McIntosh, News Desk."

"Andy, it's me."

"Are you OK, are you both OK?"

"Yes, so far. You sound concerned, I'm touched..."

He ignored my sarcasm and went on.

"As you said, the shit's hit the fan. Oslo, Dublin and Downing Street have all been talking. Emergency meetings and all that! They're incredibly pissed off at the mess, especially London. The PM's getting severe grief from the Unionists on the leaked document. Then we had to tighten the noose round his neck, by breaking the news about your escapades. In public he comes across as controlled and unflappable, but shit, you should have heard the language! It would appear that he hadn't really been given a full briefing on what was going down and now he's worried that the Norway massacre will be made public, which, coming on top of the leak, will completely derail the political process and eclipse his personal crusade for lasting peace. His security advisors are all shuffling about Whitehall, gleefully saying, 'I told you so' to the Norwegians and accusing them of interfering and jeopardising everything. Oh, and to make matters worse, by adding insult to injury it would appear that the Taoiseach knew more than him about Pedersen's talks and..."

"Do you know who's behind the hit yet?" I interrupted.

"No, not yet, there's not been a sniff. Usually by this time someone has leaked something out but, so far there's not been a squeak. On the other hand, we've also managed to keep everything out of the press...Look George is here, he wants a word."

"Hello, Paul? George Colefax, Anti-Terrorist-Branch here. How are you?"

George Colefax had been with the Anti-Terrorist Branch, formerly the ATS (the Anti-Terrorist Squad), for years and years. He was a career policeman who had come up through the ranks and I knew that Andy was on good terms with him and held him in high regard. He was leading from the front in the war against 'the gun and the bomb' and hadn't dropped his guard, even though the IRA had announced their cease-fire. He was still very much aware that the Provisionals were carrying out shadow operations on mainland Britain and in central London. He had access to all the main players in Government, he even had direct access to Rimington herself and, along with the PM, she had now been fully briefed on recent events and had requested frequent updates on our situation and had given instructions, that she be informed the minute we were safely in the custody of the Norwegians. Through perseverance, grit and results, George had attained the rank of Commander, without succumbing to the bizarre and arcane rituals of strange handshakes and apron wearing. I had seen him perform on the TV, usually after a terrorist outrage and he came across as sincere, with a tremendous commitment to the difficult role he was performing. He was at the sharp end, literally defending this country against the terrorist. I was pleased he was taking a personal interest in our case, but given the political pressure it should not have been a surprise. He continued.

"...and where are you?"

"First of all we're both fine and we're in a little village on the mountain road to Oslo, but we called Aldquist and told him that we were heading to Bergen."

"Not exactly original, but it could be effective. Do you think he's involved?"

"We're not sure. Can you find out?"

"Yes, I'm sure that won't be a problem. Keep him informed of your *progress* and I'll alert some of my Norwegian colleagues to do some checking up on him.

"Paul, take care of yourself and the girl. We need you to stay alive as much for our sakes as for your own. You see, if we can get to the people who perpetrated the attack, we will obviously expect you both to testify against them and perhaps, with whatever means are available to us, we can deal and bargain with them in such a way that they will lead us to their paymasters. We must find the group or individual who was responsible for ordering the murders at the house. To be perfectly frank, it's them we're really after and by getting your story made public, in a controlled manner, the PM thinks he'll be able to retrieve the peace process. I assume Andy has told you about the leak?"

"Yes, he told me. It certainly ups the ante on their need to get Anja and myself, but look, I don't know who these guys were or where they are, but hopefully they will be heading for Bergen. We just hope somebody gets them before they get us. Right now, to be honest, I couldn't care less whether you find the people who are bank-rolling them or not!"

"No, of course, your safe return is paramount." He paused. "Would you remember what they looked like?"

"George, I think you can relax on that point. Their faces are indelibly printed on our minds. It's unlikely we'll ever forget them!"

"Paul, I'm coming over to Norway. I'll be there tomorrow. You and Anja have to stay out of trouble and ahead of the game until we can get you both in. The Norwegians are deeply shocked by what's happened and they are coming under immense pressure from No.10 to sort it all out and they have formally asked for our help. They don't yet know that you have been in touch with us and that I have already made certain preparations, but I will brief them tomorrow on my arrival."

"It's not the Norwegians' fault for Christsakes! They were just hours away from something that was going to help end all this 'Troubles' crap, without the usual political skulduggery and treachery. I'm telling you George, Bjorn Pedersen is a bloody hero for what he achieved."

I felt angry at the attitude of the Government in London.

"I have also contacted colleagues in Lisburn and Lyons, but so far they have not come up with anything. I've had the disadvantage of not giving them a full report, as I've had to be very careful not to tell them too much, in case there is a security leak, before all the facts are known. If this was to get out now, in addition to what else was happening, the IRA cease-fire and the Loyalists' intended cease-fire might disappear down the pan and we will have a major escalation of violence as each side blames the other for what has happened."
"How will you be able to help us?"

"Keep in touch with Andy and I'll contact him periodically to find out where you are. Once I get to Oslo, I'll instruct him to arrange a rendezvous with you. In the meantime, trust no-one. By all means keep in touch with Aldquist and try to keep convincing him you are heading for Bergen...Oh! and Paul, keep your heads down."

"George, a question - why can't we turn ourselves into some local police station? Or why can't the Norwegians pick us up by helicopter or something?"

There was a short, silent pause on the other end of the phone.

"We discussed that, but the Norwegians are reluctant to send choppers up at the moment because of a severe weather warning and I also suspect that they are more than a little worried that there may be a mole in their organisation somewhere."

I trusted George - we had to - but his explanation sounded like crap to me.

"Do you want to know what I think, George...I think the bastards are using us as bait. For as long as we're out here there's a chance of us luring the bad guys to them and I think the authorities will be quite happy to expend me and Anja if it means they ultimately nail the killers. I don't know who to trust and I don't know what the fuck to

184

do!"

Again there was a short silence, then George spoke.

"Just stick to your own plan and be careful. Andy wants a word, stand by."

Andy came back on.

"Take care and keep in touch...and before you go I think you ought to know that Claire called me. She caught me off guard and I told her I hadn't seen you. She sounded really pissed off."

"Right now she's the least of my worries. I'll check in with you in a couple of hours."

I said a curt good-bye and slammed the phone down. The bastards were setting us up. I went back to the car and Anja was waiting. She was sitting on the car bonnet, the mountain breeze blowing through her hair. I sat beside her and she put her arm around my shoulders.

"Everything OK in London?"

"Yes," I lied, "I think we'll be alright."

"I'm hungry, can we get a coffee and a sandwich or something?" She sounded almost back to normal.

"Sure, great idea. Where can we go?"

"I think there is a small hotel over there, maybe they can help."

"I hope so, after all this isn't Pakistan!"

She gave me a shove, pushing me off the side of the car.

We walked hand in hand across the road to the hotel. We looked like any young couple on holiday and I wished that I could be doing this with Anja again sometime, but in happier circumstances. I wanted to see more of Norway. It's a beautiful place and I wanted her to be my guide. There would be so much to see and do. I wanted her to show me and share with me, the romance of the whole country.

The hotel was quiet, after all it was out of season and we were miles away from any ski resorts. We sat down in the lounge area and a girl in her late teens appeared and asked us in Norwegian what we would like. Anja ordered coffee and sandwiches for two. The girl soon returned with a pot of freshly brewed coffee and four open sandwiches of prawns and rare roast beef and a little salad garnish. We ate quickly. We didn't have a lot of time and besides we were both fairly hungry. After two refills of coffee and a shared Danish pastry, we both went to the loo and when I came back I asked for the bill. The young girl, who hadn't really said much, asked Anja if we had far to go. Without thinking, Anja innocently explained to her we were heading further into the mountains, heading ultimately for Oslo. The girl urged us to take care - the roads could be treacherous and almost impassable at this time of year. She added that heavy snow was forecast. I handed over the money for the snack and Anja thanked her and we returned to the car. It felt good to have eaten and freshened up. I was ready for the next stage of the journey.

The girl's advice had only served to confirm Anja's doubts and concerns about the route we were taking, but I didn't want to go back.

Soon we were travelling up again, the road a series of tight hair-pin bends reducing our speed sometimes to a crawl, as we drove higher into the mountains. The Audi handled the inclines easily and as the roads were pretty much clear of snow we made good progress. The scenery was everything I imagined Norway to be. Wild and wonderful. The mountains, bleak and unforgiving in their snow-blasted coating towered over us in every direction. We travelled on; there were few trees now, as we were fairly high up and the few there were grew in sheltered pockets, clinging to life on a thin veneer of soil, away from open exposure to the elements. Again there was water everywhere, streams, burns, waterfalls, lochs, rivers. I imagined it all to be an awesome sight in spring when the snows melt and these pretty water ways are transformed into raging torrents in full spate. I found myself day-dreaming, trying to shut out from my mind the unknown threat that was out there looking for us, tracking us, hunting us.

"Anja, I'd like you to show me round Norway sometime. The mountains, Oslo, Bergen, the islands, the Far North, everything."

"Yes, I do that, first of all I will show you all the beautiful places near Stavanger. I think I will take you to Prekestolen or Pulpit Rock as it is known in English, on the Lysefjord. It's a dramatic place, a square shaped outcrop of rock hundreds of metres above the fjord. We go there sometimes in the summer to picnic and sunbathe. It would appeal to you, I think."

We had been driving for just over an hour and as we emerged from one of the numerous tunnels, we ran into some heavy snow. Anja slowed the car, as the flakes began to settle and lie on the road surface. The sky had turned a deep turquoise. The snow continued to fall, but fortunately the wind was not too strong. I was aware that Anja had become a little agitated and was beginning to look uncomfortable with the conditions.

"Paul," Anja paused, then said reflectively, "maybe we should turn back?"

"No, I don't think that would be wise. You're doing fine."

I pulled out the road map and told her to keep going and not to worry. I studied the area where I thought we were and realised we were only several kilometres from a village. We drove on through the snow and by the time we did in fact reach the village, the wind had got up and we saw the beginnings of a full blizzard sweeping in over the summits and into the pass. The village was another one horse town, or more appropriately one reindeer town, with two small, traditional looking hotels on either side of the road, directly opposite each other. I asked her to cross the road and she pulled into the hotel on the left. There were two cars already parked there and only one car in the car park of the other hotel. All appeared to have been there for sometime as they were covered in snow and there were no fresh tyre tracks. A General Store, not unlike Ike's from the Waltons, and a handful of timber houses flanking the hotels, was all the village consisted of. There was no evidence of a police station. Probably there was no crime and I wouldn't have been surprised if people didn't even lock their doors at night. I told Anja to get out of the car and make a run for the hotel.

I retrieved our bags and secured the car, then I walked briskly over to the hotel and even in the short time I was exposed to the blizzard, I was cold and covered in snow. I brushed the snow off my head and body in the vestibule, before I entered the reception area, relieved to be out of the rapidly approaching storm.

A woman in her mid-forties was chatting cheerfully to Anja, as she filled in the registration card. The woman, who was heavy set and dressed in a red crew-neck top and a black skirt, smiled to me knowingly, as Anja handed her the card and called out.

"Come on darling, we're in Room Five."

I blushed as my Norwegian 'wife' led me through reception and upstairs to our room. Anja unlocked the door and we went in. The room was cosy. A black wood burning stove heater had been lit and its warmth radiated out to all the corners of the room. There was a large, comfortable looking double bed and through another door, which I thought was a cupboard, there was a small en suite shower room, panelled in pine. It would do very nicely.

I put down the cases and flopped forward onto the bed. Anja fell onto the bed beside me and I turned around to face her, brushing the hair from her face. I kissed her on the forehead, on the cheeks, then on the mouth.

"Would you like to have that shower with me?"

It was the second time she had asked me - our first attempt, back at the house had been thwarted by little Mette. For a split second, my mind drifted off on a tangent. Little Mette, I hoped she was safe and well, but how could she be well when she realised she wouldn't see her daddy again. Poor Einar had lost his dad, his 'coach'. I thought of Nina - what would all this do to her? I pulled my thoughts back into line and when I opened my eyes, Anja was looking at me. I turned away, the shyness I thought had gone somehow re-emerging for the first time in days.

"Yes." My reply was almost inaudible.

Anja went through to the shower room where she undressed and entered the shower. I took my clothes off in the room, deliberately folding them up neatly, anything to delay going through and into the shower. I could hear the water hitting the cubicle door, so I grabbed a towel and wrapped it around me and walked through into the en suite. I opened the shower door; her back was to me, her outstretched arms pushing up into the spray, her head tilted back. She turned to face me and I drank in the sight of her perfect honey-hued body and thought of the work of Rodin. She released my towel and it fell at my feet, then she guided me into the shower with her. The water was warm and her body was soft. Her touch excited me immediately, as her hand slipped down over my flat stomach and rested just above my pubic hair. I felt my breathing sharpen, she dropped her hand and stroked the inside of my thigh, never venturing too high. She never took her eyes off me, she was teasing me, but I was enjoying it. So was she. I moved forward and we kissed long and passionately, as the warm water cascaded over us. My hands moved up over her slender hips, her neat waist and then I cupped and caressed her breasts, teasing her nipples very gently between my thumb and forefinger. She pushed her head back as I drew my index finger down her stomach, down over her sex. It was my turn to tease. She gave into me, as I delicately touched, searched and probed. Anja brought her head forward and took a deep breath.

"Let's go to bed," she suggested in an urgent whisper.

I turned off the water and led her out of the cubicle. I lifted her up and she wrapped her arms tightly round my neck, then I carried her through to the bedroom. I carefully stood her down directly in front of the warm stove-heater and using one of the large soft bath towels I began gently to dry her wet and glistening body. I dried off most of the moisture, then I began to explore her body with my mouth, licking away the few remaining droplets on her shoulders, back and stomach. I let her fall back onto the bed and I climbed up by her and, kneeling over her, I began to kiss her. I kissed her lips, then rolled my tongue over onto her ear, down her neck and onto her hardened, swollen nipples. My tongue eased over them, barely touching them. I slipped my head down over her stomach and down onto the softness and sweetness of her sex. Her

188

breathing became more rapid, her hands grabbed and pulled at my hair, as my tongue and fingers worked in harmony, rubbing, searching, until I brought her to a frantic, back-arching climax. For a few moments I lay motionless, my head nestled on her warm thighs, not wanting to move. She pulled me up to her and she kissed me. We lay in each other's arms, me on my back, Anja lying across me, her head on my chest. It felt safe and comfortable and was a favourite cuddling position of Hannah's. We lay there and must have dozed off. I woke first and I tried to slip out of the bed without disturbing her, but she called out to me in a whisper,

"Paul."

"Yes, Anja?"

"Nothing."

I kissed her and she pulled me back onto the bed. Around a quarter to eight, we were disturbed by the phone ringing. Anja answered it nervously, but it was only Mrs Brodal asking us if we would require a meal. She put her hand over the receiver and asked me if I wanted to eat in the room or downstairs in the dining room with the other guests. I thought for a moment and was about to say that I had already eaten, but I suggested we should go down stairs to the dining room. I felt good inside. I was happy and relaxed and besides, the blizzard was still blowing fiercely outside, the gale howling south, relentless and unhindered from beyond the Arctic Circle. If anyone was following us they would be having a hellish time, especially back up on the higher stretches of the road, where the visibility would have been reduced to zero in white-out conditions. It may have been a little reckless, but I didn't want to stay shut up in the room. It would be good to relax and be sociable by mixing with the other guests. We each showered and I had to stop Anja playfully trying to grab me as I dried myself. We dressed and went down stairs. Anja just wouldn't let go of my hand. Maybe it was a fear thing and she felt safe - there again, maybe she really liked me. We sat at a table by the open fire and we chatted. We talked about her school days, past holidays with her parents and her time in the UK as an au pair. Anja looked good and was obviously feeling better, but our topic of conversation never strayed onto Andy or Bjorn or what had happened back at Manefossen. For the moment at least, we were able to forget the danger.

"Paul, you haven't told me much about your life back in Scotland."

For once, I was just about to let go and tell her everything. I wanted to give myself completely to her and was on the verge of breaking open the lock that protected the inner sanctum of Paul Robertson, when the food arrived. Our first course, surprisingly enough, consisted of a mixture of prawns, grapes and apple, dressed in a light, piquant marie rose sauce. We were offered beer or wine and we both chose to have a cold glass of beer. The menu was fairly limited, but more than adequate and as a main course we settled for a fillet steak in a bernaise sauce, with mushrooms, carrots, green beans and plenty of potatoes. We didn't order a sweet, preferring instead to go for some coffee and mints, followed by a liqueur. Anja had a cognac and I had a Glayva. I had asked for it, half expecting that they wouldn't carry a bottle, but I was pleasantly surprised that they had some behind the bar. Apparently, they had been asked for it several years earlier by a Scots tourist and they hadn't heard of it, but now they always had some in stock. We asked Mrs Brodal to join us for a cognac, but she politely refused, explaining that she had too much to do. We sat by the fire chatting, or just watching and listening to the others who were dining in the hotel that night, eavesdropping on their hushed, private conversations. A rumour had started that we were honeymooners and there were plenty knowing smiles when we finally said goodnight to Mrs Brodal and the others and we went upstairs.

Anja entered the room first and motioned to switch on the light, but I stopped her, gently moving her hand down by her side. I closed the door behind me and led her through the darkness toward the bed where I started to undress her. She wanted to do the same to me, but I pushed her hand away and I stayed in control. With nimble fingers I confidently unbuckled her belt and unbuttoned her 501s, before easing them gently down to her ankles, then helping her step out of them. She stood silent and motionless as I unbuttoned the shirt she was wearing. She had commandeered my denim Ralph Lauren shirt which was far too big for her, but its bagginess made her look wonderfully sexy. I undid the last button of the shirt and parted the soft, faded cloth. She wasn't wearing a bra and I freed her firm breasts out from the shirt. I brushed her nipples with the back of my hands, before peeling the shirt off her shoulders and letting it fall to the ground. I lowered my head and delicately teased then sucked on a nipple and she gave a little gasp as the pleasure trickled through her.

I then dropped to my knees, gently nuzzling my face in the talcumed freshness of her vee. I ran my tongue along her stomach, then I removed her panties. I stood up and sat Anja on the bed. The bedroom was warm; she was completely naked, but I was still fully dressed. I kicked off my shoes and lay on the bed beside her. I moved her on to her front and began to massage her neck and shoulders - first with only one hand, then I pushed myself up and knelt over her, freeing both hands. I worked down from her shoulders, covering every inch of her back to the base of her spine, working and dwelling on the areas that induced the most intense sighs and moans. Anja closed her eyes; she trusted me, she wanted me. I continued to knead her back, then she propped herself up on her elbows and, bowing her head, she let her hair drop over her face. I worked on her neck, then I slid my hands down her back, under her arms and then slowly ever more slowly round to the fullness of her breasts and her nipples. I tracked my fingers down her spine, over her soft round buttocks, my left hand easing between her thighs and as if on cue she parted her legs slightly for me, as if inviting me to continue. I brushed my hand over her sex, threatening, but never daring to penetrate her secret place. I could feel the excitement building up inside of me as I touched and stroked, my fingers continuing to find their target, my mouth nuzzling her neck and ears.

I seemed to be pressing all the right erogenous buttons; I felt confident and in control as Anja moaned and sighed, her body gyrating slowly and rhythmically. She let me retain control until she could stand it no more and she turned round and tore at my jeans and shirt. I ripped off my socks and lay next to her, dressed only in my boxers. She began to kiss me on the chest and then I felt her lips on mine, her mouth opened and our tongues met, searching and probing. My fingers continued to explore and touch, I pulled my head away from her kiss and carefully started to bite at her nipples. I could feel the heat of her as her inner thighs squeezed and gripped my hand. Her hand brushed down over my body and she released me from my boxer shorts and I pressed my hardness against her. She pulled my face to hers and again her tongue found mine. I pushed myself up and balanced over her, as she skilfully removed my boxers, before guiding me into the softness of her body.

We both sighed and gasped, as our bodies responded to each other's touch. It felt so good to be inside of her, but I dared not relax. I went to work and our lovemaking was long, slow and gentle. No words passed between us, but I felt her warm breath on my neck and her fingers digging into my back and I knew she had passed that point of no return. I withdrew slightly, teasing her, but she pulled me down into her, her pelvis rising up to meet mine. I slipped my hand under her, pinching the soft flesh of her buttocks, lifting her to meet me on every slow, deep stroke. Her breathing was now very rapid, her movements more urgent. She let out a muffled moan; I felt her finger nails dig into the nape of my neck, tearing the skin, in a combination of what was, for me, pleasure and pain. She shuddered, then I felt the tightness of her hold relax as I let myself go and our bodies became one.

We didn't speak. I just held her in my arms, wanting to protect her, wanting to assure her everything would be alright. I wondered if our love-making, my love-making had satisfied her, but I dared not ask and for a brief moment I was overcome with angst as I wondered how I had compared to any previous lover. The thought of her ever being with someone else tore through me. Lying next to her felt different to anything I had experienced with Claire, it was like...it was like it used to be with Hannah, in our early days - maybe even better. I eased myself off of her and propped myself up on one elbow and watched the movement of her body: her breasts rising and falling gently with the action of her breathing. I went to touch her, my fingers barely brushing over her cheek, then downward, following the contours of her body at a distance of no more than a quarter of an inch. I let my head fall back onto the pillow. We pulled the duvet up over us and her arm slipped round my waist as she snuggled into me. We drifted into sleep, but in the dark recesses of our dreams the demons lurked, cowering and shying away from the light. After the murders at Manefossen, they would always be there. They would be there when we woke. I turned my back on the darkness, my physical energy temporarily spent and slipped into sleep.

Sleep had been deep and restful, but I woke suddenly and stared into the darkness, taking some time to get my physical and mental bearings. The night was dead still, the silence and darkness almost total. I had no idea of the time, but my bladder told me I needed a pee. I rose and went through for a run off, padding over the soft, thick carpet, tentatively feeling my way through the darkness that seemed to smother my naked body. I switched on the bathroom light and, looking at my watch, I saw it was 6am. Anja was still asleep. Before going back to bed, I looked out of the window into the night to see if it was still snowing. Against the feeble orange glow of the streetlights, I could see there had been a heavy fall. Now only a few flakes were falling, individual snow crystals, stragglers, that had somehow become detached and separated from the blizzard. As my eyes grew used to the darkness it was, however, not the snow that concerned me. In the hotel car park across the road, on the shadow's edge of the floodlighting, there was another vehicle, one that had not been there when we had arrived. The small hairs on the back of my neck tingled and my stomach sank. Even though it had a layer of snow on it, I was sure it was a black 4WD. It could have been anybody's, but I instinctively sensed it was them and I felt the first tinges of an overwhelming, claustrophobic panic stir within me. I felt more frightened now than I had ever been before...Had they found us?

I took a deep breath, went back into the bathroom and splashed my face with cold water. I dressed and filled the small kettle that sat on the desk and switched it on, and I had just started packing and organising my gear when Anja began to stir, drifting on the fringes of sleep.

"Good morning," I said as I brought her a cup of Cafe Hag.

"Hi, what time is it?"

"It's just after six."

"You're up early. Couldn't you sleep?"

She cupped the mug in her hand and took a delicate sip of the steaming coffee. Then she placed the mug on the side table. She stretched and yawned. I watched as she kicked off the duvet and lay back on the bed. She still felt good and looked up at me and smiled. I stared at her naked body, and swallowed hard before I spoke.

"Anja, it's time to get up."

"Why? It's still so early. Breakfast won't be served for ages yet."

"I know, but it's time to get up."

Maybe she could tell by the tone of my voice, but she sprang up, looked straight at me, the smile dying on her lips. I could see at once that the fear had returned. I said nothing, trying hard to keep my face expressionless in a vain attempt to conceal my own fear.

She sipped at her coffee again, then insisted on having a quick shower, even though I said we didn't have time.

"Paul, I'm having a shower."

"OK, but be quick."

When she had finished dressing I called her over to the bed and sat her down.

"Anja, I don't want you to panic because I'm not one hundred percent sure, but I think the men from the house are in the village."

"Paul, are you joking with me?"

"No."

"So, where are they? How do you know it's them?" she asked, half laughing.

"I don't, I've just got a feeling they're here, so I think it's better if we leave now."

"I don't know if I can take much more of this."

"I know, I know. Hopefully I'm wrong and it's not them, but let's just get out of here."

We packed our bags, checked underneath the bed and in all the cupboards and drawers, to make sure we hadn't forgotten anything, then carefully made our way downstairs. In the hall, a grandfather clock ticked and clunked and whirred. It provided the morning's only sound. Being so early, there was no-one on reception. We left Mrs Brodal a note thanking her for her hospitality, as well as the money for the room and dinner and an explanation that we had to return to Stavanger. We placed the note in an envelope behind the reception desk.

"Give me the keys and I'll bring the car over to the door. You stay here out of sight, until I signal it's OK to come out."

I unlocked the front door and went outside. I held the bags high around me, fearing a sniper's bullet. I had dressed as if we were going for a walk in the snow - boots, fleecy, ski jacket. I didn't know what conditions would be like ahead. The snow was deep and crisp and made a crunching sound underfoot as I walked to the car. It was the kind of snow that would have rolled perfectly into a snowman, the kind of stuff I used to love playing in when I was a boy. No doubt the Inuits had a word for it. The morning was still and quiet and cold. Very cold. I put the cases in the back and jumped into the driver's seat. I kicked the snow off my boots and sat for a few moments relieved to have made it safely to the car. I turned the key and the engine started first time. I let the engine idle before switching on the back and front wipers. After four or five attempts, the windscreen was clear of snow. I put the car into reverse and slithered out of the parking place. I crunched the car into first, left the lights off and just let it crawl over to the hotel entrance. I eased the brake on, opened the driver's door and crawled over into the passenger seat. I beckoned to Anja. She stepped out of the door and down the steps to the car.

"Anja, hurry up and get in! Get in the car!" I pleaded.

She stood by the car door gazing around her.

"Oh my God!" She said as she brought her hand up to her mouth. She had spotted the jeep.

Again I called to her to get in. She seemed to take ages, but finally she climbed in. She was obviously scared and was trying to control her breathing as she switched on the head lights. The stillness of the morning was broken, as a snowplough on the early shift suddenly thundered past, attempting to clear the main road, its orange flashing light illuminating the snowy dawn. A three foot bow wave of snow spewed off its massive metal blade. We reversed out of the car park and, with a slight wheel-spin in the deep snow, we followed its tracks. I looked back over my shoulder but there was no apparent sign of life from either hotel. Nothing seemed to be stirring other than us and the driver of the snow-plough.

*****

Piers Richardson had not slept well. He had difficulty coming to terms with the fact that he was not in control of the situation he now found himself in. With the hard experience and basic gut-instinct of a former member of the Intelligence services, he suspected that his prey had not gone to Bergen, but he couldn't be sure, so he had sent two of his colleagues up North and one to cover Sola Airport, while he had backed a hunch. Just after 7am, he crossed the road to the Ibsen Hotel, taking care to navigate the rough snow wall that had been left by the plough a short time earlier. Mrs Brodal's seventeen year old son Karl was on early morning duty in reception.

194

"Good morning."

"Good morning, sir," Karl beamed in reply, pleased to be given the opportunity to try out his English. "Can I help you?"

"Yes, I wonder if you can. I'm looking for a friend of mine, a Norwegian girl by the name of Anja Andresen. A group of us in a convoy of cars were all driving to Oslo and our vehicles became separated when the weather worsened and the blizzard set in. Did she by any chance checkin here last night?"

Karl dutifully checked through the four new registration cards from the night before. He saw the name Robertson, but searched on.

"I'm sorry sir, we have had no-one by the name of Andresen staying in the hotel last night."

"Thank you very much, you have been most helpful." With these words, Piers Richardson motioned to turn and leave the hotel. Maybe he'd been wrong and she was heading for Bergen.

"One moment sir, is she an attractive girl in her early twenties?"

Karl had remembered the note Anja had left on the reception, a note he had passed to his mother, a note on which she had signed her own name, before leaving. Richardson turned slowly, grinned and moved closer to the Reception desk believing his luck was changing.

"Yes, that's right."

"Oh, she was in last night sir," the boy said, pleased with his own powers of deduction, "but they checked out this morning."

"*THEY* checked out this morning?" he questioned.

"Yes, Mr and Mrs Robertson. Are they just recently married? My mother thought they were honeymooners."

Richardson's initial look of confusion evaporated in an instant, as the pieces began to fall neatly into place. She was with someone!

"Oh, yes, of course, the newly-weds. Andresen is Anja's maiden name. What time did they leave?"

"About 6.15 am, possibly earlier. I had just come down when I saw their car leave. Their note said they were returning to Stavanger because of the weather, but for some reason, which I thought was odd, they drove off down the Oslo road."

Richardson's discipline had splintered, his grin having returned, broader than ever.

"Was it the Volvo?"

"Oh no, I think it was a German car. A BMW or a Mercedes, I think - no, it was an Audi. Yes, it was definitely an Audi."

"Thank you very much, thank you very much indeed."

He offered Karl a 100 Kroner note for his help, but the young lad refused it. He was only too pleased to be of assistance.

Mrs Brodal, who had watched the little scene unfold through the partially open door of the unlit office, crushed the note she had been left. As the main door swung shut after Richardson had gone, she stepped out into the hall and flashed her son an emphatically disapproving stare. He was completely bemused by the coldness of her glare. What had he done wrong? Surely he had been more than helpful and he had even refused the tip! Women!

*****

We trailed the snowplough up above the tree line, before it stopped and pulled into the side of the road. Territorial demarcation. This was as far as he covered. Someone else would be responsible for completing the road we were now on. Anja carefully overtook the massive yellow truck and we pressed on over the weary wastes of virgin snow. There was now a danger we would run into a snow drift, but we drove on regardless. About half an hour after leaving the snowplough, I became aware of a set of headlights high up on the mountain road some kilometres behind us. From that distance, there was no way we could confirm who or what was coming but Anja increased the speed of the Audi.

Chapter 8

CHAPTER 8

I was feeling more and more tense. My stomach - the most effective barometer of my stress levels and nervousness - was churning. I had survived major abdominal surgery in my early twenties for a burst ulcer and one or two other internal problems. Healthwise, the success of the operation had changed my life and the registrar who put me under the knife actually wrote a paper on the complications he encountered when he opened me up. For a few hours after I had been initially rushed in to hospital by ambulance, it had been touch and go whether or not I would survive, as the bleeding wouldn't stop. I was given an immediate transfusion and was wired up to a number of monitors and intentionally prevented from sleeping by the nurses, who were ordered to take my blood pressure and temperature every half an hour through the night. It seemed that, as quickly as they pumped blood into me, I was leaking it out. That was all behind me now, the fork and knife job had been a success and I was generally fit, though my stomach was still capable of giving me a problem every now and again. A reminder of how close I'd come. I was a bit of a worrier and thought about things too much.

Although my eyes were open and I was looking outside, my mind was wandering - I thought about Mum and Dad, about Hannah, Steve, my sister Victoria, my life in Aberdeen and it made me catch my breath. Surely it wasn't going to end here in Norway on a cold, lonely stretch of mountain road, with a girl I hardly knew. I'm no philosopher, but life, I thought, is so fragile and it can be snuffed out in a matter of seconds. Staying on this depressing train of thought, I wondered who would come to the Crem to see me off. Would there be a lot of people? What would they say? Would

197

their words be kind? Mind you, what can you say about almost thirty years of life in your allotted twenty five minutes, before your family and friends leave by one door and the next lot are shipped in and the whole cycle starts again. Shit, maybe no-one would come - a legacy of my life as a loner.

"Are we still being followed?"

Anja's question rescued me from the depths of self-pity and I twisted round and looked back.

"I can't see anything."

"I think we've got to assume that, if it was their jeep in the hotel car park, then they will almost certainly be on the road by now. I guess you need to phone Andy urgently and give him an update."

"Sure."

They were closing in again and, apart from calling London, I wasn't sure what else to do. The Bergen ruse had evidently failed. The road seemed to go on forever. We were still high up on the plateau and I worried that if it snowed again we would have a real problem. Exposed on the road, without shelter or cover. I thought about the capability of their vehicle and it concerned me that a 4-wheel drive would be handling the snowy conditions with comparative ease. It was only a matter of time. The road began to wind downward but so far there was still no sign of our pursuers. The headlights I had seen had gone. Anja had driven confidently over the snow and she seemed bright and alert, no longer displaying any signs of fear.

"There is another small village coming up and beyond it there are two ways we can go to Oslo. There is the new shorter way through a series of tunnels or there is a longer route that heads south to the coast, then north to the city. Which way do you want to go?"

"Are we far from that village?"

"No, we're almost there."

"OK, let's get there, as quickly as possible and I'll phone Andy. What's your thoughts ?"

"I just want to get to Oslo - you decide, you've made all the decisions so far."

"Are you pissed off with me?"

"No, of course not. I'm sorry, I didn't mean it to come out like that."

Once again, Anja eased her foot down on the accelerator pedal and the Audi began to speed up. We soon arrived at the village and Anja slowed the car to a crawl, looking for a telephone kiosk. There was no obvious sign of a public call box, other than the possibility that one might be in the premises of a small decorative candle-maker and gift shop with an adjoining cafe. We agreed it was our best bet. This time neither of us made any reference to Pakistan. Anja parked the car out of sight behind a house, a few metres from the gift shop. We zipped up our jackets against the wind chill and walked back to the cafe. Anja didn't take my hand which was unusual. I needed her touch and the insecurities that always bubbled within me worried that she was beginning to distance herself from me. A bell rang as we entered the cafe.

"Are you hungry?" she asked.

"No, not really, just get me a coffee please, while I call Andy."

I found the phone, but had to frantically search my pockets for the crumpled note with his number. I called London.

"Hello, News Desk."

"Can I speak to Andy McIntosh please?" I asked politely and calmly, not recognising the voice at the other end of the phone.

"I'm sorry, he's not here. He's had to leave the office."

"When will he be back?"

"I can't say. Can I take a message?"

"OK, tell him Paul called. It's very important you let him know I phoned; I need to talk to him."

"Paul from Norway? Paul Robertson?" she interrupted. She had obviously been briefed, and knew who I was and had been expecting a call.

"Yes, that's right."

"Can you call back in ten minutes, I'll have some information for you then."

"I don't know if I've got ten minutes!"

"I'm sorry, I'm only doing as I'm told."

"Yes, I know, thank you."

I hung up the phone and swore under my breath. I turned and walked back to Anja. I had expected Andy to be there and the disappointment induced a further evaporation of hope. Anja had taken our coffees from the counter and had sat at a table by the window. She was staring, her eyes transfixed on the road. She jumped when I touched her shoulder. I pushed my hand through her hair as I sat down, thanked her for the coffee and apologised for startling her. She reached across and touched my hand and I felt close to her again.

"What's Andy saying?" Anja asked hopefully.

"He's not there," I sighed, "I got through alright and spoke to a girl who said he's out of the office right now, but could I call back in five or ten minutes. She'll be able to update me then."

"Can we afford to wait five minutes?"

"Yes. We have no choice; he's our only contact with George and the Norwegian authorities."

Time went by slowly and we spent an uncomfortable ten minutes looking out of the window, our hearts leaping into our mouth every time a car or truck would drive past. We watched a car drive into the car park and we were relieved to see an elderly couple get out and enter the gift shop. The bell rang again. Without any prompting from Anja, I went back to the phone and called London. Shit! I couldn't believe it; all lines out of the country were busy. I looked across at Anja, shrugged and mouthed 'I can't get through'. We'd now been waiting for just under fifteen minutes. If we didn't make a move soon we could be in serious trouble.

"Come on Anja, we can't wait here any longer."

We left the cafe and ran back to the car. Anja drove to the bottom of a lane, turned into someone's drive, reversed and headed back onto the main road. There were no other cars so we drove off. I felt the first tinges of panic, but I kept them hidden. Just outside the village, Anja slowed down.

"It's decision time. Do we go to the coast or onto the tunnels?"

"Drive through the tunnels," I said, without hesitation.

"But that tunnel system is over twelve kilometres long, what happens if they catch us in there? There won't be any escape."

"Trust me, I've got an idea."

It wasn't much of an idea, more of a risk. It wasn't even a calculated risk, it was a serious risk in that we were dealing with an unknown factor once we were in the tunnel. We drove on into the first tunnel and Anja switched on the headlights, even though the tunnel was well lit. The noise of the winter tyres on the road surface sounded different, as it echoed and resounded off the hardness of the asphalt.

"Put the foot down, please," I requested, touching Anja's leg as I said it.

The engine purred and we began to cruise through the tunnel. The clear, but wet surface was a welcome respite from the rutted snow outside. The tunnel was dual laned, solid rock all round, with a continuous crash bar down the middle, much to my relief. Anja continued to accelerate. If she made a mistake at this speed, we'd be seriously hurt at best. My mind was in turmoil and I tried to free my thoughts from the limited options - death by a bullet in the head, or death by multiple injuries caused by a car smash. Soon the end of the last tunnel came in sight and we blinked and squinted as the pupils of our eyes reacted to the sharp sunlight.

"Right, turn the car around."

Anja looked at me.

"What are you up to, Paul?" she asked, obviously puzzled. I repeated the instruction.

"Turn the car around and head back up the tunnel."

"Paul, are you sure?"

"No, but if I'm right I might have bought us some time. I don't know. Do you want me to take a turn driving."

"No, having to concentrate on the road helps take my mind off everything."

"OK, you're the boss. Let's head back the way."

Anja did as she was told. She turned the car and eased it up to the tunnel entrance and stopped. She looked at me and opened her mouth as if to speak but I put my finger against her lips and whispered, "I know, I know."

Ahead of us lay Oslo and, hopefully, safety - behind us lay a malevolent force that was tracking us steadily and unrelentingly. We kissed and held each other. She pulled me tight to her body then, taking my hand, she kissed my fingers and pressed my open hand against her cheek.

"Come on, let's go."

She put the car into gear and we re-entered the unknown of the man-made caverns, heading back toward the village and the coast road to Oslo. The leaden feeling in my stomach was still there and a feeling of unease had once again invaded my thoughts. We had gone about a third of the way into the tunnel when a set of car headlights came towards us and I felt my heart race and touched Anja's hand as the car approached, but as it passed we saw it was being driven by a middle-aged woman. We chatted nervously as the tension and panic receded. Anja drove quickly, but never nearing the speed that had driven us down the tunnel. I was beginning to worry that my hunch would not pay off, that all I had succeeded in doing was wasting time and unnecessarily putting Anja's life at even greater risk, when the lights of a second vehicle came into view.

"Just drive normally and don't panic. It'll be alright," I said, trying to assure her, but needing reassurance myself.

The two sets of headlights drew closer and closer, as if they were magnetically drawn together, then they were upon each other. The black 4WD slowed right down to a crawl as we moved past, its three occupants gazing at the passengers in the racing green Audi. Anja and I kept our eyes on the road up ahead and kept going. We were past them. The other vehicle sped off and I turned round to watch them. Anja was looking in her mirror and not concentrating on the road ahead.

"Anja!" My shout startled her. "Get your foot down and for Christ's sake keep your eyes on the road."

"I'm sorry, I'm sorry."

"Never mind, there's no time for that, just get a move on."

I kept looking back, following the tail lights of the dark vehicle. It looked like our luck had held again. Suddenly the brake lights came on and they seemed to stop, then they appeared to reverse a few metres. There seemed to be some confusion and uncertainty, then the crimson glow of the reversing lights went off and their vehicle tore off down the tunnel at high speed, the eerie screech of their wheel spin echoing after us.

"I think they've sussed us. Let's get to..."

I stopped myself before I said the 'F-word'. Hannah used to hate me, or anyone else for that matter, swearing, claiming it demonstrated a lack of vocabulary or intellect - or both! I tried not to swear in front of Anja, even though her command of the language was liberally sprinkled with expletives.

"It's up to you, Anja, I need to get to a phone and then we can head for Oslo - no stops."

We were at the village in minutes and Anja screeched into the cafe car-park, before skidding to a halt conveniently at the door. I dashed out, burst into the cafe and went to phone Andy, the scribbled note with his number safely in my hand; there wasn't any time for rummaging through pockets and fucking about like that. I tapped in the digits and waited.

"News Desk." It was a male voice.

"Andy?"

"No, Andy's not here. Is that Paul Robertson?" Was this another new player on the other end of the phone? What the hell was going on?

"Yes."

"I've been expecting your call, Andy's had to go to..."

"Never mind that, just listen. I've got about ten-fifteen minutes start on them, maybe more, maybe less, but they now obviously know the car and the fact that I'm with Anja. What's the jackanory with George?"

"OK, I understand. Listen carefully."

I nodded as if to signal to the voice at the other end of the phone that they had my full and undivided attention.

"George will meet you both at the entrance to the Central Railway Station on Karl Johans Gate, in Oslo. Don't worry about the time, they will wait for you. He's picked that location because it's city centre and there should be plenty of people going about."

"How will they know us?"

"Don't worry about that, they'll know. Oh before I forget, Andy left a message to pass on to the girl - the Norwegian police have issued a warrant for the arrest of Oldfist's assistant. He said she'll know what it means."

"Oldfist? You mean Aldquist."

"Yes that's correct. He works at the University."

"That's the fella. Look, whoever you are thanks, but I'd better go."

I think the voice may have shouted good luck or something as I replaced the receiver. I smiled at the bemused owner of the cafe and rushed back out to the car.

"The Central Station, Karl Johans Gate, do you know it?"

"Yes, yes I do," she said.

"OK, that's the meeting place, let's GFI...go for it! I also have a message for you - looks like Aldquist's not involved - they're after his assistant."

"Who? Svein-Olaf?"

"I don't know, he didn't give me a name. Do you know him?"

"Yes, of course. He was involved in the beginning when we first set up the group, but I would never have believed he would have betrayed us. Having said that he is a weak man - I have never liked him."

Anja released the clutch and the car spun out of the snow-covered car park and we turned onto the coast road. Anja believed that we were no more than forty five minutes to an hour from Oslo. The road itself was relatively clear of snow, but it was banked three to four feet by the verge, piled there by the efforts of a plough or snow-blower, eventually disappearing altogether as we drove south. I said a silent prayer for our safe delivery in the hope that I hadn't screwed up. All too soon we could see the sea, away in the distance and I felt the adrenaline of the chase rush through me. On one hand, I have to admit, there was a partial excitement in the fact that we were being pursued. The chase. The hunter and the hunted, as ancient and basic as time. On the other hand it was terrifying to realise how close they were and that if they caught us it would end in certain death. There could be no last minute reprieves, mercy would not be on their agenda. There was also a great feeling of relief and anticipation that we would soon be safe. I stretched over to the back seat and opened my case and pulled out the tape I had made for Anja. I pushed it into the cassette and as the music began to fill the car, she turned and smiled at me as she remembered the music we had danced to only a couple of nights ago on the island. I sang what words I knew. I guess I was pouring my heart out to her through the words of the songs. "Will You Still Love Me Tomorrow", "What Are You Doing the Rest of Your Life", some Bacharach songs, all songs of lost love and broken hearts. I sang them all.

"Anja," I said softly, "will you come and see me in Scotland?"

"Yes. Yes of course, I would love to do that."

"It's a date then!"

She rubbed her eyes. The songs lifted us, or saddened us, but more importantly they distracted us and we were in the outskirts of Oslo in less than an hour. The headstart of the tunnel incident and the performance of the Audi had seemed to have given us an edge. I kept looking back, fearing that the grill of their vehicle would suddenly appear tight against the rear bumper of the Audi. There was no sign of it.

Oslo, Norway's capital city, formerly known as Christiania, population 460 000. I had read about it in a book, but had never been here before. Anja's knowledge took us painlessly into the city centre and she parked in a new car park by the harbour at Aker Brygge.

"This is it Anja, we're looking good. Are you OK?"

"Yes of course - I'm with you."

Anja had found a new energy and enthusiasm, whereas I was feeling drained. We were back on her turf and I was depending on her now. No, that's wrong, I was depending on her again! So far she had controlled her grief and apart from the odd tear, she had hidden it, but a time would soon come when the lock would open and her emotions would flow. Maybe by that time we would be safe and her mother or Nina would be there, as I dreaded having to cope when it happened; I wasn't very good with things like that. For the time being she was fine. She was in control. We carefully parked and secured the car and then she led me in the direction of the Central Station.

The Aker Brygge is an area of docklands renewal and although it was very cold it was bustling with people. A relatively new quayside development of cafes, pubs and restaurants, shops and clubs, it was a massive turnaround from the halcyon days of ship building and ship repair, when the place was alive with riveters, platers and gantry cranes. The popularity of the port as a stopover for Nordic and Baltic cruises was evidenced by the sleek cruise ships that lay docked in the fjord - below the Renaissance castle, the Akerhus Fort - moored there in full view of Oslo's cafe society who thronged the boardwalks. Varying smells of fresh seafood, hot pizza and other culinary offerings hung, warm and tempting on the still, late afternoon air and somewhere nearby an accordionist played a lively medley of traditional tunes; soft and gentle melodies that seemed to call out longingly for old Christiania. However, we weren't there to enjoy the atmosphere, that would have to be put on ice until a later date as Anja pushed her way through the crowds as we made our way to Karl Johans Gate. According to Steve there is no Norwegian equivalent for the phrase "Excuse Me" and what I'd noticed in the Stavanger Fun Pub was happening here again, people just barged their way past without a thought.

Daylight was fading on the streets of Oslo and I was aware of floodlights swamping a massive building, the skyline-dominating City Hall, the city's political and administrative management centre.

"Come on Paul, this way. I come down here all the time in the summer, it's a great place. There is a wonderful restaurant just over there, I think it would be the perfect place to take Nina and Bjorn for a meal when you come back over."

She pointed in the direction of a bistro, then realised instantly what she had said. That particular get together could now never take place. I thought that it might trigger the deluge that she had been fighting to hold back and for a brief second it seemed as if she would lose it.

"Keep going, I'm right behind you," I urged.

We pushed and shoved our way through the crowd with Anja taking the lead. She knew where she was going and I was happy to follow. She was now totally focused in on the rendezvous with George, like a child returning to the safety of a mother's arms. Anja obviously sensed she was nearing safety, it wasn't far now, but unlike me she had not seen two of the men who had been at the house, and who had followed us to Stavanger, step out of a shop doorway. I jerked on Anja's hand and pulled her into the entrance of a nearby cafe/theatre.

"Paul, stop it! What are you doing, we're not there yet," she said indignantly, trying to pull away from me.

"Anja, didn't you see them ? They're here, they've made us."

"No Paul, you must be mistaken, they can't know we're here. They just can't."

It was them, I wasn't mistaken. We stepped into the crowded cafe. Again we were standing on the edge of darkness. The cafe bar, which was designed on two levels, the floors linked with a wrought iron spiral staircase with old cinema and theatre posters plastered over the walls, was busy with groups of both young and old, sitting at candlelit tables listening to a middle aged couple sitting at a baby-grand piano playing Grieg. The atmosphere in the bar seemed to be very arty, very Bohemian. I recognised the tune that was being played instantly, it was the same piano duet that Nina and

Bjorn had played at the house, when we had all celebrated the handshake of Coyle and McCreery. The irony of it all was lost on me. I pulled Anja through the crowds to the bar. The bar-tender caught my eye and I felt obliged to order a drink. I ordered two beers, even though we didn't really want them. They just sat untouched on the polished granite bar top. The two from outside had followed us in and were standing near the door whispering, colluding and plotting our fate.

Anja leant against the bar, her head buried in my shoulder. I couldn't stop staring at the two men at the entrance, glowering and scowling at them in bare-faced defiance. Bastards! They weren't much older than me, but they were trained mercenaries. Killers. I had trained in Shotokan Karate about ten years earlier, but in those days my football came first and I kept missing gradings, so I never knew how good or bad I was, but in reality I wasn't a scrapper, I couldn't fight sleep. I had spent my whole life avoiding trouble and had been reasonably successful up to now. I hated violence. I had witnessed trouble in pubs and on the streets and had seen at first hand the damage that could be done. Now here I was faced with two killers and I knew I was no match for one, let alone the two of them. Maybe if I had a Desert Eagle tucked inside my jacket, that might have evened up the odds. I got the impression that the mistakes of the house and the Fun Pub would not be repeated here.

"That's them over by the door isn't it?"

"Yes, I'm afraid so."

"You're right. They're definitely the ones from the house. I'd know their faces anywhere."

"Exactly, why do you think they are so determined to kill us?"

"How did they get here before us? How did they know we'd be here?"

I couldn't provide a sensible answer, "I don't know, it beats the fuck out of me!"

For a moment there was silence.

"Do you know any 'back doors' out of here Paul?" she asked without looking at me. I smirked and shook my head.

I knew we were so close to safety and what had once been fear was now anger and frustration.

"Anja, I'm not the kind of guy who ever says much about the way I feel or what I'm thinking about, but after what's happened, there's so much I want to say to you, so many experiences I want to share with you. What I'm trying to say is I, I..."

She smiled and her index finger brushed my lips.

"It's alright Paul, I know, I know."

Like two tag-team wrestlers coming out of their corner for the final, no holds barred round, the two assassins began to walk towards us. Just then, the music stopped and the crowd broke into loud applause. Some of the audience stood up cheering and clapping. I pulled Anja forward into the crowd and we began applauding as well. The crowd began to move as the pianists took their bow and left the stage, their performance over. Some of the audience began to make their way back to the bar, while others made toward the exit. Anja and I began to move with the crowd as it bottle-necked toward the front door. I hoped to lose our two friends, but they were obviously too smart for that and one was making his way back to cover the door while the other had made for the bar. We were now trapped between them. Our options were now limited to those of instinctive action. A group of ten or twelve slightly pissed, noisy and highly excited individuals were making their way to the exit and we moved into their jostling ranks.

The gaunt, tough looking killer in the black leather biker's jacket had his eyes fixed on us, his sights locked in. He was preparing to deal with us, either by blade or by pistol and silencer. This time there would be no safety in a crowd. As we made our way toward him, he motioned to put his right hand inside his jacket and without thinking I picked up a small, heavy bar stool with my right hand and sprang at him, my first swipe catching him on the elbow as he pulled his arm from his jacket and attempted to defend himself. He was a fraction of a second too late and he let out a scream as the stool struck home, fracturing and splintering bone. I lashed out again and my second effort, more of a vicious jab than a haymaker, caught him on the cheek and the temple and he went down on his knees, dazed and in pain, a wicked cut immediately appearing below his eye. By this time the group we were walking out with had got over the shock of witnessing what appeared to be a completely unprovoked assault. Three of them grabbed me and threw me out into the street then menacingly gathered round me. I thought I was going to get a good kicking. I managed to get up onto my knees and prepared to go up against these less dangerous civilians. During the melee, Anja had slipped out unnoticed and had begun running down the street toward the station.

"Anja, find George! Find George ! Don't worry about me!" I called after her.

The group that had turned on me were suddenly distracted and they temporarily abandoned their interest, their attention diverted to the two police cars that screeched to a halt in the street a few feet away. Six armed policemen wearing flak jackets dived